The Grumpy Crumpet Club

RJ Whitfield

TSL Publications

First published in Great Britain in 2021
By TSL Publications, Rickmansworth

Copyright © 2021 RJ Whitfield (John Samson)

ISBN / 978-1-914245-55-8

All that we see or seem is
but a dream within a dream

A Dream Within A Dream
– Edgar Allen Poe

'The Grumpy Crumpets.'

'Whaaat!!'

'You are kidding?'

Sara The Bitch looked pleased with herself. Of course at that point she wasn't Sara The Bitch, she was just plain Sara Green, mother of two and wife of Oliver Green (Ollie to his friends), a fairly successful broker up in the city.

'The Grumpy Crumpets,' Sara repeated her suggestion, lifting her glass of red in a toast to her own ingenuity and looking round for agreement.

'I suppose it's better than The Beatlettes.' Jenny half raised her glass and cast a glance across at Desiree who had suggested the feminine of the Fab Four. Desiree shrugged. She obviously had no particular attachment to her idea and pronounced, after contemplating her wine for a moment, twirling it in her glass like she knew what she was doing, 'I guess The Beatlettes is a little clichéd, so yeah, I quite like The Grumpy Crumpets actually.'

'What'll Ian think of the name?' Sara asked. She was always the one to ask what the husbands would think. The truth was that Desiree would not give a toss what Ian thought. 'If it doesn't involve sex, Ian doesn't think,' she had told me once, laughing it off with a wave of her hand. But she would never have said something like that to Jenny or Desiree.

I guess I probably knew more about my three friends – band mates I should say – than they knew about each other. I was, for some reason, the one they confided in. I knew about Jenny's brief affair with Sara's Ollie, Sara's abortion when she was at uni and Desiree's situation.

'What do you think, Clair? You've been very quiet in the corner there,' Sara looked to me now and the other two turned, glasses held ready to toast the band's new name if my blessing was forthcoming.

I hated the name and the only thing that stopped me saying so was the fact that we would never pick up an instrument or a microphone, never climb on a stage in front of a crowd, never pen a number one hit. The whole thing would only happen in our minds. We did this all the time, spending our girls' nights imagining lives more interesting than the banal reality that we had to deal with day in and day out.

I gave a long contemplative pause, enjoying the irritation and expectation that built up in the group, then slowly leaned forward, picked up my glass by its stem and lifted it in a toast. 'The Grumpy Crumpets,' I said.

Name: Sara The Bitch (Bass)
Age: 51
Star sign: Gemini
Favourite food: Red wine
Celeb Hero: The man who makes the red wine
Favourite Song: Red Red Wine
Favourite Band: April Wine
How did you get your name? Well, I wanted to be Rockbitch or Rock Goddess, but Jenny told me that there was already a band called Rockbitch who apparently cavort nude on stage. I don't object to having to cavort naked, I just didn't fancy having to deal with any legal wranglings with naked woman. Rock Goddess, I decided, was just a little too pretentious and Bitch on its own was too plain. It was my hubby Ollie who suggest Sara The Bitch.

And you're still married? Yes (laughs). He's Ollie The Tosser and I'm Sara The Bitch. It somehow works for us.

Why the bass? Well, we couldn't all be lead singer, so we had to draw lots. Clair is the shy one, so she was happy to be the drummer, likes to stay in the background, but Jenny, Desiree and I fought it out and Desiree won. I then wasn't fussed about whether I was bass or lead guitar just as long as I wasn't the drummer.

Your band mates, Snog, Marry, Kill?: Snog Desiree, she's got the lips, marry Jenny she's got the money and kill Clair, sorry love, but the other two were the obvious snog and marry. Nothing personal.

Name: Jenny Jangle (lLead guitar)
Age: 50½
Star sign: Virgo
Favourite food: Steak
Celeb hero: Jackson Browne
Favourite song: Lawyers In Love
Favourite band: The Eagles
How did you get your name: I used to wear loads of bangles at uni. I was a bit obsessed with the whole hippy movement back then even though I was about twenty years too late. I got the nickname Jenny Bangles. I

thought about resurrecting that name when we formed The Grumpy Crumpets, but it didn't quite cut it. Then, when I lost out on being the lead vocalist and was handed the guitar role, I remembered Johnny Marr from The Smiths. They often referred to his 'jangling guitar' sound. Jenny Jangle has a nice ring to it and reminded me of my old nickname.

Does anyone still call you Jenny Bangles: My husband, Geoff, who I met at uni, still calls me that. It's kinda cute that he does, reminds me of our wild youth (sighs).

Why lead guitar: Well, if you can't be lead singer, it's the next best thing. You can do the guitar solos and strut your stuff out front. Even upstage the lead singer if you're good enough.

Your band mates, Snog, Marry, Kill?: Tough one. I'd like to marry them all, they are all wonderful in their own kinda way. Not too sure about snogging, that would be a bit weird. And I would never want to kill anyone one of them. (Pause) No one said they would kill me, did they?

Name: Desiree Desire (Lead vocals)
Age: 48
Star sign: Libra
Favourite food: Quinoa…just kidding. I would have to go with chocolate.
Celeb hero: Dame Judy Dench, especially when she played M in the Bond films.
Favourite song: The James Bond Theme Tune
Favourite band: The Beatles
How did you get your name: The girls always tell me that I am the prettiest of the four of us. Maybe I was back in the day, but I think that Clair is the one who has kept her looks while the rest of us got old. But they still say I'm a looker, so I guess the name is a bit of a tongue in cheek answer to that. If you're going to say outrageous things like I'm the prettiest, then you may as well go completely overboard. Desiree Desire sounded overboard enough for me.

Does your husband like your name: Um, yeah, I guess.

Why lead vocalist: Well, I was the lucky one when we drew lots. We all, well all except Clair, wanted to be the singer. I do think that I have the best singing voice of the four of us, judging by our karaoke nights.

Your band mates, Snog, Marry, Kill?: Kill would definitely be Sara. She's not known as Sara The Bitch for nothing. Snog? I guess it would have to be Jenny over Clair, mainly because Jenny's about my height while Clair is a lot shorter, so I may get backache bending over to snog her. That just leaves marry for Clair which I suppose would be right. She's the most dependable one and that's what one needs in a partner.

Name: Clair da Loon
Age: 48
Star sign: Aires
Favourite food: Anything Italian
Celeb hero: I don't really have one
Favourite song: It's a bit cheesy, but I do like 'That's What Friends Are For'
Favourite band: Cocteau Twins
How did you get your name: My dad's favourite piece of music was 'Clair de Lune' by Debussy, so it's a play on that I guess. Spelling it as 'Loon' like in looney makes it sound a little more punky and it fits in with the names the others had come up with. I'm not really a looney, I don't think.
What does your dad think of about it?: Oh, he's dead, but he would have liked it…I guess.
Your band mates, Snog, Marry, Kill?: Sometimes I would like to kill them all…Joke!

We were at Sara's the night The Grumpy Crumpets were born. It was her turn to host our girl's night. Sometimes we would watch a film, but usually it was just a simple meal, a lot of wine and copious amounts of talking nonsense. We had won the lottery on numerous evenings, been world leaders, run multinational corporations, starred in Hollywood blockbusters, won Olympic gold medals and all that was required was a few bottles of red, comfortable sofas, babysitting husbands (in the early days) and a vivid imagination.

Desiree and Jenny were the main drivers of this while Sara was a 'gotta keep up with the hip ones' kind of girl. I always got the sense that she really didn't see the point of our little games but was dead scared of being isolated by the group if she didn't partake. I think that's why she was the bitch of the group. She desperately wanted to fit in but also had a strong urge to do what she wanted and if the two did not align, then she would start with the snide comments. A number of our evenings had ended abruptly after Sara The Bitch lived up to her name.

And when things did go sour like that, it was usually me they called on to get them talking again. It did help that Sara was a borderline alcoholic. 'It was the wine talking, you know she loves you guys really,' would usually do the trick in getting them at least to agree to meet up again. Sara would be on her best behaviour for the next few evenings, volunteering to bring the wine as her gift of contrition and then partaking of it sparingly as she knew what it did to her tongue. But her fear of missing out always led her to apologise. I did think that if is she had ever been properly expelled from the group, she would have spiralled down into full alcoholism pretty quickly.

How did the name The Grumpy Crumpets come about?

Sara The Bitch: I came up with it. We had been throwing around ideas, The Groan-Ups; Freedom's Mums; Claret, Pinot, Rosé and Sauvignon – that was too cumbersome. There were some other suggestions, but nothing really clicked. I wanted a name that said something about us, you know, something that reflected our personalities. So, I asked myself, 'what are we good at?' and the only thing that came to mind was bitching. We all love bitching, okay maybe not Clair so much, but the rest of us do. But as I was planning to be Sara The Bitch, I didn't think that we could use 'bitch' in the band name, the others would accuse me of wanting to take over. So I thought bitching... moaning... grumpy. That was a natural progression, but grumpy what? I remember looking round the group and thinking, you know, we're not bad looking for our ages. I mean Jenny's still got an amazing figure and look at Desiree, I have no idea how she keeps her skin so young looking. She swears that she doesn't use *Oil of Delay* as my son calls it. Anyway, I thought we're all still pretty good looking, enough so to be regarded as a bit of crumpet. So, there is was, The Grumpy Crumpets.

Jenny and Desiree also hated the name.

'Typical of Sara to have something with a food reference, particularly something from the bakery aisle,' Jenny said when Sara was out of the room making coffee, 'I think she's been eating a few too many crumpets herself, she's been putting on weight a bit, don't you think?'

Desiree nodded, 'And I don't like the "Grumpy" bit. Yes, we have our moans, but I would hardly say that we were all grumpy. She's the only one who can get really grumpy.' And it was Sara who took on the name 'The Bitch'? They were all smiles when she came back with the drinks.

'I thought you'd bring some grumpy crumpets for us to have with our coffee,' Jenny joked.

Sara, still proud of her suggestion for the band name, glowed slightly, taking Jenny's quip as a compliment.

'Sorry, don't have any round the house. I think I might be able to rustle up some bitching biccies or moaning muffins if you want, that is as long as the kids haven't eaten them all.'

'I thought your kids were perfect, they would never do anything like scoff all the biccies would they?' It was Desiree's turn to have a dig. Sara was proud of her two but was a bit of a disciplinarian. We had occasionally been shocked at the rules she imposed on Julie and Neil, poor things. It was no wonder that they were turning into rebellious teens.

Sara glared, a look of pure hatred briefly flittering across her face and then it was gone. It was not too long after her last fall out with the other two and one could almost see her thought processes as she geared up to respond, then reminded herself to tread carefully. I swear that Jenny and Desiree knew this and would exploit it.

'They are good kids, but they're only human and my biccies, as you ladies well know, are irresistible.' She gave a smile that said, 'You know I am right'. And we knew. Sara was a good baker. If she put her mind to it, she could make a fortune selling her cakes and biscuits. But work was not an idea she entertained lightly. Ollie made more than enough for her to live very comfortably without having to join the rat race, thank you very much.

'Go on then, let's have some biccies, if you've got some. You are quite right, we can't resist.' Jenny smoothed things over and we were okay again.

If you weren't in a band, what would you be doing?

Jenny Jangle: It would have to be something that involved travel. I love going places, seeing the sights, meeting different people, experiencing different cultures. So I guess an air hostess or tour guide, or better still, a pilot. Yes, a pilot. That way I can travel and have money to spend as well.

Sara The Bitch: You're only saying that because you want to spend time in the *cock*-pit.

Jenny Jangle: Good one, I hadn't thought of that. So definitely a pilot, one that never leaves the office. Ha ha.

How about you Sara, what would you be if you weren't in the band?

Desiree Desire: Oh that easy, she'd be a baker.

Sara The Bitch: No, no. Baking is my hobby. You never want your hobby to become your work. If I had to get a real job, then I guess professional lottery winner.

Desiree Desire: Good one. I'd like to be that too, but I guess we can't all be the same, so I would have to say that I would love to be a baker.

And you Clair?

Clair da Loon: Oh, I dunno. Zoo keeper maybe. Something where I don't have to deal with people.

I don't remember which one of us suggested forming a band. I have a vague recollection that it was Desiree but sometimes, when I think about it, I am sure that it was Jenny. Who knows. I may not even have been in the room when the suggestion was put forward. One does tend to go to the loo more often when drinking a lot of wine. I do remember the evening though. Ollie was there when I arrived, but disappeared as soon as Jenny arrived, making his usual excuses about work to do and moaning about his staff not being up to the job.

I was worried about Jenny. She had not been the same since things ended between her and Ollie. I think that she was going through a bit of a mid-life crisis, doubting herself, doubting her good looks, extremely conscious of the slow rot that hits us all. But she was still attractive. I had seen the men – granted it would generally be the older ones – who would steal glances at her when we had coffee together, their eyes surreptitiously following the curves that Jenny's tight jeans would make as she sat, her one long leg over the knee of the other, pushing her neat butt out slightly, just enough to be alluring, yet not enough to be vulgar. She was classy and even got some looks from the younger guys, but it was no good telling her that.

There was no doubt that her affair with Sara's husband had left a mark on her, a wound that cut deep. I don't think that she ever stopped loving Geoff while she was seeing Ollie, it was just that she loved Ollie more for a bit. Or at least she thought she did. I often wonder if it was more the idea of having an affair, that appealed rather than the affair itself. We seldom actually left our comfort zones, preferring to do so only from the comfort of a sofa and hiding behind a wall of wine. But Jenny had done so. She had stepped out from our fantasy world and ventured into a real and exciting one. Exciting until Ollie started seeing a young intern at his stockbroking firm.

So I worried about Jenny that night when we arrived and Ollie disappeared. I watched her watch him making his excuses and disappearing so quickly. He used to spend a little time with us before letting us get down to our 'girlie business' as he called it. We had all been good friends at uni where we met, so it was nice to include the men for a bit and catch up on their news. But Jenny was staring daggers at his back as he left.

'What's the matter, Jenny?' Sara picked up on the vibe. 'You look like you could kill Ollie. Has he done something to upset you?' There was genuine worry in her voice.

'What? Oh, no. No.' Jenny, to her credit recovered well. 'It was just his comment that you can't get the staff. It reminded me that Geoff has been talking a lot recently about the new young intern they have at work. I'm worried that he might be having an affair.'

Jenny would make a lousy poker player. Whenever she lied, she would finish by delicately brushing her long hair behind her ears.

Sara would make a lousy poker player too as she fell for Jenny's bluff. 'Oh, you poor dear. I do hope he isn't. Ollie recently mentioned an intern they have just got in their team, but I think it's a young guy, so I don't have to worry there. I do sometimes wonder what would happen if they got a young impressionable girl in the office. But you know what I do then? I just remember when some of our older lecturers tried to hit on me and how creepy that felt. I then think that any self-respecting young intern would feel the same about Ollie…and your Geoff. So, there's no cause for worry. Come on, dinner is ready. You know my lasagne will make you feel better.'

There have been stories about wild parties after your shows. Are they true?

Desiree Desire: That would be telling, now wouldn't it?

Jenny Jangle: No need to be coy, Desiree, yes, we do have some parties. Not sure I would call them wild though. Clair usually makes the tea and Sara brings along the cookies and we relax by sitting around dunking our biccies in our tea and nattering about how the gig had gone.

Sara The Bitch: Don't believe a word Jenny says, the parties are definitely wild. We get a lot of younger men coming to the gigs and the bouncers are under instruction to let a few hand-picked ones backstage. Our agent is the one who picks them.

Your agent?

Sara The Bitch: Yes, my husband. He knows what we like and choses the best looking guys for us. Then, you know, well anything can happen.

What do you say Clair, afterparties, wild young guys or tea and bicces?

Clair da Loon: (Pause) Wild.

The lasagne, as always, was really good. Sara is a better cook than she is a bitch. But even her lasagne could not settle Jenny. Sara's comments about the intern, rather than making Jenny feel sorry for her friend's naivety, seemed to rile her more. 'How can Sara be so stupid?' Jenny's looks seemed to say, not realising that that same naivety or stupidity or whatever you want to call it, had prevented her and Ollie's little affair from being discovered. I truly believed that Sara was as unaware of her husband's infidelity with Jenny as she was about his office affair with the intern.

But Jenny didn't want to let it go and started to take her anger out on Sara with snide comments. Fortunately, she was one of those who mellow with wine and as the meal progressed, the sharpness of the comments dulled.

'What's up with her?' Sara asked when Jenny went to the loo. She had been a little riled by the comments but had not risen to the bait. In fact, she had seemed in a very good mood that evening.

Desiree shrugged and the subject was dropped. Jenny returned a calmer person and dessert, a lovely lemon meringue pie, was relaxed, pleasant even. Later, when we were trying to come up with a name for the band, I thought back to our pudding and nearly suggested that we call ourselves The Tarts, but just in time I remembered Desiree telling me about how her husband, Ian, had accused her of being a tart recently during one of their rows. He had called her worse things, but that one seemed to hurt her more than any of the others. Despite her libido, she had never once been unfaithful and, god knows, she had had many opportunities to be so. Although the number of good looking men who had tried to chat her up at parties was not insignificant, she had always been polite but firm in turning down their advances. Unfortunately for her, Ian was a bit of the jealous type and often after such parties, I would find myself consoling Desiree, reassuring her that it was not her fault that she had looked stunning at the party and that men were just pigs.

'Except Ian,' she would say, 'he's just insecure.' I did wonder if he ever got violent. There was something about him that never sat easily with me. But Desiree never showed any signs of physical abuse. Mental, yes, but physical, no. All I can say is that if it was happening, he was pretty good at how he went about it. She never had the awkwardly explained black eye, or bruised forearms. Despite the lack of evidence though, I couldn't help feeling that it was going on.

Jenny's Geoff was the complete opposite. He was a real sweetie, devoted to his wife. If they had asked the snog, marry, kill question about the band member's husbands then Geoff would definitely have been marry, Ian kill and Ollie as snog, but I would probably have needed mouthwash after the latter to get rid of the bad taste.

There was a time at uni when I thought that Geoff and I might get together, but then he met Jenny and that put paid to any chances I may have had. I ended up with a string of dud boyfriends and once we left uni and started working, I lost interest in trying as I was left rather disillusioned by the whole dating thing and it very quickly became too late as I built up an independent life. I still held a little bit of a flame for Geoff, but I'd never let Jenny know that.

How would you describe your music?

Desiree Desire: I would call it dramatic pop. It's not your normal boy meets girl sweet meaningless stuff. We like to include swoops and peaks in the sound. I'm a big fan of the works of John Barry, you know, the guy who did the *James Bond* and *Persuaders'* theme tunes. We like to incorporate that seventies instrumental sound into our music. I did suggest we call ourselves The Bond Girls but someone, I think it was Sara, said we would probably have legal issues with that, so I suggested The Spy's Girls which I though was pretty clever, but Sara was still worried about what our lawyers would say. They make the world a dull place do lawyers. Sorry Geoff. Jenny's husband is a lawyer.

Jenny Jangle: It's a mixture of sounds really. Kind of like Suzi Quatro meets Kate Bush in Kylie Minogue's lounge. Sometimes I think we're not quite sure exactly which way the sound is going. We can be esoteric, girlie and hard rock all in one song. We can do tight leather catsuits, wild freaky hair and skimpy revealing numbers. But it's important, when we start writing a song, that we know which one we are trying to be. We've had a few real dud numbers that did not get past the demo stage because we never really knew which style we were aiming for. It's no good if the styles are fighting one another. Our songs are best when we go with one and stick with it. Unlike some men I know.

Sara The Bitch: Definitely punk, but not the modern rubbish that they call punk these days. No, we've gone back to punk roots, you know. The Exploited, Sham 69, UK Subs, those sorts of bands. Not the Sex Pistols, they were punk's pretty boys who sold out. Maybe a little bit like The Clash, you know, intelligent punk, but a little more thrashy than them. There's a bit of anger and violence in our music. We're a bit feminist but not O.T.T. We just want women to be treated with respect and the violence in our music is a backlash against the violence some men show towards women.

Clair da Loon: It's difficult to describe the music. Our sound varies, but it's all about love, unrequited love, passionate love, violent love, infidelity, you know the kind of love you see, or don't see in real life.

I didn't think that The Grumpy Crumpets would last beyond that first night at Sara's. Most of our little fantasies were short lived and soon forgotten. The only other one that lasted more than a couple of evenings was when Sara was PM, Jenny the Home Secretary, Desiree the Education Minister – she could teach us a thing or two, she had said – and I was designated the Chancellor of the Exchequer because I was usually the one who did the sums to split the bills when we went out. And was usually the one who would chip in the extra when someone didn't pay enough. It was always easier just to put in the extra fiver or tenner where necessary than to try and get one of them to admit to having underpaid. It was usually Sara, who was probably the wealthiest of all of us, who short changed the pot the most, but I never dared mention it.

I think the whole 'government' thing lasted a couple of months as Sara clung to power like a tinpot dictator. Eventually we ousted her through a coup. Jenny emailed me and Desiree and we agreed to all arrive early to the next night at her place and have a new theme already going before Sara arrived. Desiree was the director, Jenny was the lead actress and I was in line for the best supporting actress Oscar by the time Sara arrived.

'Ah, I see my cabinet has already assembled,' she said as she blustered into the room.

'Nope,' Desiree informed her, 'We've quit the government and started a film company, 21st Century Foxes. We've already started casting. We're still looking for the male lead.'

Sara was pissed off, but she took it well. Later when she and I met up for a coffee she confessed that the power of being the PM had gone to her head and that it was probably for the best but don't tell Jenny and

Desiree that she had said that, they must still think that she was upset. She was also getting into this male lead role thing, it was interesting having to be a man. 'I think I may suggest that we have a sex scene between the male and female lead, just to make Jenny feel awkward, especially if I say that we need to act it out. It'll be fun to see her back-pedal from that.'

The sex scene never happened as when the next girlie night came around, Sara had twisted her ankle badly and we ended up fussing over her and spent most of the time in the kitchen cooking while she sat with her foot up in the breakfast nook barking instructions at us to the extent that we started calling her Gordon Ramsey and that set us off opening restaurants and having our own TV cooking show.

I do think that Sara would still have liked to have tried out the 'sex scene' thing on Jenny just to get a reaction, but of the four of us, Jenny was certainly the most experimental when it came to that sort of thing. Sara had once told me that one night when she and Ollie were round at Jenny's, Jenny had got very drunk and started suggesting a foursome. She would have had more luck with Ian than Ollie for that sort of thing I would have thought, but I was sure that neither Sara nor Desiree would be interested.

I get these headaches sometimes, really bad ones. Ones that feel as if someone is drilling into your skull, mining for your soul. It is like one's head is encased in a claustrophobic crash helmet. It makes one want to rip one's head off one's shoulders to get away from the pain. And with the headaches comes the nausea. You want to be sick but are too scared to move your head. The light hurts, as if it is piercing your eyes with white hot pins. Even when you close them, it bombards your eyelids with its prickly heat.

When the headaches come, so do the voices. Demonic voices that mock and scorn, that make me feel like I am nothing. I am an uninvited guest in normality. 'You are not welcome in humanity; can't you see how everyone hates you?'

But I fight the voices. I fight them with everything that I can. My eyes squeezed tight, my nails digging into the palms of my hands, sometimes drawing blood, trying to distract the pain from my temples, luring it down to my hands where it is more bearable.

And I fight against the voices to be who I am. I am Clair da Loon, the drummer in the Grumpy Crumpets. I am Clair da Loon, the drummer in the Grumpy Crumpets. I am Clair da Loon...

You had to cancel you last concert. What happened?

Desiree Desire: We are really sorry that we had to pull the gig, but Clair fell ill in the afternoon. We will be giving a full refund to all ticket holders and we are working with the venue to reschedule.

Is Clair okay now?

Jenny Jangle: Yes, she has fully recovered and is up and about. She'll be ready for our next gig.

You don't seem too sure.

Sara The Bitch: No, we're sure that she is fine.

Could you not just have got a replacement drummer?

'We missed you last week, sweetie,' Jenny pushes her hair behind an ear with her long elegant fingers. Just one side, not both ears, so only half insincere.

'What was wrong? Another migraine?' Sara asks, slightly more sincerely and I nod.

'Poor thing. I sometimes get headaches as well,' she says putting a plate of homemade hummus and carrot sticks down in front of us as an appetiser before dinner. Never tell a migraine sufferer that you 'sometimes get headaches'. It's a bit like telling a drowning person that you sometimes swim underwater.

Even Ian musters some sympathy although coming from him it is without substance, the hollow sound of a tree falling in a deserted forest.

I get the feeling that he resents us being in his house. He feels threatened, as if we might stumble on some evidence of his abuse of Desiree, as if we might rip up the patio and find the bodies of five previous wives that no one knew about. Oh god, please don't let Desi be the sixth.

We don't often go to Desiree's, none of us, not even Desiree herself, feel comfortable there if Ian is around. Most of the time when we are there he is away or going out. He is late in leaving this evening but eventually, after patting my shoulder to show that he cares, he gives

Desiree a light peck on the cheek and a 'see you later' before heading out the door, dragging a weight of tension in his slipstream.

'T-shirts. We need to design t-shirts.' Sara is the one who brings up The Grumpy Crumpets. We had eaten well, our dinner time conversation light and carefree. Sara had been moaning about the state of her teenagers' rooms but was comparing that to her own room when she had been a similar age. She had started referring to her two as Tango and Sprite, feeling that Julie and Neil were far too plain for the children of Sara The Bitch. No one pointed out that naming them after your favourite soft drinks was hardly more rock 'n' roll than naming them after your grandparents.

Jenny had started calling her Tracey, Bombhead which was much more punk than Tango and Sprite. The funny thing was that Tracey was such a lovely girl that the nickname bordered on the ridiculous.

Desiree had decided that she needed sophisticated names for her two, so Anthony (Ant to us when we weren't in the band) became Antoine and Peter became Pierre.

'Shouldn't we release an album first, then we can just do something with the record cover for the t-shirts?' Jenny asked.

'We could, but I was thinking of putting the band's logo on the shirt to start with, a limited edition. We have to do things the old school way, none of this X-Factor leap to stardom. We have to do the hard graft, gigging in some real dives, performing in front of a handful of loyal fans, gaining a following before an indie label signs us. Then we get enough attention for the major labels to show an interest in us and then there's the whole big press thing about us selling out, but we manage to stay true to our roots and maintain enough artistic control to still produce quality albums. Or do you want to go the X-Factor route?' Sara explained.

We all agreed that X-Factor was for the Tangos, Sprites, Bombheads, Antoines and Pierres of this world. We wanted to do things the way our stars had done so back in the day.

'I was thinking of a picture of two crumpets with *Grumpy* written on one and *Crumpet* on the other, but the writing bent like a frown, you know what I mean? Sara had given it a lot of thought and given that none of the rest of us had, we all agreed with her, although Jenny made a vain attempt to get the album released before splashing out our meagre funds, for we surely had to be skint if we were going to do this the old school way.

'I like the idea,' Desiree sounded genuine. You could always tell when she was enthusiastic about something, she would lean forward with her elbows on her knees and her hands clasped as if in prayer. 'The only suggestion I have is that we put the crumpets next to each other with a cherry in the middle of each, giving the suggestion of boobs.'

'Whaaat! What are you like, Desiree?' Sara managed to speak over the giggles.

'Well if you've got 'em, flaunt 'em.' Desiree sat back and thrust her chest forward giving it a bit of a wiggle.

'You're incorrigible,' Jenny said, although I think there was a bit of boob envy going on there as Desiree certainly had the biggest pair of the four of us. Not that I'm saying that hers were huge, but they were...oh, stop it Clair. One would think you were obsessed with breasts. They are just appendages designed to make women spend more on underwear than men.

There have been suggestions that your logo has sexual undertones. How do you respond to that?

Desiree Desire: When we designed it, we were talking about the cherry on top and how in life we all love that cherry. It's like a little bonus that you weren't expecting.

Jenny Jangle: Well, I wasn't really thinking too philosophically like the others. I just love cherries, especially the glazed ones like in the picture.

Sara The Bitch: We were more concerned about getting the writing right. The words *Grumpy* and *Crumpets* are meant to look like scowls. Nobody talks about that. All they focus on is the fact that the cherries make the crumpets look like breasts. And as a band we're not like that. We don't use sex to sell our music. We want people to buy our records because it's good music.

Clair da Loon: I hate the logo. I think it looks like a pair of tits.

The voices scare me when they come. Sometimes, when the migraine has subsided, echoes of the voices still linger, and I find myself shaking uncontrollably. My boss never believes me when I say I have a migraine, you can tell by the way he looks at me the next day. I am sure that I would have lost my job by now if I hadn't agreed to 'work late' with him every now and then.

The logo stuff went on for a couple of get togethers. The initial crumpets with cherry nipples was discarded in favour of square writing of the band name with the letters being in golden brown crumpet colours. This was ditched, mainly by Jenny and Desiree who were ganging up on Sara, and an interlinking 'G' above a 'C' was suggested along with the title for the album, *Easy Peasy, We're the GCs* which Jenny came up with. We all loved the album title but were unsure of the logo. In the end we got Jenny, who was the best artist of the four of us to sketch the various options and then, as we were at Sara's place, we got Ollie to give his opinion.

It was not the first time we had consulted with the men. Ian had been asked for his opinion on the title of our Hollywood blockbuster and Geoff had given us input into the company structure of our multinational corporation. I wasn't surprised when Ollie went for the first suggestion, the crumpets that looked like breasts, he was a guy after all.

Sex always leaves me feeling adrift, like flotsam, or is it jetsam, I can never remember which is which. It's jetsam isn't it that is deliberately thrown overboard to lighten the load. You jettison things, so it must be jetsam. Sex always leaves me feeling like jetsam. A discarded something of no value, ejected to make the load lighter.

It was a particularly rough 'working late' session with my boss and I just wanted to feel wanted again. I needed to forget, not just the latest episode, but all those stretching back, every time a man touched me, manhandled me.

Sara said she would love to join me for a drink, but had to take Neil, sorry Sprite, to football. Ian answered when I tried Desiree, so it was no good me even asking and Jenny's phone went to voicemail. I don't like drinking on my own, I am afraid of what might happen if I overdo things. Who will protect me from myself? Who will ensure that I get home safely if I overindulge? I want to overindulge. I want that warm fuzzy comfort of obliterating memories, if only for a short while, just to get me over this one.

The pub was busy, but not busy enough for me to go unnoticed. Why can't a woman have a drink on her own without being constantly bothered? I had barely been served my G&T before a guy came over, obviously being egged on by his mates, and starts trying to chat me up. He's not even good looking but has this swagger as if he believes he is George Clooney or Brad Pitt.

'Buy you a drink, love?' His voice is marginally less ugly than his face.

'No thank you,' I indicate that I already have one and put on my 'go away' face.

'No need to be like that, love. I was just trying to be friendly. Come on, just one drink.'

'No!'

He looks across at his friends then back at me. He cannot back down now, he has to keep face with his mates. Probably there's some money riding on whether he and I walk out of here together or not and this angers me. But he is getting annoyed as well as if I somehow owed it to him to accept his offer.

'Look, darling, it's just a bloody drink,' he puts his rough hand on my forearm.

'Do not touch me,' I hiss.

And he just laughs. Just laughs, like it means nothing.

I have no choice but to throw my drink in his face and storm out. It takes a long time for the shaking to stop.

There is a lot of anger in some of your songs, 'Putty In my Hands' and 'Scratch Your Eyes Out' in particular. Are you angry people generally?

Sara The Bitch: Bitchy, yes, but not angry. Well me anyway.

Desiree Desire: I guess those ones are a bit angry, okay, they are pretty darn angry, but we also do love songs too. 'My Husband, My Friend', which Jenny wrote for example.

Jenny Jangle: We like to cover all sorts of emotions. You know, we're trying to capture all aspects of life. People are complex, not one dimensional. You can't look at our songs in isolation, you have to look at the body of work as a whole.

Clair, you were the one who wrote the songs I mentioned. Were you angry when you wrote them?

Clair da Loon: It was more a metaphorical anger then a real anger that I was trying to capture. A bit like watching the rage in someone else, someone that you are not. It's a bit like venting your anger through the actions of another. You know that you will never actually scratch another person's eyes out, or smash them flat like putty, but the idea of someone doing so is a substitute that calms one's own anger. It's as if the revenge has been meted out without you having to raise a finger.

'Sorry I couldn't meet up with you last week, but you know what it's like being a mother and a taxi.'

No, Sara, I don't know what it's like. I don't have kids or a husband. 'No problems,' I smile.

'Were you going drinking last week? You should have asked me.'

'I rang, but Ian said you were out,' I lied.

'I got your voicemail, but it was too late by the time I did, sorry Sweetie,' Jenny brushes her hair behind her ears.

'That's okay, it wasn't important. I just fancied a drink after work but ended up on the sofa at home with a good bottle of red and watched *Ghost* on TV.' I hate the film *Ghost*.

'Now that's a good night in,' they all agree, and the conversation moved on to Patrick Swayze and how he was better in *Dirty Dancing* and how sad it was that he died so young. No one mentions *Roadhouse*, my favourite Swayze movie, where he ends up ripping the heart out of the baddie's chest.

We're back at Sara's as her foot has healed and the dinner is top notch again. I wish I could cook like her. We don't talk about The Grumpy Crumpets much although there is a little bit of joking about touring the country in a beaten-up van and having our equipment stolen.

Jenny remembers a story that David Bowie told about having to use the washbasin in the dressing room as a loo in some dive venue as there was no toilet. But, as David had gone on to say, if it was good enough for Shirley Bassey, it was good enough for him.

'Well it wouldn't be good enough for me,' Desiree was adamant, and I was with her on that one. The conversation drifted back to having our equipment stolen. You can't be a good band unless someone has nicked a guitar or an amp from the tour van. 'Why is it that no one ever steals the drum kit?' I wanted to ask, but don't.

'It's sad though that a band can't tour these days without having their equipment nicked,' Sara's comment moved the conversation away from The Grumpy Crumpets and on to crime and soon we found ourselves talking about knife crime and how scarily close it had become. It used to happen on the other side of London, but there had been a stabbing near my tube station the other night. I don't like talking about it. The story had scared me as that was the night I had gone drinking on my own. I ended up walking past the tube station to get home and had one of my headaches, so was not as aware of my surroundings as I usually am.

'We could have a stabbing at one of our concerts,' I suggest.

The girls are shocked at the suggestion, but it has the desired effect of moving the conversation away from crime and stabbings and we start talking about the different venues we could play, remembering those from our youth, The Astoria, The Half Moon in Putney, The 100 Club, Water Rats. How many of them still exist? Knife crime was forgotten as a haze of nostalgia descended.

Ollie and I had sex once. It was not long after Jenny called things off with him. I suppose it wasn't really having sex, it was more a case of indecent assault. Jenny and Desiree had left, Julie and Neil were out clubbing, and Sara had been hitting the red wine rather heavily. She kept begging me not to go. She had something to get off her chest. She always drank extra when she wanted to confide in me. She drank too much, then insisted that I stayed when the other two left.

'You're my best friend, Clair. Of all three of you, you're the best.'

I had heard that one a few times, and not just to me. Jenny and Desiree had been her best friend when she wanted to bitch about me. Best friend in Sara's books usually meant anyone who would listen when she wanted to moan.

But this time she had miscalculated and by the time I got back from seeing Jenny and Desiree out, and assuring them I was fine, I could deal with whatever nonsense Sara was going to come up with, she had passed out rather inelegantly. Her skirt, as she slid off the sofa, had hitched up too high and her somewhat flabby legs had ended up lying limply apart. I managed to close them and pull her skirt down just enough to be semi-decent before heading upstairs to find Ollie to help.

He was in his office looking at porn on his computer, so I silently retreated to the stairs and made a second effort, this time making enough noise and giving him time to sort himself out before I got there. I was not sure if he was annoyed that Sara had passed out or if it was having been disturbed in what he was doing, but he was irritable as he came downstairs and grumbled and cursed Sara as we struggled back upstairs with the dead weight of my friend between us.

'Help me get her out of her clothes,' he said after we had unceremoni-ously dumped her on the bed. That was awkward, but we managed to get her down to her knickers then tucked her in.

Ollie then had sex with me in the lounge. It was unexpected and slightly rough. I had been getting my things together to leave when he had grabbed me from behind and the next thing I knew, we were doing it. I was so surprised that initially I forgot to resist and by the time I had thought to do so it was practically too late. This left him thinking that it had been consensual, and, I guess he knew I had seen him looking at porn so assumed I therefore understood. I went home with one of my headaches.

LIVE REVIEW:
THE GRUMPY CRUMPETS @
THE WAYWARD CLUB, LONDON

After creating a name for themselves, playing at various small pubs round the capital, the GCs as they are becoming affectionately known, landed their first gig at a venue of note. The Wayward Club, known for being the springboard from which such acts as The Rolling Stones, Culture Club and Blur launched their careers and where Jackson Browne had his first UK gig, was heaving and the anticipation was palpable. Old rockers and youngsters rubbed shoulders, reflecting the generational appeal of the band. They are mean mothers and winsome wives. The crowd was patient and generous with their appreciation for the support act, The Beatlettes, an all-girl tribute band. But as the time draws near for the GCs to appear, the tension gets cranked up a good few notches and a chant goes up, 'GCs! GCs! GCs!' Pandemonium erupts as the girls strut out on stage. Desiree Desire wears a silky floral summer dress, hardly more than a slip that shimmies over her curvaceous hips as she swishes across to the mike. Jenny Jangle is in her trademark tight blue jeans and 70's chic white shirt and denim jacket. Sara The Bitch has gone for an eighties punk rock look, black lipstick, heavy dark eyeliner, ripped jeans and a string vest over a white t-shirt with 'anarchy' written across it in what has the appearance of blood.

They launch into their first number, 'Putty In My Hands' and the audience responded.

Putting Jackson Browne into the review and the made-up venue name was Jenny's doing. She's always been a fan of Jackson and his ilk. Sara wanted The Stones in there for credibility and although not a fan of Blur – I prefer Damon Albarn's work with Gorillaz more – we had to note the band that he rose to fame with.

I didn't like the review much. It felt too much like a *Times* article rather than something one would have read in the *NME*, but Sara insisted on writing it, we just gave her some input. She printed off copies and presented them to us when we met at Jenny's.

Geoff read it over Jenny's shoulder and chuckled. 'I'm guessing Jenny got you to put Jackson Browne in there?'

She smiled and took his hand in hers, holding it to her cheek, then kissing it fondly. I had noticed that they had been more touchy-feelie since Jenny ended her fling with Ollie.

'You know me too well,' she said, and he gave her a peck on the cheek.

I must have been staring a little too much as, spotting me, she gave a quizzical look that was not the most friendly, a sort of 'what you looking at?' threat contained in it.

I held her glace for a second, then turned and started talking to Desiree, sensing that she had been going through a particularly bad patch with Ian lately. Her smile did not have that same sparkle that it did when things were good.

'How things going?' I asked. That was our code for, 'do you want to meet up and talk about it?'

'Same old same old.' Yes, she did want to chat.

We arranged a coffee for the following morning using our coded talk and when I glanced back at Jenny, she was still giving me a look. Not quite daggers, but certainly it wasn't friendly and I couldn't for the life of me work out why.

'Ollie told Jenny that you came on to him the other night at their place,' Desiree said when we met up for coffee. We had dealt with her troubles and the sparkle had returned to her smile. But she was now quite serious.

'Whaaat?' I was shocked. How dare he.

'She seemed quite pissed off about it too. Almost as if it had been her husband. But you wouldn't do anything like that would you?'

'Why would she say such a thing?' I asked. I wasn't going to let on that it was Ollie who practically raped me.

'Oh, I don't think she was making it up. I am sure that Ollie actually said that. The question is why would he say that?'

I really wanted to blurt out the truth, but it was not fair on Sara.

'Oh, you know what Ollie's like. He's always had the hots for Jenny and she wants none of it. Maybe he thought that if he made out that I found him attractive, then she would too. You know what men are like, always trying to get into our pants. They'll try anything.'

Desiree nodded slowly, but I could tell that she wasn't completely convinced. Not about whether I came on to Ollie or not, my reputation as the goody goody of the group was too strong for her to contemplate that I could ever do such a thing, but rather, she was not sure that my explanation of Ollie's behaviour really held water.

'What state was Ollie in when he told Jenny, do you know?' I tried a different approach.

'How do you mean?'

'Had he been drinking?' the unspoken question in that was, 'had he taken any cocaine?'

'Jenny didn't say, but she did mention that they had been at a pub, so it's possible, I guess.' I could see that Desiree was beginning to accept this as an explanation of Ollie's behaviour and pushed my point home.

'Well there you go, drunken boasting to inflate his ego, that's all. You know that he likes to think he's god's gift to women.'

Desiree was placated, but I wasn't. I was furious with Ollie. How dare he. I could feel one of my headaches coming on, but I fought against it, forcing myself to relax as I had to go back to work and did not fancy having to 'work late' that week.

Ollie's accusation did, however, explain Jenny's angry looks at me. She obviously still had a thing for him even though they were no longer seeing each other. Despite her telling me that she was the one who called it off, she had followed that up with pushing her hair behind her ears with both hands, so a complete lie.

I still could not fathom out what she could possibly see in Ollie when she had someone as nice as Geoff. She was lucky to have him and I had been very good to not let him know about her infidelity. It would not have been difficult to drive that wedge between them and then been there for Geoff when he needed someone. But we were friends, we don't do things like that to each other, do we?

Tell us about your debut album, *Easy Peasy, We're the GCs*.

Desiree Desire: Well, it's due out next week. We've been working on it for about six months. The record company have been very patient. We wanted to get it just right which I think we have manged as we're pleased with the final product.

Sara The Bitch: Yeah, it's got the fan's favourites along with a couple of new tracks that we haven't performed live yet. I think people will enjoy them. 'Scratch Your Eyes Out' is going to be the first single.

Jenny Jangle: I think we've managed to capture the raw energy of our gigs on the record. It was quite difficult at first to translate that same vibe into a studio setting, but Clair and I had a bit of a fall out and that anger infected the others. The beauty of it was we that took all our differences out in the music and we're best friends again, aren't we, Sweetie?'

Clair da Loon: Yeah, best friends.

It was a little far-fetched saying that the record company would be generous with studio time. We were supposed to be a new signing. No record label gives too much latitude to an untested act, but Desiree argued that we had made such an impression with our live shows that people were prepared to take a risk with us.

I also wanted to question having a single out. That doesn't happen anymore, but then I guess we were doing the fantasy the old school way, so an old 7" single made sense. I loved collecting them as a teenager and still have boxes sitting in the attic. Some are probably quite collectable I would guess.

I tried to picture the label we would have. I used to love the old record labels, especially the indie ones, Mute, Cherry Red, One Little Indian, Creation. But my favourite had to be the sophisticated 4AD. The problem was that 4AD had all that ethereal stuff like Cocteau Twins, This Mortal Coil and His Name Is Alive. They even did that Bulgarian choral stuff. From how we had described The Grumpy Crumpets' music – punky and energetic – we would not really have fitted in on the 4AD rota at the time I was thinking of. Maybe later when they started to sign acts like The Pixies and The Throwing Muses, but that was more nineties, we were meant to be an eighties band. We would have been more at home on Beggars Banquet which had acts like Bauhaus, The Lurkers and Gene Loves Jezebel. But hey, this is our imaginary world and we can do what we like, so in my mind The Grumpy Crumpets' debut album was released on the classy 4AD record label. The rest of the girls didn't really care about labels, so long as we were signed. I was the only one to bother about the actual label so never discussed this with them.

Jenny's antagonism towards me over the Ollie incident evaporated with his sudden death. I had to feel sorry for Neil – or Sprite in GC world – as he was the one who found his father. There was a long wait to find out what really happened, but eventually the coroner concluded that his cocaine had been contaminated, causing a massive heart attack.

Poor Sara. Apart from having to deal with sorting out everything that one has to – funeral, wills, death certificates, bank accounts – she also had to allay the suspicions of a particularly nasty cop whose questions more than hinted at the possibility that she was the one who had contaminated the cocaine.

I didn't like the detective and Desiree, Jenny and I rallied round Sara, supplying glowing character references till eventually bad cop gave up and went off in pursuit of real criminals.

The Grumpy Crumpets were put on hold while we all grieved for our band mate's loss. Even Ian seemed to go easy on Desiree, or should I rather say that Desiree showed less signs of being abused. In fact, Ollie's death seemed to bring out a more tender side of Ian. Geoff was very supportive, helping Sara with a lot of the legal and financial stuff that needed doing. It almost appeared that his willingness to help stemmed from a solidarity he felt with Sara as a fellow innocent party in the Jenny/Ollie affair, but I was still convinced that neither he nor Sara had had any inkling of the goings on of their respective spouses.

I had to 'work late' the day after Ollie's funeral to make up for the time I had taken off to attend. I barely made it home that night as the headache that ensued was one of the worst I had ever experienced. It left me completely drained, but I dragged myself to work the next day and forced myself to concentrate as I knew that if I slacked off, I would just have to 'make up the hours'. The talk in the office was all about the vicious stabbing that had occurred near the pub where we sometimes went for drinks after work.

THE LOON RANGER

Clair da Loon, the drummer with The Grumpy Crumpets, has announced that she will be putting out a solo album on 4AD. She has enlisted the help of Nick Cave's Bad Seeds and legendary producer Flood. The album is rumoured to be a dark gothic affair, flavoured with the hard synth sounds of industrial rock. A source close to da Loon has said that her voice could be described as 'poisoned honey' and that the album 'sounded amazing', prompting rumours of the split of The Grumpy Crumpets just as their career was about to take off.

Da Loon insists that this is just a side project and that as soon as Sara The Bitch has recovered from the tragic loss of her husband, the band would put all their efforts into regaining the GCs' momentum. She added that the grief of the loss the whole band felt was what drove her to write the songs which make up, *A Lost Heart*, the album which is due out next week.

I didn't tell the others about my solo side project. I was missing the Grumpy Crumpet talk as that was all put on hold. I was not sure if we would ever resurrect it but had been enjoying the whole music career fantasy too much to just give it up. I now spent my evenings when I was not with the girls or 'working late', developing my solo career as a precaution against The Grumpy Crumpets being completely forgotten.

I had introduced Sara's Julie to Nick Cave's music just before Ollie died and she was now really getting into him which prompted me to listen to his back catalogue again, hence my having the Bad Seeds on my album. I also dug out Depeche Mode's 'Music For The Masses' along with my Nitzer Ebb and Front Line Assembly records which made me want Flood as producer and steered me towards the harder industrial sound.

I started wearing more black and darker eyeliner and make-up. The others seemed to take this as a sign of mourning and in an effort to keep up had followed suite with surprising side effects. A couple of days after Desiree had painted her fingernails black and put on heavy eyeliner and dark crimson lipstick, she confided in me that she thought that her new 'goth' image had been turning Ian on. She was considering dyeing her hair jet black.

Jenny took to wearing tight black denim jeans as opposed to her usual blue ones, but this seemed to have the opposite effect on Geoff as she moaned that ever since Ollie had died, Geoff seemed to spend more time with Sara than he did with her. Of course it wasn't true, but it obviously felt so to her.

It was only Sara who didn't go down the 'black' route. If anything, she seemed to become more colourful in her dress, but her mood for months after was unsurprisingly dark and the flair of her outfits just about managed to neutralise her feelings to the point that the overall effect was bland. The side effect was that she was far less bitchy, but I think that was more from the shock of Ollie's death rather than her choice of clothing and make-up. She had also cut back on her drinking and seldom got even tipsy when we met up. Perhaps she now felt more responsibility for Tango and Sprite as she continued to call them.

The cop who had harboured suspicions about Sara made the news about a month after Ollie's funeral. He was found stabbed with a large quantity of cocaine on him.

My solo album was well received by the fans. They all saw it as a stop gap, something to tide them over till we could get The Grumpy Crumpets back on track. That is the joy of imaginary fans, they are as fickle or not as you want them to be.

A Lost Heart scraped the lower positions of the Top 100 albums chart and reached number 4 on the Indie charts. I debated about sending it to the top of the indie charts, but felt that would be upstaging The Crumpets, but more importantly, I did not feel that the thrill of success was quite as much fun when you couldn't share it with your friends.

I started to imagine what it would be like discussing our indie number one hit with the rest of the band and the fun we would have giggling about this highly improbable thing happening, but I knew it would have to wait. Sara needed time to get over Ollie.

THE GRUMPY CRUMPETS TO RE-UNITE!

All girl punk-rock band, The Grumpy Crumpets, have announced that they are ready to resume their career together. A spokesperson for the band has said that, following a six-month hiatus to mourn the death of the husband of bassist Sara The Bitch, the group were ready to pick up where they left off.

Their debut album, *Easy Peasy We're The GCs*, was pulled just before it was about to be released as the band felt that they were unable to promote it while they dealt with their loss. This will now come out next Monday and the band will be playing a free gig at the HMV Megastore in Oxford Street to promote the record.

'It's been a difficult time,' Jenny Jangle, the band's lead guitarist said, 'but we are stronger for it. Sara has been through hell, but she is ready to resume playing and we are quite excited about going on stage again.'

Questions have been asked whether the band's fan base, which had been growing steadily before the tragedy, would still be loyal, but Fleur Flowers, the secretary of the band's Fanclub, thinks otherwise.

'There is a lot of excitement about The Crumpets getting back on track and especially about *Easy Peasy* finally being released. There have been some bootlegs of their gigs doing the rounds and some silly money being paid for these. But the true fans are dying to get their hands on the album. We're all going to be at HMV on Monday.'

At a short press conference, the band expressed their gratitude to their fans for sticking by them. 'We have the best fans in the world,' lead singer Desiree Desire said, 'They have stood by us through thick and thin. We are going to go out there on Monday and give them something special.'

The funk that Sara fell into after Ollie's death seemed to melt away overnight about six months after the tragedy. We had continued to meet up for our girls' nights, but they had become sombre affairs, often spent giving Sara pep talks about how everything would be all right. Ollie had left her well provided for financially, she had two lovely kids and she needed to be there for them as much as they were there for her.

Ollie's work colleagues saw him as a victim. There were no judgemental comments about his drug use, probably because they were all taking something themselves. Sara did find the tennis club crowd she saw on Thursdays initially a bit off-ish with overheard whispers of, 'How could she not know that her husband took drugs.' Jenny, who also went to the club, brought the group round. She knew a thing or two about the habits of most of the husbands and dropped heavy hints about revealing them which eventually shut everyone up. She had gained her knowledge by sleeping with most of the husbands, I presumed.

We were all quite delighted when Sara invited us to hers for the girls' night. We had been going to Desiree's or Jenny's and occasionally mine in the interim, not wanting to burden Sara with having to cook and she had been happy to accept that. Now we all looked forward to enjoying Sara's culinary skills again.

'You guys have done a good job of the cooking,' Jenny had said, brushing her hair behind her ears, 'but you have to admit that Sara is still the best.' Sometimes Jenny's hair brushing was just to stop her hair tickling her ears. It was not always easy to know if it was her 'lying tell' or not, but I think this time it was just a comfort thing.

Our happiness at enjoying Sara's good cooking turned to delight when, after diner, as we sat around a bottle of red feeling mellow, Sara said, 'Remind me, did we ever release our album?'

It was that simple and the game was back on. We worked through the details of our re-launched career with Sara insisting that Fleur, Ollie's sister who had been a great help and support recently, got a look in. Translating her unusual first name into English made her Fleur Flowers, a much cooler nom de plume than her rather boring married name of Fleur Smith. Despite Fleur being there for Sara, there was no question of her joining the band.

'She's lovely,' Sara said, 'but she's got no imagination. She'd never understand what we do. She's too real-world rooted.'

It was a good evening despite Sara drinking a little too much and getting a bit teary. We were back on track and not only that, we were doing a gig at the big HMV on Oxford Street. I had spent hours in that great establishment during my teens and seen a number of album launch sets from famous acts there. I must admit that I cried a little bit when I heard that it was closing down, I mean it had been heaven to any music lover, that and the little specialist record shops down Berwick Street. It had taken a bit of persuading for the rest of the band to agree to the HMV gig. None of them felt as nostalgic about the place as I did. They were all for a private party at the offices of the record label with a few journos and some music world celebs.

'A Whammy George Michel could attend as a fan of this upcoming band,' Sara suggested.

'Or a Spandau-ey Tony Hadley,' Jenny said.

'What about a Duranny Simon le Bon,' Desiree added.

And they called themselves punk rockers. Despite all being into bands like The Clash, The Stranglers and The Skids when we were together at uni, I could not believe that they all resorted to the pin-up poster boys of our era when considering which celebs would attend the album launch.

'What about a Jammy Paul Weller?' I said trying to restore some dignity to the fantasy. 'I once saw him do a gig at HMV in Oxford Street. He played a few songs, then signed copies of his new CD. The crowd was massive, sprawling out onto the street. It was so cool.'

I don't often put my foot down with the girls, but doing HMV was one detail I felt most passionate about and argued my case.

Eventually they capitulated, and we had our venue.

It was around that time that I had my first episode of the nightmares. A vivid dream of being attacked by an unseen assailant came visiting one night. Strong arms held me from behind while I felt the sharp prick of a knife blade at my throat. I wanted to kick out and scream for help, but fear prevented me from doing either. So I stood paralysed, waiting for the knife to slice my soft skin.

I woke in a cold sweat and struggled to go back to sleep. The next night it happened again, the details exactly the same, the roughness of the hands, the faint whiff of gin and tonic and dismissive laugh of my attacker all creepily sticking to a detailed script.

For a full week this dream returned every night and each time I would wake up with a start just as the cold sharpness of the blade began to cut into me.

I was left exhausted but managed to drag myself into work. It didn't help that my tiredness and mental state meant that I could not concentrate properly so mistakes crept into my work and mistakes led to 'working late' and 'working late', I'm sure, fuelled the dreams.

'You look dreadful,' Desiree said when I met her for a quick lunch about a week after the dreams started, 'you okay?'

'I'm fine, just been hectic at work,' I lied. I didn't fancy sharing my problems with my friends. It was almost as if the attacker in my dreams had this unspoken threat that if I told anyone I would not wake up in time when he next visited. But I needed to do something. I could not continue like this. The vicious cycle of nightmare, mistakes, 'working late', nightmare was obviously beginning to tell.

I resolved to sleep on my couch that evening, thinking that a change of scenery may also change my dreams. It didn't help that there was a leery guy sitting opposite me on the tube as I was heading home from work, late again. He was trying to undress me with his eyes and when I pulled my coat tighter, he gave me an angry look as if to say, 'how dare you spoil my fun'. I tensed up when he got off at my stop but breathed a sigh of relief when he headed off in the opposite direction.

There was a lot of blood in my dream that night, but it was not mine. It seemed to flow from behind me as I stood waiting for my attacker to come. I did not feel the rough hands or the sharp blade, just a warm sticky sensation as the blood flowed over my feet and between my toes. I woke as daylight started to crawl through the curtains, feeling refreshed, although this didn't stop me carefully washing my feet in the shower. I didn't have to 'work late' that evening.

CRUMPET ALBUM LAUNCH MARRED BY VIOLENCE

Violence erupted at The Grumpy Crumpets' album launch at the HMV flagship store in Oxford Street today. The upcoming band attracted a large crowd and, as the gig got underway, the police became aware of a scuffle in the crowd. Officers quickly made their way to the area of unrest and calmed things down, but not before one fan had been stabbed.

The fan, who has been identified as Guy Dunne (45), is in a critical conditional at St Mary's Hospital, suffering from multiple stab wounds and loss of blood. A police spokesman has said that Mr Dunne was lucky to have survived and praised the efforts of an off-duty paramedic who was at the gig and who probably saved Dunne's life.

No arrests have been made and the police are following up on some leads.

A spokesperson for The Grumpy Crumpets said that the band are horrified at the incident. 'We wanted people to enjoy the gig and to enjoy our album. Our hearts go out to Mr Dunne and his family. We hope that he pulls through.'

They also urged fans who have any information about the stabbing to come forward to the police.

'People should feel safe coming to our gigs. This is clearly the work of one bad individual. Our fans are good people just out to enjoy themselves. A gig should not end in tragedy like this.'

The band had been unaware of the incident and continued to play to an otherwise receptive audience.

Mr Dunne has a wife and two young daughters who have been at his bedside since he was admitted to hospital.

The others wouldn't be happy with that story, so it was one that only happened in my head. I suppose it was a bit of payback to my boss, Guy Dunne, for making me work late. I do wonder if his wife and daughters would stand by him in a moment of crisis if they knew what he got up to after hours.

Running through the stabbing scenario somehow made coping with 'working late' easier. As I was helpless to do anything to my boss in my real life, at least I could take it out on him in my fantasies. I could not, of course, bring this up with The Grumpy Crumpets. They would not understand. Their version of the launch gig would be very different.

THE CRUMPETS WOW HMV

HMV in Oxford Street was heaving as The Grumpy Crumpets took to the small stage in the store today to launch their debut album, *Easy Peasy We're The GCs*. Every aisle was packed with fans craning their necks to get a glimpse of the Glam Four.

Desiree, Jenny, Sara and Clair wowed the audience with their tight playing, belting out crowd favourites 'Putty In My Hands' and 'Scream Till You Bleed' before slowing things down with 'My Husband My Friend'. They ended the short set with the catty 'Scratch Your Eyes Out'.

The crowd were euphoric and copies of the album flew off the shelves while fans queued for nearly two hours for autographs.

This was a notable launch for a band who are just beginning to unlock their potential. Expect to see them on the album charts at the end of the week.

This was the launch gig that the girls went for and I guess it was the better version. Despite my unshared version helping me get my revenge on my creepy boss, I had to admit that a stabbing at a Grumpy Crumpet gig would seriously damage our prospects and I didn't want that. Besides there had been another stabbing in the neighbourhood not too far from the tube station again and bringing a similar violent death into The Grumpy Crumpet fantasy would have been in poor taste just then.

I was in a better frame of mind that evening at Jenny's when we came up with the HMV gig details. The nightmares had ceased, I hadn't had a migraine in a while and had not been required to 'work late' for a bit as my boss was away on leave. The evening was, however, spoilt by Sara overdoing it on the red wine, something she had not done since Ollie's death, and then she started on Jenny.

'You never did like Ollie, did you?' she slurred.

'What are you talking about?' Jenny had also had a fair amount to drink. 'Of course I liked him.'

'No you didn't. I could tell by the way you spoke to him. You had something against him, but he was a good man, my Ollie, he was a good man.' Sara was starting to get weepy now.

I glanced at Desiree, but she was looking as helpless as I was feeling. We would just have to let this one play itself out and then try and pick up the pieces later.

'You're drunk, Sara. You know that Ollie and I got on well. I never had any problems with him.' Jenny pushed her hair behind her ears with some force. It had obviously been Ollie who broke off their relationship and Sara was half right. Jenny had like Ollie, liked him too much. It was only after the affair that things changed so the 'never' in the accusation 'you never did like my Ollie' was not, strictly speaking, correct.

'I am not drunk,' Sara insisted and took another large slug, as if this would prove her contention. 'See,' she said, holding the wine glass up like an Olympic torch, 'not drunk.' She swayed slightly as she sat trying to keep her back straight and her dignity intact.

'Why did you hate Ollie? He did nothing to deserve that,' she was near to full on tears now, but Jenny was a little too far over the limit to see Sara's outburst for what it was and geared up to defend herself, anger flaring in her eyes.

'Okay, enough of this, enough!' Desiree intervened and indicated to me with an incline of her head to deal with Sara while she would handle Jenny. I was not really in the mood to put up with this nonsense from either of them, but one on their own would be better than having to cope with a full-blown screaming match so I moved over to Sara while Desiree ushered a protesting Jenny into the kitchen. This was the usual tactic when two of us started on each other. The other two would separate them. If one was the host, they went to the kitchen while the other was taken home. If the two were both guests, the one left in the lounge would be taken home first and once they had left, the other would be transported off.

But Sara was having none of it this time. Just as I got near her she launched herself at Jenny who was being physically dragged away by Desiree.

I had to piece together what happened next from what others told me because in launching herself at Jenny, Sara knocked me over and I hit my head on the corner of the coffee table and was knocked out cold. In the scuffle that ensued, no one noticed that I had not got up from my fall.

According to Desiree there was a lot of screaming as Sara tried to scratch Jenny's eyes out while Jenny was trying to throw punches, one of which ended up giving Desiree a black eye. The two combatants then engaged in a tussle which had them rolling on the floor.

Jenny's daughter Tracey, or Bombhead if you are in Grumpy Crumpet mode, arrived back from a date at that moment and between her, her boyfriend and Geoff who had come downstairs to investigate what all the screaming was about, they managed to separate the two.

'It was only then that we saw that you were out cold,' Bombhead told me later.

Poor Jenny. She ended up having to replace her carpet what with Sara's spilt wine and the blood coming from my head wound. All I remember was briefly waking up in Geoff's arms as he picked me up to put me on the sofa while we waited for the ambulance to come. I remember feeling safe in his arms.

DROPPED CRUMPET LANDS BUTTER SIDE UP

Grumpy Crumpet, Clair da Loon, had a narrow escape when she was dropped during a crowd surfing incident at a recent gig. The 45-year-old drummer had dived into the crowd at the end of the show but ended up hitting the ground head first as a surge amongst the fans caught a few off balance and unable to properly support the diving star.

'We tried to hold her up, but the crowd was pushing us, and we just couldn't,' Amanda and Leigh, fans of the band who had come down from Leeds to see the show, said. 'We were like, oh my god, because we thought she might be dead, there was so much blood.'

Staff from the venue were quick to react and managed to clear a space around the fallen Crumpet so that she could get medical attention. Da Loon suffered a nasty head wound, some bruising and a mild concussion, but miraculously no major damage was done.

'I guess you could say that I landed butter side up,' she laughed from her hospital bed the next morning. The doctors

kept her in for two days for observation before discharging
her.

It was a very sheepish Jenny and Sara who greeted me at Sara's a week
later. I had spent a couple of days in hospital as they stitched me up and
did some tests, but eventually I was given a clean bill of health and sent
home to nurse a very bad headache.

Desiree and her black eye came around a couple of times, once with
Ian, to check on me. She told me that Jenny and Sara had made up the
following day, both consumed with guilt at what had happened to me,
but neither had plucked up the courage to face me in person.

The knock, the headaches and the pills they gave me, conspired to
create some pretty horrific dreams, most involving my father strangely.
It had been a long time since I had last thought of him. The dreams were
not kind to him as they tortured him in all kinds of ways, both physical
as well as mental, his limbs were contorted at strange angles while his
face twisted up in fear and pain as it bobbed in and out of focus.

The dreams left me disturbed, or was it the pills? Perhaps it was that
soon after getting home Clair de Lune came on the radio, dad's favourite
piece of music and the one I had used for my Grumpy Crumpet nom de
plume. It brought back the memories I knew had caused my mind to
punish my dad like that. The dreams of dad didn't last too long but the
headaches did. The doctors told me to expect them to continue for a bit
and that I should take things easy.

My boss accepted the news that I would be off for a while with a sullen
silence, followed by a 'well just make sure you're back on Monday'. I
hoped my headaches would disappear by the time I had to go back to
work as the 'overtime' I knew I was going to have to do would not be
pleasant if I still had a pounding head.

The week off did, however, give me some time to think about the spat
between Sara and Jenny. Had Sara somehow found out about Jenny's
affair with Ollie? The passion and rage in Sara had been like nothing we
had seen from her before and that was the only conclusion I could come
to, although the fact that they seemed to have made up all too quickly did
not rest well with this explanation.

Things became clearer later when Sara came round to mine a few days
after our first get together as a group following the incident. She fussed
over me, constantly asking if I was all right and insisting on making me

dinner. It had been a long day at work, so I was glad that I didn't have to cook. After dinner, she became serious.

'I don't know why I went at Jenny like that the other week. I really don't know what came over me. I know I had had a bit too much wine, but that shouldn't have caused such an outburst,' she said, studying her teacup. 'I had been thinking a lot about Ollie that day and was really missing him. But it wasn't that either.'

She paused, unsure whether to go on or not. I waited, knowing that she would continue when she was ready.

'I had been thinking about…well about what I did at uni, you know, the abortion.' She said the word as if it were some sort of poison, something that one had to jump back from. She looked up at me, checking my reaction, possibly double checking her memory that she had already told me about the abortion.

I nodded slowly and leaned forward, taking her hands in mine, as I had done when she had first told me about it.

'I never told you who the father was, did I?' It was rhetorical, but I shook my head anyway, suddenly burning with curiosity, but making sure my outward appearance said, 'you don't have to if you don't want to.'

'Well I guess that's what triggered it all because it was Jenny who introduced me to him. I was feeling guilty about it. I was already going out with Ollie at that time and I guess I blamed Jenny for causing me to be unfaithful to Ollie. Do you think the dead know all our secrets?'

I shrugged, a momentary panic running through me at what the dead may know. 'I don't know. They're dead aren't they? Does it matter what they know?' I replied more for my own comfort than for Sara's, but she relaxed a little at my response.

'I suppose you're right,' she sighed, then went on, 'Well you remember how it was at uni, really discovering oneself and enjoying the freedom of being away from home?'

I wasn't sure what she was talking about, and it must have shown as she burst out, 'The sex! You remember, the sex. Sleeping around, being with different guys. Come on Clair, don't tell me you've forgotten all that!'

It's difficult to remember something that never happened, but I nodded. 'Oh that. Yes, of course I remember.' I remembered it happening to others, so I wasn't lying, but Sara didn't pick up on the subtle difference.

'Well the guy Jenny introduced me to was Geoff.' She paused for effect then went on quickly, 'this was about a month before they started going out.'

EASY PEASY WE'RE THE GC'S – TRACK BY TRACK

1. *Scratch Your Eyes Out:* The opening track and a firm favourite of the fans. The song is an angry, thrashy punk number that sees Desiree Desire's venomous delivery pitted against Jenny Jangle's vicious guitars, Sara The Bitch's thudding bass and a barrage of drums from Clair da Loon. It's a song about betrayal, hurt and revenge. Jangle's arrangement perfectly accompanies da Loon's vitriolic lyrics. Hell hath no fury.

2. *Shout! Don't Shout!:* After the dramatic thrash of the opening track, the girls settle into a rockabilly groove that'll have you tapping your feet to the beat. They bring a modern glitz to the retro-sound, at times veering into semi glam-rock territory. The Bitch supplied the lyrics which on the face of it are about having fun but could easily be a call to primal scream therapy.

3. *Putty In My Hands:* Scheduled to be the second single after 'Scratch Your Eyes Out', this is another fan favourite with its 'girl power' message wrapped in a poppy punk sound a-la The Go-Gos. Words are once again by da Loon and Jangle has created the perfect accompaniment that weaves a spell over the listener, making them…well, the clue's in the title.

4. *Down And Dirty:* Another one that does exactly what it says on the tin. Prince would have been proud of the lyrics which Jangle supplies, and which bring a strange kind of respectability to promiscuity. '*I love you and what you do/It touches me deep inside/I love the next one too, what they do/When my love for you has died*'. Heavy breathing accompanies a funky strut beat. This one will have a few adolescent boys in turmoil. Whoever said that older women can't be sexy.

5. *My Husband, My Friend:* Written before the tragic death of Sara The Bitch's husband, this song takes on a new meaning. It is the album's only straight up love songs and it's a stonker. Coming straight after the infidelity of 'Down And Dirty', it is a heartfelt song of devotion. Desire's ethereal vocal delivery

brings a gentleness to the track which evokes memories of the film 'Ghost' where love conquers death.

6. *Don't Stop Loving Me For My Body Because My Mind Is Too Tired:* Jangle again supplies the lyrics for another sex-laden song. However, the funky strut of 'Down And Dirty' is replaced by the more punk oriented sound that The Crumpets have built their following around. Desire's girly vocals bring an innocence that is directly juxtaposed to the almost graphic lyrics and makes for a forbidden fruit feel to the track.

7. *A Dagger In Your Heart And A Knife In My Back:* The Crumpets delve further into the theme of betrayal in this thrashy number. Jangle's frenetic guitar is in a race with Sara The Bitch's bass on this track which clocks in at just under two minutes. But it is a two minute sprint from the first note to the last. The words supplied by da Loon are angry and vengeful. *'You put a knife in my back so I stuck a dagger in your heart'* is the chanted chorus. My advice is don't ever cross a Crumpet.

8. *Quiet Time:* Ironically this is probably the noisiest track on the album. The mad drumming teeters on the chaotic, the guitar screeches a semitone below irritating while Desire, who supplied the lyrics, implores us in a growl that can't quite make up its mind if it is a sexy purr or a whiney whinge, to give her a little quiet time. The song lives on the edge, but never quite takes you over it. It has a car crash fascination to it. You can't bear to listen to it but can't help wanting to hear it again.

9. *Your Kisses Hurt:* There is something a little disturbing about this one as Desire's lyrics work on two levels. It's either a song about the aching desires of those madly in love, or it's about the violence of an abusive relationship. The gloomy, somewhat menacing gothic verse suggests the latter while the jangly upbeat chorus tends towards the former, leaving the listener deliciously confused.

10. *I Know Who'll Be Next:* Fans of Rodriguez's 'Cold Fact' will know the line in his song, 'I Wonder' which asks how many times one's had sex and if you know who'll be next. Well The Crumpets are not going to die wondering. They have their sights clearly on their next conquest, but in true Crumpet style,

you are not sure if he who is next is a willing partner or a victim. The answer perhaps comes in the last seconds of the album when the music stops with a dramatic beat, there is a pause for breath, then Desire's echoey voice intones, 'I know who's next and he'd better watch out'.

I must have been unable to hide the anger I felt at Sara's bombshell. She presumed it was because of Geoff's infidelity to Jenny and quickly reiterated that it happened before Geoff and Jenny became serious.

'They weren't seeing each other at that point, Clair. They had just met, and Jenny never said anything about being interested in him. You know what she's like, she would always let you know as soon as she had her eye on a guy. She always gave you the 'hands off' notice. But she had said nothing at that point. It was only a few weeks later that she sent out that message about Geoff. Anyway, it was nothing serious between me and him. We only did it that one time. I was a bit drunk and to be honest if I had been sober, I probably would have said no to his advances. It was just that one time and just my rotten luck that I ended up pregnant. I was usually so careful on that front, but my guard was down that day. I would never have done it if I had known that he and Jenny were together, you know me.'

It was not Geoff cheating on Jenny that had caused my anger, it was the fact that a month before he started going out with Jenny, I had been dating Geoff. Sara, in her usual self-absorbed way, had not even noticed that. Her only concern had been about Jenny. I felt as if the air had been sucked out of my lungs and I was gasping for breath as the pain of Sara's confession hit home. I struggled against it, not wanting to show my feelings. I have been pretty good at not letting on what is happening in my mind and quickly wrapped up the emotions that had ambushed me, neatly putting them away until I was on my own and could take them out and study them properly.

'Does Geoff know about it, I mean the abortion?' I needed to move the conversation on in order to protect myself.

'Whaaat? Oh god no. And he must never find out. Never. Promise me that you'll never tell, promise me.' Suddenly Sara was regretting having shared her secret with me, but I quickly consoled her.

'Of course not. You know me.' I was good at keeping my word and Sara knew that. All the girls knew that. This was how I knew so much about them all, they had the courage to confide things in me that they wouldn't with the others. She relaxed visibly as I reminded her of my discretion.

She smiled. 'Yes, I know I can trust you.'

I smiled back. 'Just please don't take it out on Jenny. I know it still upsets you after all these years, but it wasn't her fault. I want you two to be friends.'

This moved the conversation away from Geoff's infidelity and Sara and I were soon reminiscing about the good times we had had at uni and how she and Jenny had been such good friends.

'Any idea how I can fix things properly with Jenny?' Sara eventually asked, 'We've sort of made up, but things are not quite right between us, not what they used to be.

'I'll see what I can do,' I said.

HOW HAS THE SUCCESS OF *EASY PEASY WE'RE THE GCs* AFFECTED YOU?

Sara The Bitch: At first we struggled with the attention we were getting, you know, being recognised in the street or pub. It's a funny feeling really. It did cause some problems initially. Being lead singer, Desiree gets most of the attention. She's also the most attractive of us and it's not only the men who she gets a lot of attention from, but also some of the women.

Desiree Desire: I'm not sure about being the most attractive, personally I think Jenny's the sexiest of the four of us and she gets her fair share of attention from the men. I think that it's more about being the lead singer than being the lead guitarist which means I get the most attention. They're always the two most recognisable members of any band aren't they? I mean take The Stones for example. Mick Jagger and Keith Richards. You'd know them anywhere. But I would probably walk right past Charlie Watts in the street and not know. Morrissey and Johnny Marr of The Smiths, know them, but can't even remember the names of the other two. And no one remembers the drummers, do they?

Jenny Jangle: Except Phil Collins.

Clair da Loon: And Stewart Copeland of The Police. I had a huge thing for him back in the day. Cuter than Sting. Do you think we could get him to guest on our next album?

Sara The Bitch: Mike Joyce, wasn't he one of the other Smiths? And the other guy was Andy Rourke, wasn't he?

Desiree Desire: Show off.

Our next get together was at Desiree's. Ian was out of town on business for a week, so she was relaxed and her two boys, Ant and Peter – sorry Antoine and Pierre – joined us for dinner. They were both quite subdued boys. Ant was home from uni for the holidays while Peter was just finishing school. They would answer questions politely, but never really contributed to the conversation. I couldn't help wondering how much their withdrawn natures were a result of Ian's treatment of them. As with Desiree, there were no outward physical signs of abuse and I had never witnessed any mental abuse, but there was something there, one could sense it.

The boys disappeared quickly after dinner, Ant headed out to 'meet with friends', but he, like Jenny, would never make a good poker player. His 'tell' was a shifty look to his right. Peter skulked off to his room with a mumbled, 'enjoy your evening'.

'I can't believe how big your boys have got,' Jenny said after the two had left.

Desiree nodded, but didn't seem to want to take the conversation any further. Most mothers are always proud to talk about their kids, even comments on how big they've got engenders some sort of an acknowledgement, but Desiree clearly didn't want to talk about them. I got the sense that it was not because she wasn't proud of them, but rather it was a sort of protective measure. If Ian started hearing that the boys had got big, he may feel threatened. Silly, I know, but that was the feeling I got and it saddened me. Neither Sara nor Jenny seemed to pick up on this.

Desiree had done well on the dinner front, but her speciality was her choice of wine. For some reason she had a nose for a good vintage although she swore blind that she just grabbed the ones where she liked the labels. She is either a pretty good liar or always tells the truth as I have never been able to catch her out, a skill probably learned from years of living with Ian.

Sara took it slowly with the wine, her recent outburst had once again made her realise how easily she could turn into Superbitch in a matter of glasses and Desiree's black eye and my concussion must have still been playing on her mind despite the physical manifestations of our injuries having all but disappeared.

'I was thinking,' Sara said, after our usual session of moaning about life was starting to wind up, 'Are we really grumpy? I mean we moan a bit, but by and large, aren't we happy? We have good friends, lovely children and, well, you two,' she indicated Jenny and Desiree, 'have great loving husbands. And Clair, you seem happy being single. So, should we be calling ourselves The Grumpy Crumpets. Shouldn't we call ourselves The Happy Crumpets or at a bare minimum The Contented Crumpets?'

Well, this certainly kicked off the debate. It first revolved around simple brand awareness. We had created The Grumpy Crumpets name and people were beginning to take notice of us, albeit only in our fantasy world. To change our name now, just as we were beginning to be noticed would be committing 'careericide'. I came up with that term and was rather proud of it even if the others gave me a weird look.

'But we could say that an established American group called The Grumpy Pancakes were threatening legal action and we were forced to change our name,' Sara counteracted.

'I don't want to be forced to change our name because of some dumb American band,' Jenny retorted, 'besides, Grumpy Crumpets has a ring to it that Happy or Contented Crumpets doesn't. Anyway, if we were to change our name to either of the ones you suggest, we would have to change our music style, wouldn't we? And all our songs.'

'What makes you say that?' Desiree, who had not really been paying attention, asked.

'Well, you couldn't have a song called 'Scratch Your Eyes Out' by The Happy Crumpets, now could you? It just doesn't fit.'

Sara wanted to argue against that, but she was struggling to come up with something, leaving her frustrated and, dare I say it, grumpy. Jenny looked smug, which was probably not a good idea given Sara's recent penchant for violence. But Sara had learnt her lesson and remained calm, so I ventured into the conversation.

'Well, Sara looks a bit grumpy now,' I said, a little nervous of the reaction the comment could provoke.

CRUMPETS TO TOUR

The Grumpy Crumpets have announced a nationwide tour to promote their debut album, *Easy Peasy We're The GCs*. They kick off at King Tut's Wah Wah Hut in Glasgow and will work their way down the country, playing in major towns and cities, including Manchester, Blackpool, Nottingham, Birmingham,

Derby and Cambridge. They will also, rather obscurely, be playing at a festival in the little town of Crowland.

'It's where my husband, Ollie, came from and the gig is in memory of him,' the band's bassist, Sara The Bitch, explained. The tour is expected to last 2 months.

We didn't meet up as a foursome for the next two months as Jenny had to go to Glasgow for work, Desiree and Ian and the boys went off to Blackpool for their annual holiday, I had to go to Cambridge with my boss for work, to 'look after' him, and Sara went to the little town of Crowland to visit Ollie's parents for a couple of weeks. None of those trips coincided so we were always at least one short of a quartet on our usual meet up nights. That didn't stop us meeting up as a trio or duo, but it seemed unfair to talk Grumpy Crumpets when one of our number was not there. So while our fantasy selves were living the high life on a nationwide tour, taking drugs and having wild parties, smashing up hotels and such like, the reality was that those of us who did meet sat around moaning about the state of the world, the youth of today and what pigs men could be. I found myself envying our fantasy alter egos as all the moaning and grumpiness was boring. I started to plot our progress through the country on a map that I stuck up in my spare bedroom, eagerly awaiting the end of the tour and the grand homecoming gig in London.

I wasn't sure if the others would want to start the tour again when we were all back together, or whether we would move on and just sort out the details of tour by way of memories rather than living it in real time so to speak.

But I missed having the whole gang together. It was not the same following our progress without them. I had a lot of headaches during that time, the worst being just after I got back from Cambridge. It didn't help that my boss' wife came into the office on our first day back and gave me some really dirty looks as if she thought I had been seducing her husband. The headaches brought dreams of my father again, nasty disturbing dreams that had me waking up in a hot sticky sweat that felt like blood. I would spend an age in the shower trying to wash it off as it seemed to cling to my skin.

When I was not escaping into The Grumpy Crumpet nationwide tour, or trying to wash the bloody sweat off me, I found myself fixating on Geoff and how he cheated on me way back in our uni days. Sara's aborted foetus sneaked into my dreams, taunting me like a nasty little Chucky, you know, that scary doll from the horror movie.

It wasn't easy shifting the dreams from my waking thoughts, but I would force myself to do so while at work as lack of concentration led to mistakes and mistakes led to 'working late' and 'working late' led to more dreams and migraines.

I told Jenny about my boss' wife and the looks she had given me. She just laughed and said, 'Well, are you sleeping with him?'

'Of course not,' I retorted. He was the one sleeping with me, but I couldn't say that.

'Why not?' Jenny asked, 'He's kinda cute. I'd sleep with him if I had the chance.'

Well, that was Jenny for you. She'd sleep with anyone given half a chance. She had briefly met my boss once when he had taken me to lunch and she had been in the same restaurant, after which she had asked me all about him, making it clear that she thought he was good looking. I couldn't see what she saw in him and I wasn't going to feed her promiscuity by arranging for her to meet him as she had repeatedly asked me to do for a couple of weeks after she first saw him. Back then it was partly for Geoff's sake that I kept her from my boss. I used to feel sorry for Geoff.

There were more stabbings in the area, three in the week that I got back from Cambridge. I was sure that this was not helping me with my dreams as if the blood from the stabbings was seeping into them. Things were quite tense by the end of the week and the police had upped their presence. 'Working late' didn't help as I would arrive back at my tube stop after dark and have a nerve-racking walk home. Even the police presence didn't help my nerves as I had a nasty feeling that it was actually one of them who was the psychopath.

THE CRUMPETS ROCK THE HUT

The Grumpy Crumpets kicked off their nationwide tour with a scorching gig at King Tut's Wah Wah Hut in Galsgow, putting paid to any thoughts that the band's fan base was limited to London. The gig, which sold out within hours of the tickets going on sale, was one of the most eagerly anticipated that Glasgow has seen in a while. Touts did a roaring trade with some tickets changing hands at...

'What do you reckon, are we using current prices, or prices back in the eighties?' Jenny asked.

'Surely eighties prices,' Sara said.

'But isn't all this supposed to be happening in the present? We should use current prices,' Desiree waded into the debate and it wasn't long before she had persuaded us.

'What then? £100? Is that too much for a small gig these days?'

'I don't know. I reckon the face value of the tickets would be around £25 to £40, so £100 would probably sound about right, not too excessive.

'£100 to £150?'

'£150 sound too excessive.'

> ... with tickets changing hands at around £100. Plenty of disappointed fans had to be turned away.
>
> After a blistering set, during which The Crumpets played every track from the album as well as a new song called, 'Can't Run Away From Myself', Desiree Desire yelled, 'We love ya Glasgow, do you want us to come back?' The answer was a resounding yes.

I was quite happy that the girls wanted to go through the tour blow by blow. It was going to be a completely different tour to the one I had imagined. For a start, my version of the Wah Wah Hut gig had been that it was a relatively low-key event, tickets selling well, but with a few still available on the door. My tour had built up our following as news spread about how good our gigs were, and it was only as we headed south that we saw more sell out shows and disappointed fans having to be turned away. I didn't have the overpriced tout tickets, even at the London gig which, in my mind, we had overcome by adding an extra two dates as soon as we realised that we would quite easily sell out due to demand.

Still, I went along with the girl's version even though I thought they were peaking too soon.

Sara had calmed down a bit. Her confession about Geoff seeming to have done her the world of good. I half thought about starting another fantasy thread, one where the Catholic Church allowed women priests and I became known for my hearing of confessions. People would come from all over the world just to tell me their deepest darkest secrets because I had the power to make them feel truly forgiven in a way no other priest could. I would hear all sorts of secrets, stories of sexual escapades, infidelity and such like. People would tell me about crimes they had committed and times they had overeaten, describing in detail the type of food they had binged on. Drug users and alcoholics would admit their addictions. My favourite would be the child molesters. Not because of what they did, that sort of behaviour appals me, but it would be the fact that after their confession, they would be cured of wanting to commit such atrocities. In the end though, I decided not to go with that fantasy. I think I was worried about what my real self may confess to my fantasy self.

I was pleased though that I had helped Sara get that secret off her chest. I can never begin to imagine the feelings she would have had regarding the abortion. I remember when she first told me she was pregnant and that she was going to abort. I was really shocked. But back then it was a much bigger deal than it is now, and we had to find some seedy back street place to arrange it. Sara was not in a good way afterwards and for about a week she feigned a bad flu while she recovered. For the next few months she really wasn't herself. The others kept asking me if she was all right. I would reassure them and say that she was struggling with her studies, but that she'd be okay.

I smiled at her now as I watched the relaxed way in which she added to The Grumpy Crumpet fantasy. We did two gigs that evening – The Wah Wah Hut one, then moved on to Sneaky Pete's in Edinburgh. I had never been to Glasgow but did visit Edinburgh once as a young child. It was when my mum was in the hospital for a week and my uncle and aunt came to collect me to go and stay with them as dad was unable to look after me on his own. I have good memories of that time. Not the tourist attractions or any of the places we went to, I can hardly remember those. I just remember how well my aunt and uncle treated me. They spoilt me rotten. I remember how they kept asking me if I was okay, kept asking me if daddy was treating me well.

I dreamed that I ended up in a threesome with Geoff and Ian. It was disturbingly erotic. Disturbing because I know I have no feelings for either man other than my anger towards Geoff for his betrayal and a wariness of Ian. And yet in my dream I enjoyed the experience and awoke strangely aroused with my body tingling. I tried to shake the feeling, reminding myself over and over that both men repulsed me. It was still the early hours of the morning and I tossed and turned till eventually I could take it no more so got up and climbed into the shower, blasting my body with freezing cold water, gasping at the pain the coldness inflicted on me.

I forced myself to stay under that cold stream of water for as long as I could. My teeth started chattered, goose bumps broke out all over and my skin started to take on a blue hue. The cold hammered at my head, causing it to ache, the water slowly chiselling the dream from my mind, chipping away at it till I could visualise it heading down the drain.

At last, when I felt nearly ready to pass out from the cold and the dreadful pain it had created in my head, I reached out a hand, shaking violently, and changed the settings, feeling the water turn quickly from icy cold to almost scalding. I think I may have screamed at the sudden shift in temperature and the way my body stung as if millions of red-hot needles were being simultaneously shoved into every single nerve ending.

I attacked myself with the soap, vigorously rubbing every part of my body, wanting to be cleaner than clean. Slowly I began to feel again and with it came a sense of calm. I slipped to the floor of the shower where I sobbed uncontrollably. I had rid myself of the dream, but one little piece of it stayed and I knew I would never be able to wash that bit away. In my dream I had seen my father standing at the end of my bed, watching and grinning.

Dinner the following evening was difficult. Instead of our usual girlie night, we had agreed that Geoff and Ian join us at a restuarant. My work had suffered during the day as a result of my shaky mental state, and I ended up having to stay on an extra hour after everyone else left. It meant getting home late and I had to shower again before going out. The others had already finished a round of drinks by the time I arrived.

'Sorry, had a crisis at work,' I said as I sat down.

Ian looked annoyed while Geoff gave me an empty sympathetic glance. The girls fussed a little bit, moaning about my boss's cruelty in keeping me late.

'I'm sure you don't mind, do you Sweetie?' Jenny said, 'He is after all really good looking.'

If only she knew. Ian gave her a disapproving look while Geoff feigned hurt.

'Not as good looking as you, of course, my love,' Jenny quickly made amends, pushed her hair behind her ears and snuggled up to her husband.

I had thought I had washed away most of the memory of the dream but it now played games with my mind as I sat there, reminding me of what Ian, Geoff and I had been up to in that other world. If I had really wanted to fantasise about threesomes – which I didn't – I would have chosen two completely different men to be with, probably some celebrities, or better still, characters from films or TV, perfect men whose darker side one knows nothing about. All people have darker sides and when you know, or even suspect what they may be, it taints them.

The only seat left when I arrived had been next to Geoff and, as the restaurant was quite small, we had to sit so close that I could feel the heat from his body near mine. I found myself lusting after him yet at the same time wanted him dead because of what he had done to me at uni.

He was, of course, completely oblivious to the emotions that clashed, smashed and bashed around in my head, and he even seemed to cut me out of the conversation by leaning forward all the time to obscure my view of the other girls, leaving me with just Ian opposite as the only option to have any sort of interaction with.

He is not the most talkative and we had stilted conversations about his work, his boys, the weather and I even lowered myself to have a chat about football, knowing he was a fan. I had picked up enough from the office talk to have some idea of what was happening in the Premier League. But even that didn't help the conversation and the conversation didn't help me forget the dream.

I felt betrayed by the girls as none of them noticed my discomfort or even made an attempt to converse with me. To be fair to them, which I was later when I got home, it was as difficult for them to start up a conversation across Geoff as it was for me to talk to them. I'd like to think that Geoff's playing human barrier was unintentional and that he was unaware he was doing so. And he probably was, but my mind kept telling me that he was doing it on purpose, but I had no idea why he would.

THE BEATLETTES PLAY THE CAVERN

History repeated itself as The Beatles were resurrected at their old stomping ground, The Caven Club in Liverpool. However, instead of John, Paul, George and Ringo we had Joan, Pauline, Georgina and Inga Starr. Calling themselves The Beatlettes, this all-girl tribute band opened for The Grumpy Crumpets and went down a storm. Wearing mop top wigs and the natty black suits that were the trademark of the early Fab Four, they played a set of near perfect covers.

'It was like being back in the 60s,' one old rocker who had come primarily to see the Crumpets, said. 'I had the privilege of seeing The Beatles here in their heyday and these girls brought back loads of memories.'

The Grumpy Crumpets delivered a blistering set but even they knew that they had been outdone. They were, however, gracious in defeat and invited The Beatlettes back on stage for a final encore where they played covers of 'She Loves You' and 'Please Please Me' together.

'I guess we were up against history, Crumpet Desiree Desire said afterwards. 'We always knew that The Beatlettes were a great cover band but hadn't realised what the effect of them playing The Cavern would be. They were brilliant, gave me goose bumps. We're really proud of them, they're great girls to hang out with.'

'I just really like the idea of an all-girl Beatles tribute band rocking The Cavern,' Desiree said. She had been the one who had originally suggested that we call ourselves The Beatlettes and allowing them to upstage us had been her idea. We took some convincing as no one likes having their limelight stolen. Sara was the most stubbornly opposed while Jenny and I eventually succumbed to Desiree's passion.

'But surely that undermines The Grumpy Crumpets if they are up-staged by their support act,' Sara said. 'If we are going to be the biggest band in the land, we can't have The Beatlettes outshining us.'

'Yes, but the attention The Beatlettes get, if they are as good as we're…sorry, as I'm making them out to be, would help get the gig noticed, particularly by the local press and The GC's would be men-tioned. Then, if we're gracious in admitting that The Beatlettes had a better gig, we get kudos. You know that The Beatles are like a religion to Liverpudlians. We respected their gods, so we would therefore be accept-able, don't you see? There is no such thing as bad publicity.'

'And it's just the one gig, you know, at The Cavern.' Jenny was fully on Desiree's side now. 'It's quite a powerful statement for women if an all-girl tribute band were to rock the same venue where The Beatles started out. Think about it.'

'Okay, you guys win. But I don't want The Beatlettes mentioned too much for the rest of the tour.'

We agreed and the famous Beatlettes gig at The Cavern was officially entered into the annuls of our fantasy history.

'Where's the next gig?' Sara asked once we had sorted out the Liverpool one.

'Manchester, surely,' Jenny replied.

'Yeah, but where in Manchester?'

'The Hacienda Club? Was that around in the eighties or was that a nineties thing?'

'Yes,' I said, 'It's been around since the early eighties but wasn't big until later. Factory Records was certainly around in the early eighties. *Blue Monday* by New Oder was released on Factory so was Joy Division's stuff.'

'What's Factory got to do with The Hacienda?' Sara asked. Of the four of us, I would say that Sara was the least clued up on the music scene.

'The boss of Factory Records, what was his name again, Tony something, Alan Partridge played him in that movie. Anyway, that Tony bloke started The Hacienda club.' Jenny replied.

'Tony Wilson. The Hacienda opened in 1982 and it even had a catalogue number, you know like records have a number. FAC51 I think it was.' I sometimes can't help myself.

'Of course, I forgot we have our own resident music encyclopaedia in Clair,' Jenny said pushing her hair behind her ears.

I hadn't told them that I had missed a small detail earlier on. It was only when I Googled it that I found that King Tut's Wah Wah Hut in Glasgow only opened in 1990, so wouldn't have been around in the eighties when our supposed Grumpy Crumpet career was meant to be taking place. I could have kicked myself for missing that, but I loved the name of the venue too much to suggest that we revisit our Glasgow gig and anyway this was a fantasy so in our fantasy world King Tut's existed in the eighties.

'So, The Hacienda then?' Desiree looked round at us and everyone nodded, although I did so a little reluctantly as I had bad memories of the place.

None of the girls had wanted to go up to Manchester to see New Order at The Hacienda, it was only Ian and some of his mates, guys I didn't know, who were keen. We drove up in Simon's car. Simon was probably the best looking of the group but was from a rich family and had an ego the size of an elephant. I got stuck in the back seat of the car, squashed between Digby and Toby, two rather lecherous guys who kept brushing their hands against my breasts as they pretended to point out things along the route. They made out as if they hadn't noticed the contact they made, but it was clearly a juvenile game to them, each one trying to outdo the other in how far they could go. I almost felt like pulling my tits out and telling them to go ahead and have a good grope, embarrassing them into stopping and putting an end to their bullshit but I suspected that they might well have taken me up on the offer and I did not want to give them that satisfaction.

Apart from their attention to my boobs, they practically ignored me, and if they did speak to me at all they addressed me with the condescending 'love'.

'You okay in the middle, love?'

'Ever been to Manchester before, love?'

Drove me mad, I was not their 'love'.

But they were mild compared to Simon once we got to the gig. He somehow thought that, as he had given me a lift up, I owed him sexual favours even though I had paid my petrol money in advance. He stood close behind me at the gig and before New Order came on, he had grabbed my bottom a few times, grinning lasciviously at me each time I turned and glared at him. And then he had grabbed my breasts. When I tried to remove his hands, he leaned close, his beery breath hot in my ear and nearly shouted over the music, 'You and me tonight, love. My room, otherwise you walk home.'

I glanced across at Ian for help. He was staring at the stage, but it was a too intense stare, as if he was deliberately not wishing to make eye contact. I wasn't sure, but I could swear that he knew exactly what was going on and approved.

I did not have enough money for a coach fare home, so when we got back to the B&B after the show, I dutifully went along to Simon's room. I didn't have a choice. It left me numb for the journey home and I hardly noticed the antics of Digby and Toby, which resumed with less subtly, but seemed to diminish as I completely ignored it. I was trying to cope with the nausea that accompanied a migraine.

I struggled to listen to my New Order records for months afterwards. Then I heard one day that Simon had died. Apparently he fell down a flight of stairs at uni. While it was a tragic accident, and I felt really sorry for his girlfriend who was in one of my classes, it somehow lifted the curse on New Order and I listened to their *Power, Corruption And Lies* album non-stop for a month.

FOOD FIGHT @ THE HACIENDA

The Hacienda Club in Manchester has seen a lot in its short life, but last night it probably witnessed one of its most bizarre scenes yet. Music gigs are renown for strange things happening and invariably it is initiated by the audience. In a show of appreciation for The Grumpy Crumpets, the crowd last night ended up in a food fight.

'We were halfway through our second number when I saw an object come flying onto the stage,' lead singer, Desiree Desire said. 'It landed at Sara's feet. At first I thought people were throwing bottles but I carried on singing, then I looked at the object out the corner of my eye and thought oh god, someone has thrown their underpants. The next one landed just near me and that was when I realised that it was raining crumpets.'

It is unclear how the crumpets got into the venue but, judging by the number of them, it is likely that a group of fans smuggled them in as the cakes began to fly back and forth amongst the crowd.

'I've never seen anything like this before,' Neil, a Hacienda regular said. 'I've seen scuffles between guys, women getting groped, glue sniffing and loads of other weird stuff, but never a food fight. Fortunately, crumpets are soft.'

The gig itself was once again a top-notch performance from The Grumpy Crumpets who are causing waves as their nationwide tour gains momentum.

It was Desiree who suggested the crumpet tossing crowd and we all loved the idea. It was something quirky, but not too outrageous nor beyond the realms of reality. In celebration of the gig, we toasted some crumpets and sat around nattering, drinking red wine and eating. It was a mellow evening, spoilt only by the early arrival of Geoff to pick Jenny up. It wasn't anything he did, other than send a sharp reminder of my weird dream and of how he had cheated on me at uni.

I hadn't seen him for a few weeks and that had eased the pain of betrayal I had been feeling ever since Sara's confession and I had all but erased the memory of the dream. Seeing him again at Desiree's and noticing the way he hugged Sara, I couldn't help feeling that there was still something going on between them, a small spark that they had kept alive all these years.

I tried to push my feelings aside, telling myself that Geoff's 'closeness' to Sara was just a gesture of care, just checking that she was coping with Ollie's death. It was seven or eight months since the event and you could occasionally see that something had triggered a memory with Sara as she would go quiet, or get a bit bitchy as was her way. If it was the latter reaction, I would usually send a subtle reminder to her of what happened the last time she let her tetchiness get out of control. I would rub the back of my head where I caught the coffee table the time she had pushed me and, even though she showed no outward signs of making the connection, a subliminal message must have got through each time as she would calm down.

There was no sign of Sara getting irritable that evening though, in fact it seemed to be the opposite. She was cozying up to Geoff a little too much, making the most of his sympathy and, dare I say it, possibly trying to subtly seduce him, to the extent that Jenny even gave her a sharp glance.

I couldn't help chuckling quietly to myself about the irony. Jenny, who had had an affair with Sara's husband, was getting upset when Sara was trying to get it off with her hubby. In the days before I found out about Sara and Geoff, I would have intervened somehow, probably distracting Geoff with a comment and then inviting Jenny for a coffee and talking her through it, saying that Sara was just a little lost at the moment and that things would be all right, we just needed to distract her, maybe introduce her to some men. But in my current frame of mind, I didn't want to help. I was quite happy to let this one play out and watch.

It was Ian who came to the rescue, albeit completely by chance as he walked in just as Jenny looked about to make a comment.

'I thought I heard your voice,' he said to Geoff, 'glad I caught you. I was wondering if I could pick your lawyer's brain for a moment?' And he led him off.

Sara looked momentarily peeved, then seemed to realise what had transpired as she caught Jenny's glare. She picked up her glass of wine, started to take a sip, then thought better of it.

'I think I've had a bit too much again,' she announced. 'I should get going. Clair are we going to share a cab?'

It didn't completely placate Jenny, but it helped. She relaxed a little, although her goodbye hug was not as warm as usual. I was almost out the door when she said, 'Clair, sweetie, you want to do a coffee tomorrow?' I knew she had been expecting me to ask her if she wanted to meet, but I had resolved not to. There was a feeling of hurt in her tone when she asked, as if she were saying, 'what's wrong with you, didn't you realise I needed to chat?' It irritated me that I ended up feeling guilty for not asking her first.

Sara was quiet in the cab on the way home, feigning tiredness brought on by the wine. But she was pensive, presumably thinking through her earlier actions.

'I overdid things a bit tonight, didn't I?' she said as we neared her place. I nodded. The Sara of old would have gone on to defend her actions, tried to justify herself to me, but in a post-Ollie world, she had become more self-critical and she just nodded and then stared out the window. As we turned into her street she said, 'I don't know why I feel guilty, after all Jenny had it off with my Ollie for months, so why can't I get a little from her husband?'

Jenny has a birthmark on her left buttock, one of those wine stain blotches. I saw it when we went on holiday to Spain once, just us four girls. The first day on the beach she was in a skimpy bikini – this was in our uni days when we could get away with wearing such things – and there it was for all to see. She had apparently taken a lot of teasing over it at school but it no longer bothered her.

'They used to call me beetroot butt,' she said when she caught us all staring. 'Used to annoy the hell out of me, but then one day a guy said to me, "you know, with a body like yours, it would be unfair on all the other girls if you didn't have at least one little blemish" and ever since then I've not cared what people say or think about it.'

It shocked me a bit that a guy at school had seen her birthmark and shocked me even more when she later admitted that said guy had been one of her teachers, even though she swore that he had only seen it like we had, when she was wearing a costume for school swimming. That was what she said, but that was when I first realised that she would brush her hair behind her ears when she lied.

It was the way the old guy at the next table kept staring at Jenny's still shapely butt that reminded me of her birthmark, especially as the bloke was old enough to be her school teacher. It was more than her birthmark that I was reminded of, it was also her sexual appetite which, by all accounts, went way back to when she first became sexually aware at twelve or thirteen. She was one of those who, back then, we would have said 'had a reputation'.

I found it difficult listening to her moan about Sara's behaviour the other evening. 'Doesn't she respect boundaries. I mean yes, I do feel sorry for her that Ollie is dead and all that, but he's not that long gone, she should have a bit more respect for his memory and should not be going round trying to steal her friend's husbands. Anyway, Ian is more her type if she wants to be a marriage wrecker.'

Despite my anger at Geoff, which still lingered, I found myself thinking that Jenny did not deserve him, not the Jenny who seemed so oblivious to her own hypocrisy. Even cheating Geoff deserved better than that.

'Oh come on Clair, Sweetie, don't give me that look. I never set out to wreck Sara's marriage when I was screwing Ollie. We were just having fun. It was never serious,' she pushed her hair behind her ears with some force, her long delicate fingers trembling slightly as she did so. 'It was just a fling, nothing serious. But the moves she was making on Geoff, that had husband stealer written all over it.'

'Oh, I knew you and Ollie weren't serious,' I responded and resisted the temptation to push my hair behind my ears as a mocking gesture, 'but I think you're reading too much into Sara's behaviour. I don't think she's after your Geoff. When you lose a loved one it can hit you unexpectedly at any moment without warning, months and sometimes even years later. Something just triggers a memory and you find yourself aching for that loved one to be there and you end up doing silly things. You'll see, Sara is unlikely to behave like that again. She had a moment and will be over it by now. She probably won't even have realised what she did, her mind would have been somewhere else completely.'

Jenny stared at me for a bit, looking unsure whether to believe me or not, then said with some venom, 'Oh yeah, little Miss Psychology, and how do you know all this. You've never lost a husband before.'

'No, but I did lose my mum when I was fourteen.'

CRUMPETS RETURN TO THE STUDIO

Following their hugely successful national tour, The Grumpy Crumpets have returned to the studio to begin work on that difficult second album. There are high expectations of the band and rumours that a contract with a major record label beckons if they can pull it off.

'After being on the road for so long, we are excited about getting down to recording new material,' Jenny Jangle, the band's lead guitarist, said. 'We've got a number of great songs ready to go, songs we wrote while on tour.'

'We were inspired by people we met and places we visited,' Sara The Bitch added.

When asked about signing with a major label, Desiree Desire replied, 'We've had no offers and 4AD are looking after us very well. We have no reason to want to move. If they stay loyal to us, we'll stay loyal to them.'

The band are hoping to have the as yet untitled album out in the spring of next year.

I don't like talking about my mum, and I was annoyed with myself for mentioning it to Jenny. My mum and my memories of her were private and not for sharing. But Jenny's comment about me never having a husband had hurt and I had retaliated using my secret weapon. I could see that I had shocked her a little but did not give her a chance to respond saying that I had to get back to work which wasn't a lie. I put in two hours 'overtime' that evening for being late back from my lunch hour and a migraine started to crush my skull. It left me feeling drained for the rest of the week and I nearly cancelled going round to Sara's for the next instalment of The Grumpy Crumpet Saga.

It was a bit of a strained evening as Jenny seemed to avoid talking to me and she had not yet forgiven Sara, so she cozied up to Desiree. Sara was feeling a bit guilty about her antics with Geoff at the previous meeting so was happy not having to engage too much with Jenny, but as Jenny had paired up with Desiree, Sara was left with me to talk to and I wasn't much company that evening.

Even Sara's cooking – a lovely Moroccan terrine – didn't do much to break the ice. I felt sorry for her. She had clearly gone to a lot of trouble, possibly seeing it as a peace offering to Jenny, but it was not having the desired effect.

Desiree sensed the tensions but was at a bit of a loss as to how to overcome them. She looked uncomfortable being monopolised by Jenny and gave me a few questioning glances. When she did manage to break free from Jenny's clutches for a moment, she asked me the coded question, 'So how things going with you, Clair?'

'Same old same old,' I said, thinking yes, I do want to meet up with Desiree, even if it was just to talk about something other than the Jenny/Sara issue. She nodded and scratched her nose, telling me in the gesture that she would call.

No one was in the mood for a proper Grumpy Crumpet session, but the atmosphere was so forced that I think we were all grateful for the distraction when Sara suggested we return to our fantasy world. We started with a recap of where we had got to on the tour. Desiree asking about venues in Derby where we could play, but there was very little appetite amongst us to continue touring.

'Maybe we should just move on to going back to the studio to record our second album,' I suggested after a while and in a great show of lukewarm enthusiasm, they agreed.

The evening ended early and I was rather relieved to head home. In the cab, I began to wonder if the rifts in our friendships would ever heal. Sara had offered an olive branch to Jenny and Jenny had offered one to me, but neither had been accepted. It was not often that we came away from an evening still holding on to the grudges that we had arrived with and every time this happened, I feared for our friendship. The headache, which had been a nagging, dull background pain all evening, began to get worse and was heading for another migraine when I got in.

My dreams that night, when I eventually got to sleep, were again drenched in blood. They were sticky, cloying dreams that threatened to suffocate me. A ghostly image of my mother's face floated in and out of focus, sometimes rippling across a pool of crimson blood, sometimes seeming to bubble up to the surface from within a bath full of the stuff. Sara's unborn child – I can only presume that was what it was – also scuttled across my vision, a scary alien imp that had the face of Geoff. There was a voice too, someone talking to me. But the me they spoke to was not me, or rather not me as I know myself. It's hard to explain exactly what it was like.

When I woke the next morning, the sheets were soaked in my sweat and my body felt like lead. I struggled to move my legs off the bed before plodding heavily to the shower where I didn't really wash myself, rather just let the water, which I had set at lukewarm, pour over me.

I was busy drying myself when my phone rang. It was Desiree telling me that Geoff had been stabbed and killed last night.

Jenny was a wreck when I got to her place that evening. Sara and Desiree had been there all day and Tracey, who could not be called Bombhead on a day like that, sat quietly in the corner with a couple of her friends, talking quietly amongst themselves.

There was very little I could do after offering my initial condolences. Sara and Desiree seemed to feel as if they had sympathy rights as they had been there all day and Sara even gave me a bit of a glare for daring to set Jenny off crying again. It wasn't my fault that I had had to work all day instead of being there for my friend, but they wouldn't understand. I had never told them about my boss and how he treated me.

'Thanks, Sweetie,' Jenny said as we hugged, but then she turned back to Sara because, of course, Sara had lost a husband, so Sara knew what she was talking about. I stood around like a spare part for a bit, then joined Tracey and her friends. I suppose I had more to offer there as I knew what it was like to lose a parent when in one's teens. Not only that, but I knew what it was like to lose a parent to an act of violence.

Tracey seemed to be handling the situation better than Jenny. She looked grim, but there was no trace of tears. She spoke quietly, shooting occasional glances across at her mum. It was through her that I found out more of the story. Geoff had been for drinks after work. His colleagues had said that it had been a quiet session and that he was quite fine when he left, not even tipsy. One of his workmates got off the tube at the same station but, after a short chat, they went their separate ways. The police had found his body a block away, dumped in an alley. None of his belongings had been taken. His wallet, watch and credit cards were all still on him.

I later found out that the stabbing had been particularly brutal, seventeen knife wounds in all. The police had been reticent to go into any details, presumably trying to spare Jenny the distress, but the press had no such sympathies as the gory details were spelt out on the front page of one of the less salubrious papers.

I stayed fairly late, but Sara and Desiree showed no signs of leaving so I never really got a chance to speak to anyone except Tracey and her friends. They were a good bunch and reminded me a little of what we had been like at that age, the difference being that I was into New Romantics with big hair and big make-up, where they were into the re-emerging goth scene with black clothes, pale faces, jet black hair, dark lipstick and nail polish. Despite the different fashions, they still talked of the same things I had when I was that age – boys, other girl's fashion sense, the latest music. They did have mobile phones to talk about too, but Tracey and her friends did not seem as addicted to them as the press would have us believe.

Like us at that age, these girls also talked about serious matters, the big one obviously being about how Tracey was coping. They were hugely supportive of their friend and I wondered if in thirty years' time, this group would still be friends, the way Jenny, Sara, Desiree and I were. Would there be a Grumpy Crumpets II?

I somehow doubted they would do the music thing that we were doing. When we grew up, music was an integral part of our lives, but to them it was peripheral. Maybe they would have a sort of Facebook fantasy group when they got to our age, remembering and laughing at what they had got up to on social media. I found myself hoping they would have something that they could look back on with affection although I knew that today would not be one that held good memories.

I felt quite depressed when I got home, and I must admit that part of my mood arose from the realisation that The Grumpy Crumpets' career would once more be put on hold, or possibly even forgotten. I recalled the hiatus we had when Ollie died. I knew that it was selfish, but the group had become the one thing in my life that I really enjoyed and the thought of losing it saddened me. I was, of course, also upset about what had happened to Geoff. It was horrible and, despite my feelings about his betrayal back in uni, I was still very fond of him.

I decided to have a bath before going to bed and ran the water very hot so that the bath salts I used created a heady perfumed steam while the water stung my skin and turned it pink-red. It relaxed me both physically and mentally, blotting out the memories of the day.

I woke up in very cold water with my body shaking uncontrollably. My skin had shrivelled up as it had soaked in the water. At first I didn't know where I was and looked round in a panic. Then, as my thoughts became clearer, I pushed myself up and climbed unsteadily out of the bath. The cold seemed to have pierced right through to my bones and the dreams, which had distracted me so that I had not woken as the water had cooled, clung to my mind like barnacles on a ship's hull.

Somewhat dazed, both by the cold and my dreams, I staggered into the shower and turned the hot water on. Slowly it burnt the cold off my skin and prised some of the dream remnants from my brain, but my bones still felt frozen and the core of the dreams still poked sharply and painfully at my mind.

In my bedroom, I saw that it was only three in the morning and I felt dead tired, but knew that I would not sleep, that I did not want to sleep. I had to exorcise myself of the dreams before I could face sleep again. I dragged my duvet into the sitting room, wrapped it round me and turned on the television, trying to immerse myself in the banality of the shows. It was nearly 6 o'clock by the time I finally felt warm again and the bloodied body of Geoff that had haunted my dreams was now just a faint echo in my head.

A RADIO INTERVIEW

'We're pleased to have Clair da Loon of The Grumpy Crumpets in the studio with us today. The Crumpets have been hard at work on their second album. How's it going, Clair?'

'Hello, John. It's going very well. We're making good progress, but its hard work. We want to produce something special so we are taking our time. 4AD have given us a generous budget to work with and that's really helped We're immensely grateful to them.'

'And Jenny Jangle, how's she holding up? I should remind listeners that Jenny's husband, Geoff, was recently a victim of the wave of knife crime that has plagued the city. How is Jenny recovering from what must have been a huge shock to her?'

'Well, John, it was a shock to all of us. We're a very close-knit group, like family almost. Geoff was like a brother to the rest of us. We feel his loss just as acutely. But Jenny is doing well under the circumstances. She has good days and bad ones, but she has thrown herself into her song writing and we've put together some great tracks already. It'll take some time before she gets over this. It'll take us all some time.'

'And, of course, you had to put the release of your first album on hold because of another death.'

'Yes, that was Sara's husband, Oliver. But we came back stronger from that experience and we will be even stronger after this.'

I hoped we would come back from this second tragedy but was not convinced that we would come back stronger. The radio interview was my own doing to keep the Crumpets going while it became a forgotten topic with the others. The effect of Geoff's death was in some ways like that of Ollie's but it impacted on the group dynamic in a way that Ollie's hadn't. The Grumpy Crumpets' career was put on hold, as it been with Ollie's death, but where Sara had felt a little isolated and unable to relate to the rest of us who had never lost a husband, she was now the expert and took Jenny under her wing, explaining to her how she should be feeling and what she should be doing.

I expected Jenny to get annoyed and push back, especially when Sara was telling her all the emotions she should be going through, but she didn't. I could only put this down to shock as it was not in Jenny's nature to be told what to do, especially not what emotions she should be having. The two of them grew closer and at times almost seemed to shut Desiree and me out of their conversations because we 'would not understand'.

I worried for Tracey though. She was also being excluded by her mother who seemed to wallow in self-pity when Sara wasn't around and then would ignore her daughter when Sara was there. I arranged to meet up with Tracey after work one day and we went for a pizza over which she told me that tensions were high. Jenny would lose her temper at the slightest thing, screaming at Tracey that she was a useless daughter and once even blamed her for Geoff's death. Tracey stayed out all night after that, sleeping over at a friend's place. The next morning Jenny had been all weepy and contrite, begging Tracey to come home.

'I had to go, she's my mum after all, but I don't know how much more of this I can take,' she confided in me. There were two things I knew I could not do. I couldn't make excuses for Jenny and I could not tell Tracey it was all going to be fine. She was too smart for either approach, so I told her if she ever needed to chat or if she needed a place to stay over a night or two, to call.

'Thanks, Clair,' she said, 'it's nice to have someone talk straight with me. I know that in time things will improve, I know that mum's going through a very difficult time. I don't need people to tell me that. I'm not stupid. I guess I just need someone to talk to. My friends are okay, but they skirt around the issues, they are too scared to talk about it in case they upset me. I don't hold that against them. If it had been one of their fathers instead of mine, I probably would have been the same.'

She's a smart girl that Tracey. We chattered for a bit about her friends and her school work, then she suddenly asked, 'What is all this stuff about Grumpy Crumpets?' The question took me a bit by surprise. I had sort of assumed that the other three in the group would have shared a least some of our nonsense with their families. I knew that the husbands knew, or had known in Geoff and Ollie's cases, but hadn't realised that the kids were not included.

I explained as best I could, telling Tracey how it was just a bit of fun to help escape from reality. I wasn't sure how she would react and ended by saying, 'You probably think that it's a bit silly.' But she smiled and replied, 'It actually sounds like fun.'

It was around this time that things got a bit over the top with my boss. I was still dead scared of losing my job, so went along with his perversions, but I did not feel comfortable with them. He was pushing the boundaries and I did not know how to stop him. There were evenings when I arrived home with serious pains resulting from what he had done, and this added to my feelings of loss that came with the lack of Grumpy Crumpet talk. My nightmares intensified and things from my past haunted me in tortuous ways, often causing me to sit up suddenly in bed, gasping for breath and feeling like the sweat that covered me was actually blood. It would take me hours to calm myself enough to dare to face going back to sleep and the voices continued, talking to a me that was not me.

Neither Jenny nor Sara seemed to notice, they were caught up in their mutual mourning and had grown so close that I suspected they had started turning to each other for physical as well as mental comfort.

Desiree was less sure when I mentioned my suspicions to her but didn't rule it out. She did, however, take some notice of my condition and kept checking that I was okay. I managed to lie enough to convince her that yes, I was going thought a bit of a rough patch, but that things would be fine.

Tracey was also concerned. She and I were meeting up quite regularly now and it often ended up with her comforting me rather than, as one would have expected, me consoling her. When I articulated this, she just laughed and said, 'You *are* helping. By having to worry about you, I've got less time to wallow in my own misery.'

I never told her everything, but I could sense that she knew that. She would give me a look as if to say, 'and what aren't you telling me?' but she never pried further. I told her about the dreams, the blood and violence that haunted my sleeping moments, but I never mentioned the role my father played in the dreams, nor what my boss was doing which,

I was sure, was what was bringing the dreams on. Nor did I tell her about the voices.

Talking to Tracey helped, especially when we got on to The Grumpy Crumpets and I was able to escape reality for a bit as I told her in detail about our imagined group and all it had got up to. The nights after meeting with Tracey were always quieter and I managed to sleep through a few of them.

We would also talk about music in general. She was into some of the more obscure groups, War on Drugs, Frightened Rabbit and Panda Bear. She had also taken a shine to a guy called Rodriguez who she had seen at Glastonbury and kept telling me I needed to see the movie about him. Other than Rodriguez I knew nothing about the bands she spoke about, but we made a pact that she would listen to some of my favourites from when I was growing up – Kissing The Pink, Cocteau Twins, New Order – and I would try out her stuff. It did surprise me how good some of it was and I enjoyed rediscovering the forgotten thrill of coming across great music.

BOMBHEADS AWAY

Clair da Loon, the drummer with The Grumpy Crumpets, has announced a new side project. She has teamed up with a young singer who goes under the name Tracey Bombhead. Very little is known about Bombhead. She is reputed to be 'just sixteen years old, has the voice of an angel and an ear for a tune second to none.'

'We've recorded a couple of tracks and have a couple more demos ready to record, then we'll put out an EP and test the water,' da Loon said. She described Bombhead's voice as 'ethereal, similar to Elizabeth Frazier of the Cocteau Twins' and has said the music brings together old and new sounds.

Da Loon insists that this is a side project and that work on The Grumpy Crumpets' as yet untitled new album is continuing slowly in the wake of the death of Jenny Jangle's husband. The EP is expected out next month with da Loon and Bombhead going under the name of OCD See?

Tracey came up with the band name after a discussion we had about my obsessive compulsive behaviour. I was commenting on how I liked everything in its right place and struggled to leave things alone if everything wasn't just so. I wasn't completely obsessive about it and I could cope with things being out of place but always had a strong urge to correct them. I liked the name even though I was not a huge fan of AC/DC who our band's name played on.

Tracey understood that it was a side project but pleaded with me to keep her up to date with any Grumpy Crumpet developments if we ever continued our imaginary career. I was less confident about this happening as we had not been meeting up as regularly. Sara and Jenny were practically a couple, something Tracey confirmed after hearing 'noises' from her mum's bedroom one evening. I wasn't sure how I felt about this. I liked to think of myself as open-minded and liberal with such things, but that was when it didn't affect me. When it was this close to home, it left me feeling a little uncomfortable. However, as they never made any public displays of excessive affection, I was able to cope with it. Tracey seemed completely unfazed. 'As long as she is happy,' was all she said of Jenny.

The unwanted attention from my boss was put on hold when his youngest daughter went missing. She had been abducted from a park near where they lived. I felt sorry for his wife. A picture of them appeared in the local paper as they appealed for help. She looked exhausted, dark rings under her eyes which were red from too much crying. He looked in total shock, but I couldn't muster any sympathy for him, especially as he stood in the picture with his arm around his wife as if they were a perfect couple. I did wonder if she knew what he got up to at work.

After a week during which there was no news, he returned to the office, but he was too distracted to concentrate. He sat in his office staring at his computer screen most of the time. Some of the other women in the office fussed over him. Making him tea and checking that he was okay, but as far as I know, he had never made any of them 'work late'. I kept my distance, not sure how this crisis would affect him. I was in constant fear that all this tension would result in a sudden flare up of violent lust and found myself wishing that he would just get on with it and get it out of his system. But he just threw himself into his work after a period of inactivity, although he always left the office at 5 p.m. sharp. The other women saw this as a sign that he was supporting his wife, but it just made me uneasy.

After two months during which the police had not made any progress, the storm I had seen brewing broke and I left work very late that evening barely able to walk. I refused to give him the satisfaction of crying as I straightened myself up afterwards and left but struggled to keep my emotions to myself as I sat on the tube going home. The tears started as I reached my front door and didn't stop till the early hours of the morning. I ran a scalding bath which I lay in until it began to turn cold.

Two days later the police found the body of his daughter. They said that she had obviously been held captive all the time and only killed the night he reverted to his savage ways.

CRUMPET COMEBACK

After months of silence, there have been signs of life emerging from The Grumpy Crumpets' studio. A leaked track is doing the rounds amongst fan club members. No official title to the track had been given and fans are referring to it as 'Lusting For A Friend'. The lyrics again have the ambiguity that The Crumpets do so well. Are they just looking for a friend or do they already have the friend and are after an intimate relationship?

A fan who did not wish to be named, told us of the excitement surrounding the new track. 'We're all really stoked by hearing something new from The Crumpets and this taster of what is to come is telling us that we're in for a real treat when the new album comes. People are having 'Lusting' parties when the track is played over and over again all night.'

There has been no comment from the band or their management although a record company executive said he was disappointed that the leak had occurred, and they would be investigating how this happened. When pushed for a comment, he admitted that the death of Jenny Jangle's husband had set the recording timetable back a good number of months, but that things were moving forward again, and he expected the new album to be completed soon.

Jenny and Sara finally 'came out' about their relationship. It was about nine months after Geoff's death. Our regular get togethers had become less regular and Desiree and I were just beginning to wonder if they would ever return to normal when Sara rang and invited us round to hers for 'dinner and maybe some Crumpet chat'.

She had laid on a real treat with the dinner, doing starters, mains and pudding, all of which were Michelin Star quality. She had also turned the lights low and resorted to candlelight. It was between the main course and dessert, while we were finishing off an excellent glass of red, that Jenny tapped on her glass and said that they had an announcement to make. I think she was a little disappointed when Desiree said that we had suspected this for quite a while now. She was hoping to shock us.

Something in Sara's demeanour, though, told me that she was not completely comfortable with things and I strongly suspected that it had been Jenny who had coerced her into the relationship. Jenny had always been promiscuous to the degree that I would almost class her as a sex addict.

We talked a little bit about it, both of them seeking assurances that we were okay with the relationship. We both said that we had no problems and Desiree asked if their kids knew, wanting to know how they had taken it.

'They're all fine about it,' Sara said. 'The kids today are far more accepting of this than our generation. Neither of us have said anything to our parents, they come from a different era. They wouldn't understand.'

The two of them began to relax as the evening went on and they realised that Desiree and I genuinely had no issues. After dessert we moved into the lounge with our glasses and a couple of bottles of red. Jenny and Sara sat together on the sofa holding hands and looking like teenagers on that first night when you bring your other half round to meet the parents.

'So,' I said once we had settled, 'do we bring your relationship into The Grumpy Crumpet story? It's up to you how you want to play it.'

That started off a discussion about whether it would be good or bad for the band's image. We all agreed that in this day and age it wouldn't really have much of an impact, but our fantasy was supposed to be taking place back in the eighties and back then it would have had a bigger impact. Eventually we decided to leave it out of Grumpy Crumpet world.

We then got back to the business of The Crumpets and worked out where we had left off. They were all for picking up with the release of that difficult second album and I was about to agree when I had the inspiration to have a leaked track. Everyone thought it was a great idea as a way of re-starting The Grumpy Crumpets.

As the evening drew to a close, Sara asked Desiree to help with the dishes because Jenny wanted to have a quick chat with me. I was unsure what she could possibly want, but when the other two left the room, she dived straight in.

'I'm worried about Tracey. I don't think that she's coping with Geoff's death. She never says anything about him, in fact we hardly talk anymore. I know she's been hanging out with you a bit lately. Is she okay?'

'She's fine,' I smiled. 'She's really strong. Got her head screwed on right.'

Jenny's smile was sad. 'Yeah, she was always Geoff's child.' She cuddled her nearly empty wine glass, staring at the blood red remnants as she contemplated her next question. 'Do you think you could put in a good word about me to her?'

'What?' I was quite taken aback with the question.

She looked at away, then down at the floor for a few seconds before eventually raising her eyes to me.

'I miss her. She's my baby and, I don't know, I guess I feel like I'm losing her. I am just coming to terms with having lost Geoff, I don't think I can handle losing Tracey too. But I'm worried I may already have. Clair, sweetie, please help me get my baby back.'

It was not really what I wanted to hear. I was enjoying my relationship with Tracey and had begun to feel a little bit like she was my own daughter. I didn't like the idea of Jenny stealing her back. But I knew, deep down, that Tracey Bombhead really did want to return to being Jenny's daughter and I couldn't deny her that.

'I'll see what I can do,' I assured my friend.

My boss took three weeks off after receiving the news about his daughter and we closed the office for the funeral with all the staff attending. It was a dreadful afternoon. There was a torrential downpour and most arrived at the church drenched. A wet and musty smell filled the packed sanctuary which did little to help. To add to this, the vicar was useless, his attempt at sympathy came across as false as he tried to drag God into a godless situation. The press intruded with their usual sense of self-righteous importance getting annoyed with the mourners who got in their way of a shot of the grieving parents.

His wife looked as though she had been slapped hard across the face by life, bewilderment darting across her features like a trapped animal seeking an escape route. He was serious in a sombre black suit, trying to keep his composure as he comforted her.

Their other daughter was there too in a suitable black dress with white lace trimmings. She was uncertain of what was happening and stared wide-eyed around at everyone, her young mind trying to understand why everyone was so solemn and I wondered if she had been told yet that her sister would never be coming home.

I had to figure that out for myself when my sister Cathy died.

After the funeral things were quieter on the 'working late' front, although there was a build-up of frustration that I watched with dread, waiting for the storm to break. I don't even remember getting home the evening when it did. I was in a complete daze, my body and mind had been pummelled by both a verbal and a physical attack, the brutality of which I had never experienced before with him. There were four stabbings that evening.

SINGLE OF THE WEEK
REMEMBRANCE OF MEMORIES – OCD SEE? (4AD)

OCD See?, the side project of The Grumpy Crumpets' Clair da Loon featuring little known singer, Tracey Bombhead, have produced a gem with their debut EP. There are four polished tracks that combine pop sensibilities with sublimely surreal lyrics and lush echo-y orchestration to astonishing effect. Opener, 'Colourfall', glides from the speakers like a burbling brook of satin while, 'Water Wash' and 'Wonderblast' sparkle, gurgle and hiccup across wide vistas of pristine desert. The closer, 'Time Taken Aback' is an 11-minute epic that starts as a whisper and ends as a scream, building and swelling as it grows till it seems to fill the entire universe. The emptiness that follows the last crashing note is so intense that it hurts, yet you immediately feel compelled to start the journey all over again.

Tracey deserved a good review for the debut. We had decided that we would be a studio band only. There wouldn't be any touring or nonsense like that, perhaps the occasional rare live gig in a small club somewhere. Tracey did not want to upset The Grumpy Crumpets, so this way we could have a little fantasy world of our own without impinging too much on the one I had with my friends.

The song titles were all Tracey. She has a really arty side which is quite surprising as neither Jenny nor Geoff showed any real inclination in that way. Ian was the only one in our group who was artistically talented. He painted in his spare time, although he never liked showing us his work. I once saw some when he left the door of his studio open. I peeped in quickly, always worried that he would catch me and be cross. I am no art expert, but I would say that he was technically pretty good, capturing expressions, moods and colours well, but the subject matters were disturbing. There was violence and anger in the paintings. Distorted figures, clearly in some pain, writhed against hellish backgrounds that burned vehemently on the canvas.

I never said anything to Desiree and wondered if she ever saw any of Ian's work. I know I would have been worried had my partner displayed such psychopathic symptoms, but I was sure Desiree would never talk about it if I had ever said anything. I did sometimes wonder if my memories of those paintings fed my dreams as they were not too dissimilar and that made me even more wary of Ian.

I debated talking to Tracey about it but, despite being very mature for her age, she still had an innocence that I felt I could not spoil by dragging her into this ugliness. Besides, I had a job to do and that was to try and convince her to re-connect with her mother.

I suspected it wouldn't be too difficult. The conversations we had regarding her mum always seemed to indicate that if Jenny would just offer an olive branch, Tracey would snatch at it straight away.

I'd like to think it was a kind of tough love I showed Jenny in that I took my time letting Tracey know that the olive branch was there. That way Jenny would appreciate the reconciliation more if she had to wait for it, but if I am honest with myself, it was more from a selfish point of view that I delayed things. I knew that once the two of them reconciled, I would lose Tracey back to her mum. So, I strung Jenny along, feeding her stories that Tracey wasn't quite ready, but there were signs, she just needed time. Meanwhile, I let Tracey know that her mum was slowly coming round to making up.

We were struggling to come up with a title for the new album and we also had some preliminary discussion about the cover although we all acknowledged that covers can often be inspired by the album title. There were a few ideas thrown around – 'GCII', 'Still Grumpy', 'The Dark Side Of The Grump' and a not too subtle reference to Jenny and Sara's relationship, 'Blonde on Brunette' – but none were put out there with any real enthusiasm or emotional attachment and we all felt a little frustrated that good suggestions weren't forthcoming.

When I mentioned our problem to Tracey, and she came back the next day with 'Beyond The Loss' which alluded to both Sara and Jenny coming through the bad times they had suffered with their respective husbands' deaths. Everyone liked the title, and I felt a bit guilty not letting on that it was actually Tracey's idea. She had made me promise not to say anything, she did not want Jenny knowing that she knew all about The Crumpets.

With the album name now settled, we launched into the debate about the cover. I was thinking of some sort of dark, desolate landscape looking towards a beautiful sunrise which linked in with the title. Desiree was with me on that one, but Jenny and Sara weren't convinced.

'It sounds a bit bland, something you'd find on the cover of a Yes album,' Jenny said, and Sara agreed. 'We need something with a little more spice.'

As the debate raged on and the wine flowed, Jenny and Sara began to gang up on Desiree and me, shooting down any ideas either of us had and in return we closed ranks on them and disagreed with anything they came up with. Surprisingly, this was all done in a civil manner and started to become a bit of a joke with either side deliberately coming up with things they knew the other side would not like. This resulted in a lot of giggling as we tried to outdo each other.

Then, in typical Jenny fashion, she suggested we do a 'Calendar Girls' with the cover. 'You remember the movie,' she said, 'those old women who did tasteful nude shots for a charity calendar? How about a tasteful nude shot of us playing our instruments, but everything, guitars, drums etcetera are strategically placed to cover up where needed and our arms can manage the rest.'

'A mike stand is hardly going to cover much for me,' Desiree said.

'That's a point,' Sara agreed, 'but what if you were in a sort of side pose, or even had your back to the camera?'

'I suppose,' Desiree nodded, 'It doesn't really matter though as we don't actually have to do it, we don't actually have to pose naked in real life, so I'm up for it.'

'I'm in,' Sara added and looked at me.

'I guess,' I said. I wasn't overly keen on the idea of using sex again to sell our imaginary album but had grown tired of the debate. 'As Desiree said, we don't actually have to…'

I stopped as I caught the gleam in Jenny's eyes and I knew what was going on in her mind.

'No, Jenny, no no no,' I said.

'What are you like?' Sara said catching on, but she had a big grin on her face.

'We don't have any instruments anyway to do a real shoot,' I said in desperation.

'I'm sure we could hire some,' Jenny said waving a dismissive hand.

'We would have to hire a professional photographer too' Desiree said, which I read as her attempt to dissuade Jenny.

'Your Ian's pretty good with a camera, isn't he? We've all seen his holiday shots and he's got one of those big professional ones...no camera, Jenny...a big professional camera.' Jenny had already thought this through. 'What do you say, Des? Will you ask him?' she was not joking. We had gone from a silly idea about posing nude in an imaginary world to arranging for a real photoshoot in the real world and I could not recall us all agreeing to actually doing this, but it felt like a done deal and I could not back out now without looking like a woosie.

'It's not like Ian hasn't seen naked women before now is it?' Sara prompted.

'Yes, but you're my friends, he hasn't seen you naked before.' Desiree's reticence seemed fake.

'I suppose not,' Jenny pushed her hair behind her ears with both hands, 'but I'd rather have him than some stranger.'

Both hands! I thought to myself. Had Jenny also screwed Ian?

INDIE TOP 20 SINGLES

1. (N) Remembrance Of Memories (EP) - OCD See? (4AD)
2. (1) Blue Monday - New Order (Factory)
3. (2) Somebody - Depeche Mode (Mute)
4. (8) Desire - Gene Loves Jezebel (Beggars Banquet)
5. (N) Chenko - Red Box (Cherry Red)
6. (3) Pearly Dewdrops Drop - Cocteau Twins (4AD)
7. (9) Bela Lugosi's Dead - Bauhaus (Beggars Banquet)
8. (5) Scratch Your Eyes Out - The Grumpy Crumpets (4AD)
9. (N) The Singer - Nick Cave (Mute)
10. (4) Putty In My Hands - The Grumpy Crumpets (4AD)

I probably got some of my years mixed up as I think Depeche Mode's 'Somebody' came out a year or two before the Cocteau Twins' 'Pearly Dewdrops Drop', but that wasn't important. We wanted OCD See?'s EP at 1 and Tracey said to fill the rest of the top 10 with some of my favourites from around that time. We also threw in the two Grumpy Crumpet tracks to tie in with the other fantasy. Again, it's what Tracey wanted.

I made a printout of the top 10 and when we next met we had a good laugh over it. Tracey asked me to tell her a bit about the other songs and I let her listen to them on my phone. She quite liked 'Blue Monday' and 'Bela Lugosi's Dead' but wasn't that keen on 'Somebody' or 'Chenko'. She thought she may have heard the Gene Loves Jezebel one before, possibly in a movie, but she wasn't sure.

'It would be great if we could listen to The Grumpy Crumpet ones as well,' she said once we had gone through the real tracks. 'The titles are so cool. Don't you ever wish you could make the fantasy become real?'

I put the pending photoshoot out of my mind and nodded. 'That would be fun, I suppose. Problem is in real life you can't direct what'll happen the way you can with a fantasy. I know you can influence things, but you can't force them to happen in a certain way.'

'I guess,' she said sadly and looked away for a moment.

'You're thinking about you and your mum, aren't you?' I asked as innocently as I could, knowing full well that my previous comment had been designed to get exactly this reaction.

She nodded.

'It'll work out, trust me. She's coming round to realising that's she's treated you badly. She talked about you the other day.'

Tracey brightened. 'Did she? What did she say?'

'She was saying how much of a mess she was when your father died and how she wished she could be more like you about it all.' That was true. Despite her relationship with Sara, Jenny still struggled with her loss and could get weepy at the oddest things.

'Really?' Tracey's smile was tinged with sadness. 'I feel for her, but I can't be there for her if she keeps shutting me out.'

The next evening I had arranged to meet Jenny for a drink after work. Fortunately my boss was less rough with me and I arrived only a few minutes late and in a relatively decent frame of mind, decent enough that is for Jenny not to notice anything amiss.

She started talking about how she was getting along with hiring the instruments. She had found a shop that sold the stuff and was negotiating with the owner about hiring some equipment for an evening.

'He says that he doesn't usually do that, he only sells the stuff, but I think I may have charmed him into agreeing. He says he'll think about it.'

'Charmed him,' in Jenny speak usually meant some form of sexual favours were offered and I found myself hoping that she hadn't promised him copies of the photos once they were done.

'I know what you're thinking, Sweetie, but I didn't sleep with him,' she brushed her hair behind her ears, 'but I did say he could have a copy of the final shot that we decide on for the album cover.'

I hoped that we didn't have to pay too much extra on top of what Jenny had offered.

'Can you do Saturday evening for the photoshoot? Ian and Desiree are available, and Ian has said we can use his art studio. Their youngest is sleeping over at a friend's so we won't have to worry about him.'

I nodded without enthusiasm. I really wasn't looking forward to this.

'Good, then it's settled,' Jenny said, not noticing my reluctance.

We moved on to talking about Tracey.

'She wants to be there for you, but feels you won't let her in. She's still smarting from when you blamed her for Geoff's death.'

'Whaaat? I've never blamed her. How could she...' Slowly a memory seemed to come to her and a horrified look came over her face. ' I might have...' She looked away, her eyes welling up. 'But I didn't mean...She must know that I didn't mean...'

I touched her arm to comfort her. 'I know. I know you weren't thinking straight at the time. You had just lost your husband. I know that Tracey knows that. But you have never gone back to her and told her, you never confirmed to her that it was just your grief speaking. She needs you to confirm to her that you didn't mean it, otherwise she will always have a nagging doubt that you really do think that it was her fault.'

I took a tissue out of my handbag and offered it to Jenny. She wiped her tears away, sniffed loudly then blew her nose.

'You are a good friend, Clair Sweetie, you really are.'

'Oh, I don't know so much,' I replied.

As Saturday drew near, I grew more nervous about the photoshoot. We had agreed that Desiree would help with our make-up as she was pretty good with that sort of thing. A message had also come through from Ian saying that we shouldn't wear underwear beforehand, just a loose dress as tight underwear would leave marks on our skin that would take a while to disappear. He had apparently read that somewhere. It made sense I suppose, but the idea of sitting in a cab with just a flimsy dress on, did not appeal.

'You can always bring something to put on afterwards,' Desiree said.

The man from the instrument shop was carrying the last bits of equipment into the house when I arrived and he gave me a rather lascivious smile.

'I told you my friends were hot,' Jenny giggled as she saw him off. Thanks Jenny, as if it wasn't bad enough having to do the shoot.

Desiree was also nervous, as was Sara. But Jenny was in her element and really excited, turned on even, by the whole thing. It was decided to do the photoshoot first and then have dinner which was just as well because I don't think I could have eaten anything just then.

I don't remember too much about the session except that I felt very exposed and vulnerable, not too dissimilar to the evenings at work when my boss told me that I had to work late, and we were just waiting for the last of my colleagues to leave before he would start.

Things that did stick out in my memory were the birthmark on Jenny's bottom which bounced around like one of those Pac Man ghosts in front of me as she danced about, and Ian constantly telling me to lift my hands up to cover my breasts. I was sitting behind a small drum set and was meant to hold the two drumsticks up as though I was about to pound the drums. This was also designed to have my arms obscure enough of me to be decent.

I couldn't help wondering how we had let the fantasy creep into reality. This was not what the whole thing was about, and it worried me that this would ruin things.

Sara and Desiree got over their initial nerves as Jenny's enthusiasm rubbed off on them. They were having great fun so the whole ordeal seemed to drag on. All I wanted was to put my clothes back on and feel decent again.

But I had one last humiliation to endure as Ian suggested a shot of the four of us standing huddled together as if about to take a bow at a gig. This left us completely exposed and it took a lot of cajoling from the others to get me to join in. I felt that he was also enjoying himself a little too much and was having a field day eyeing me up in particular.

'I didn't realise you were such a prude,' Jenny said laughing. 'Come on, don't be so uptight. Relax!'

Eventually I agreed as long as they promised it would be the last shot and we could get dressed afterwards.

Dinner felt like a bit of an anti-climax. We ordered an Indian take-away to be delivered and, although the girls were still buzzing from their excitement, the adrenaline was slowly draining away. It was boosted a bit when Ian showed us the pictures on his iPad and we looked through them. I had to admit that the one we chose for the album cover was actually not too bad. You couldn't see too much of my body and what had been fear and embarrassment in most shots had, for the split second when the camera shutter was open, made me appear as if I was enthralled and lost in the music. Jenny and Sara were also caught with an air of wild abandonment to the Rock 'n' Roll. Jenny's guitar was slung low to cover her nether regions while her arm was flung across her body, covering her breasts, as if she had just played a dramatic chord. Her long hair flew off in the other direction.

Sara had lifted the neck of her bass right up to cover one breast while the other one was sort of squashed by her other arm. Her head was thrown back slightly as if nodding to the beat. Her mouth was slightly open in a half pout which looked quite alluring, especially with the dark red lipstick Desiree had put on her and the whole look was enhanced by a naughty glint in her eyes.

But it was Desiree who stole the limelight. She was at the mike in an Elvis type pose, her one knee bent across her body maintaining her decency, her arm nearest the camera was flung across her chest and held the mike stand at an angle. Her head was turned to the mike and her mouth and eyes were wide open as if yelling some essential lyric.

'That's just perfect,' Jenny enthused, 'you've really captured the energy in that one, Ian. Desi, you look amazing. You could crop it and that in itself would make an excellent cover for your solo album,'

We all agreed that that was the shot, but continued to look through the pictures, our excitement waning as we did so. No one else seemed to notice it, but there were a lot of shots that zoomed in on me, most of them catching moments when I was not covering myself properly.

In the weeks after the photoshoot I saw less of Tracey and that saddened me. I was glad that she and Jenny were patching things up, but I missed our chats. Sara and Jenny's relationship also meant that I saw less of them outside our girlie nights. I suppose they both feared that the other would become jealous if they spent time with me. I did see a little bit of Desiree, but she was acting a little strange. She kept trying to lure me into conversations about Ian and what I thought of him. Eventually I realised that she had also noticed the number of photos that he had taken of me.

I started to hang out with Carol, a woman at work who was painfully shy. She was pretty with curly blonde hair, bright laughing eyes and a cheeky smile which was at odds with her personality. The problem with her was that she thought the world of our boss. She kept going on about how kind he was and how dreadful it was about his daughter.

She envied me, she said one evening when we had gone for a drink after work.

'Why?' I asked.

'Because you're Guy's favourite. Everyone knows that. Tell me,' she said suddenly gathering up all her courage in her small frame, 'are you having an affair with him?'

'A what?' I suppose I should not have been surprised that she, and probably everybody else in the office, thought that. But I had never actually considered it and my surprise was genuine.

She seemed to crumple at my answer, back-pedalling quickly.

'Is that what people think?' I asked as kindly as I could.

'Well. I guess. Maybe. You know. Well some of...I don't know. But. Well, you know how people talk. But I never...'

I shook my head slowly, partly to stop her babbling and partly to start answering her question. What was going on between me and my boss was not an affair. I had no doubt in my mind on that front and had no qualms telling Carol that.

'No. But I can see why people might think that. I can tell you the truth, but then I will have to kill you,' I grinned. She gave me the 'go on' look that I had expected. 'Okay, but not a word to anyone else. Promise?' She nodded so I continued. 'We do work late quite a bit, but it's not what people think. There's a lot of stuff going on behind the scenes that keep the business going. I can't say too much, Guy is a bit paranoid about industrial espionage so there are some things that he only trusts me with. In his previous business he was burnt by a partner who stole all his ideas and made a fortune. Guy got nothing, in fact he lost everything, his business, his house. Everything.'

'Oh, the poor man,' Carol was clearly upset by this.

'He rebuilt his life, but he trusts very few people now, understandably so. I stuck by him when his first business went under. You could say that I helped him get back on his feet, so we have this bond. But it's all professional. He's madly in love with his wife and would never do anything to jeopardise that relationship.' I was amazed at how easily this nonsense flowed. 'But not a word of this to anyone else in the office please, Carol. It would break his heart if he found out I had told anyone. He's a very proud man and hates people knowing about this.'

'Not a word, I swear,' Carol said, her pretty eyes sparkling.

Two days later Carol was tragically killed in a hit and run accident. They found the car, it had been stolen earlier in the evening. The police believed it was kids who had nicked it and their joyride had gone tragically wrong. They appealed to the culprits to come forward, but no one did. I was sad about this as I had begun to like Carol.

NAKED CRUMPETS!!!

Rumours have been circulating amongst Grumpy Crumpet fans that their new album, provisionally titled *Beyond The Loss*, will feature the all-girl group in the nude on the cover. It is believed that the photos, supposedly taken by a close friend of the band, have the girls cavorting naked with their instruments. There are apparently some copies of the photos changing hands between fans, although this story has not been substantiated. The band have remained tight-lipped about the rumours, neither confirming nor denying them. It will be remembered that their first album, *Easy Peasy We're The GCs* featured a cover with two crumpets with cherries in the middle, suggestive of a pair of breasts so it is not that great a leap to believe that they have gone that little bit further with their second album. *Beyond The Loss* is due out in June when, dare I say it, all will be revealed.

'As long as the real photos are not leaked to the public,' I said. I didn't really like the story which Jenny had suggested, but she made a case for it being a good way to promote the album.

'Have a bit of intrigue that builds the anticipation,' she said. 'People will be curious, even if they don't know the music. They will give it a listen just to hear what these saucy girls are all about.'

She was probably right so we all agreed to the 'leaked photo' story.

'And don't worry about the real ones,' Desiree said, 'Ian knows what'll happen to him if they are ever leaked.' She gave me a look which made me feel in the wrong for having mentioned the real photos.

Jenny giggled. 'Oh, you're such a prude, Sweetie.'

That annoyed me, mainly because she was right. I sometimes wished I could have the confidence about my body that Jenny had about hers. But then she had the figure to be confident about.

I smiled weakly at Desiree as a thanks for her reassurance and pulled a half-hearted face at Jenny.

'Oh come on, Sweetie, I only said that for your own good. You need to be proud of yourself, Clair. You always look amazing, doesn't she?' Jenny looked at the others who nodded, although Desiree's nod was not as affirming as Sara's. 'There, you see.'

She was just trying to be nice since I had helped her and Tracey make up, but I played along and gave her the necessary smile which satisfied.

About a week after that get together, Ian and Desiree were burgled. Amongst the things that were taken were Ian's laptop and camera. Jenny was suddenly not as confident while Sara and Desiree fretted that the person who had stolen them would put the pictures up on the internet. There was a lot of squabbling and Jenny took the brunt of it as she had been the one who had persuaded us to do the photoshoot.

After a lot of accusations being thrown around I said, 'Surely whoever stole the laptop and camera would erase everything on it so that it can't be easily traced. They were after them to sell them and make some money. If they got caught with someone else's data and pictures on them it would raise suspicions. And if they put the pictures on the net, then it'll give the police a way of tracking the thief.'

This seemed to placate everyone a little and slowly they calmed down with the aid of a very good red.

That night I re-looked at the photos. They were not actually that bad. I shut Ian's laptop and went to bed.

It had been quite quiet on the 'working late' front for a while. There had been a bit of a spike in 'overtime' after Carol was killed, but that hadn't lasted long, and I found myself beginning to look forward to the end of the day. Then for a couple of evenings in a row my boss said those dreaded words, 'Clair, I'm going to need you to work late tonight.'

He was unusually gentle these nights and I wondered what had caused that. It did not, however, stop me from seeing my father's face in his, although it was less recognisable in this gentler form.

My dreams, which had eased off as well, came back with some force. I found myself thrashing around in a pool of wet, sticky blood while my father watched over, laughing at my distress. Usually my mother made an appearance, but as a helpless waif, distress etched across her pretty face at her inability to help me. This angered my father and he lashed out at her while I seemed to drown in the blood.

I woke up suffocating and in a blind panic till I realised that the cloying sensation was the bedsheets which had wrapped themselves around my head. They were drenched in sweat and it took a while to untangle myself.

As I lay in the bath, ridding myself of the sweat, Bruce Springsteen's song, 'I'm On Fire' came into my mind. Not only had I woken up with the sheets soaking wet, but I did feel like there was a freight train running through my head. Bruce must have had similar experiences, but his had been brought on by his love and desire for his girl who had left him, leaving him with an unquenched fire in his soul.

I wondered how any woman could leave Bruce. The man was so sexy and, given the way he had sung songs like 'I'm On Fire', he must undoubtedly be a very passionate man. I began to fantasise about being there for him when he woke up in the song, fretting about his lost love. I shared that soaking wet sheet of the lyrics and that freight train he sang about, set up a rhythm while the pumping pistons became an obvious metaphor for what we were up to. I was cooling his desires.

But all that cooled with the bath water and when I surfaced from my fantasy I found myself thinking of the rest of the song which is actually quite disturbing as it seems to tell the story of a creepy man taking advantage of little girls. There are also lines about sticking knives into people. It is not easy to carve a 'six-inch valley' into a head. That would require a huge amount of brute force.

'Blunt force trauma isn't that what they call it?'

'Oh, Sara stop being so morbid,' Jenny chided.

'I'm not being morbid, I just think it sounds better than smashed his skull in.'

'Can we stop talking about this, please?' I pleaded.

'Sorry, Sweetie. You're such a sensitive soul you know,' Jenny smiled gently.

We had just heard that the guy who had rented us the instruments for our photoshoot had been bludgeoned to death in his shop. It all sounded pretty morbid and it was not helped by Sara sharing all the gory details she had picked up from the papers and a friend of hers who was in the police.

'They are worked off their feet,' she said, 'not only with all the stabbings, but there was that hit-and-run not so long ago and now this. They haven't got the manpower to cope.'

I could tell we weren't going to get any Grumpy Crumpet business done that evening and was a little annoyed, although I knew I should be more concerned about what was happening in the real world. But that was so unpleasant that I really wanted to run and hide inside our fantasy.

'Do you know if Ian sent him those photos?' Jenny suddenly asked Desiree. Her concern spread rapidly as we realised the possible implications.

'Oh my god, Jenny, I don't know, but what if...'

'Calm down, Desi,' Jenny sounded anything but calm. 'We don't know what, if anything, has happened. We don't even know for sure Ian sent the photos across. I know I promised the guy a copy, but I can't remember if I told Ian to send him one so why don't you just call him and find out before we start to panic, okay?'

'Does it matter?' I asked quietly.

'What?' The others couldn't understand why I was so calm.

'Does it matter? Even if he has the pictures,' I had picked up on Jenny's use of the plural which the other didn't seem to have noticed, 'what's the worst that can happen? The police may search his computer, or his wife might find them, but all they will think is that the guy was sent some porn from a friend and will probably just delete it.'

'It wasn't porn,' Jenny insisted, brushing her hair behind her ears, 'it was art.'

'You know what I mean. Porn, art, saucy pics. Call it what you like, the point is that whoever finds the pictures will just see it as something like that, saucy pics sent from a friend and they'll delete them. Worst case is that the cops link us to the photos. Did you pay the guy by card or cash?' I asked Jenny.

'Cash,' she said again brushing her hair behind her ears.

'So only in kind then,' I thought to myself.

'Well, then how can any of this cause us any problems? Even if by some remote chance the police do connect us to the photo and come and ask us about it, they can hardly link us to the guy's murder, can they? All that will happen is that it may be a bit embarrassing.'

It was a little odd that I was the one thinking rationally about this. Usually I would be the one worrying, and the others would be calming me down.

'I guess you're right,' Sara said, and the others nodded, but without much conviction.

The evening ended rather sombrely as the spectre of the photos hung over us, but as the weeks went by and nothing happened, the whole thing was forgotten.

CRUMPETS IN LUST

The long-awaited new single from The Grumpy Crumpets will finally be released next week. 'Lusting For A Friend' is already getting serious airtime on all the major radio stations and it is expected to be a top 20 hit. The raunchy track powers along at pace in fine Crumpet style. The lyrics have courted some controversy as it hints at a lesbian relationship and some questions are being asked about which of the band members this may relate to. The band have not responded to these questions but Jenny Jangle, who wrote the lyrics, has been quoted as saying that it is a song about the need for having good friends around you, especially in times of crisis when the need is acute. The single is due in the shops on Monday.

'Back then it was a big deal if you were outed, although it was mostly the guys. For some reason there wasn't much concern about women's sexuality. It did seem there were no lesbians in pop music in the eighties.'

We had got on to a discussion about the meaning of 'Lusting For A Friend' and had all agreed that we would be rubbish at actually writing lyrics, so coming up with titles of songs was the most we would attempt, only adding the occasional line from a song if we came up with a good one.

Jenny was lecturing us on the eighties because, apparently, none of us had been there. Okay I was feeling a little sarky that evening. I don't know why. I had just come from a rough session with my boss. That usually left me feeling disconnected and disengaged, but that evening I just felt grumpy and annoyed. I think it was because I had actually had an orgasm while 'working late'. This was a first time it had happened, and I am not sure who was more shocked about it, me or my boss. Usually, when everything was going on after hours, I would clear my mind and try and creep into a mental vacuum. Sometimes I would count the panels on the ceiling then maybe try and calculate how many panels there were in total in the office. I had also tried to work out how many squares I could find in the ceiling like one of those puzzles you get in newspapers. But this time I made the mistake of wondering what was behind the panels. That was okay as I started imagining the network of air conditioning ducts and such like but suddenly Bruce Willis appeared in one of them, crawling along like he did in 'Die Hard' and the next thing I knew my mind was telling me that Bruce had dropped down into the office, landed on top of me and, well, Yippe-ki-oh-ay-motherfucker!

That was the last thing I needed. I never wanted my boss to think that I enjoyed what was happening, I only went along with this because I was dead scared of losing my job. I never signed up to enjoy it. I expected him to smirk and perhaps make some comment about how I was finally thawing, but I was wrong. Instead he was angry. He stopped, slapped my face and screamed, 'don't ever do that again', then proceeded to go hard at me until he was done after which he dismissed me with a wave of his hand. That was the most humiliated I had ever felt when leaving the office. I wasn't even capable of just lying there and taking it properly.

I wanted to call the others and tell them that I had a migraine, go home and curl up into a small ball and disappear. But the thought of releasing our new single spurred me on. It had been delayed for so long that it felt I could not be the one to be blamed for further problems. So I had a shower and headed off again. We were at Sara's and she had made a delicious chilli which perked me up a little, but I was still smarting from what had happened.

I bit my tongue, knowing that an outburst of sarcasm from me was not fair on the others.

'There were some, weren't there?' Desiree picked up on Jenny's comment about lesbians in the eighties, 'wasn't k.d. Lang one?'

'She was more nineties, wasn't she?'

'I don't know. Maybe late eighties, early nineties,' Jenny responded.

'Her first sort of success was in 1988,' I waded in as usual. 'But apart from her there was also Phranc.'

'Frank? That's a guy's name.'

'No, Phranc, P-H-R-A-N-C. She was around in the eighties.'

'Never heard of her,' Jenny said.

'She was definitely around in the eighties,' I insisted.

'But hardly mainstream, was she?' Jenny seemed annoyed that I was trying to prove her wrong about lesbians in the eighties.

'Oh well, pardon me,' I snapped. The self-control I had been exercising was waning. 'I didn't realise we were only talking main-bloody-stream,

I'm sorry if my music tastes are not mainstream enough for you. I was only trying to tell you what I know but if you're not interested that's fine. I'll just go home, and you can carry on wondering about bloody lesbians in the bloody eighties without me.'

'Woah!' Jenny sat back, her eyes wide in shock. I never lost my cool with anyone.

'Clair, honey,' Desiree who was next to me took my hand. 'Are you okay, I've never seen you so angry like this before. What's the matter?' Her voice was soothing.

Sara just stared at me as if I was some sort of alien creature.

'What's the matter?' Desiree repeated gently, giving the others a warning glance.

I looked round at my friends and my anger crumbled, being replaced by an intense irritation at myself for letting my emotions show. I shook my head to try and evict all emotions.

'I'm sorry,' I said, trying hard not to cry. 'I had a really rough day at work and guess I'm just tired and irritable. I'm sorry Jenny, I didn't mean to go off at you like that.'

Despite the sympathetic looks I was getting, I needed to get out of there so excused myself and went to the loo where I splashed cold water on my face and took a number of deep breaths before I felt up to facing them again. I paused outside the living room door, bracing myself to go back in and reminding myself not to show any emotions.

'She'll be all right, I'm sure,' Desiree was saying.

'She needs a man.' That was Sara.

'Maybe that's her problem. Maybe she tried to seduce that boss of hers and he turned her down. I would also be tetchy if he turned me down.'

'What are you like Jen?' Desiree chided but they were all chuckling.

I felt as if I had been punched in the guts. The last person on earth I would want to try and seduce was my boss and, as I stood outside the door, I could almost feel his hands groping at me and I wanted to scream. I walked back into the room, made my excuses – a migraine coming on – and left.

The next morning I woke up feeling strangely good. Even the news of three more fatal stabbings in the neighbourhood the previous evening did not dampen my mood as I had slept with Bruce Willis all night. He had come into my room in that blood and sweat-stained vest that he wore in 'Die Hard'. He was limping from where the glass had cut into his bare feet, although strangely he left no bloody footprints. His muscular arms glistened with sweat and he was all man. He was gentle with me despite the violence of his appearance. And he stayed all night, not suddenly drowning in a pool of blood like so many other night visitors had.

He also did not wilt when my father came into the room to watch as he always did. No, Bruce was cool. Without missing a beat in what he was doing with me, he just casually reached over the side of the bed and picked up his gun, pointing it at my father, his face suggesting to dad that he would be advised to leave. It angered my father, but I was safe in Bruce's arms and after dad stomped out of the room, Bruce and I made passionate love again.

At work they were all talking about the stabbings.

'Three in one night. No one is safe.'

'It's like Jack the Ripper all over again.'

'Well, not really. This guy is not targeting prostitutes,' I said.

'You know what I mean though. A serial killer on the loose and the cops have no idea who he is.'

'Or she,' I added.

'Whaaat?'

'Or she. Who says the killer is a man?'

'Oh come on. Women don't do that sort of thing.'

'Who says?' I was playing devil's advocate.

They all looked at me as if I was mad, but I held my ground.

'Women have been known to carry out acts of violence.'

'Yeah, but not like this. How many serial killers are women? Hardly any and those that are usually use poison. They don't stab people. Don't you watch TV?'

'Maybe it's a woman making a point. Maybe she's saying that if a man can do it, so can I. It's genius. The police are looking for a man, but if it is a woman, they'll never find her because they keep looking for a man.'

'How can you call it genius? People are getting killed. Wasn't your friend's husband one of them? How can you even defend the killer?'

'I'm not defending. I'm just saying that the cops will struggle to catch a woman as they all automatically think it's a man.'

'You're weird, do you know that Clair?'

I just smiled and they all went back to work shaking their heads.

None of them came back and said, 'I told you so,' when later that day, after receiving an anonymous tip-off, the police found a bloodied knife in my boss' office and promptly arrested him.

'I still can't believe it,' Jenny said. 'Doesn't it freak you out knowing that your boss was going round stabbing all those people?'

'It is kind of weird,' I said.

'Kind of weird! Clair sweetie, you are the master of understatement. It's not weird, it's creepy, it's nasty, it's horrible, it's...it's...' she ran out of words and shrugged slightly. 'It's downright scary is what I would say.'

'Were there any signs?' Sara asked. 'I mean did he seem like the violent type to you?'

'No. He was a perfect gentleman. That's what I meant when I said weird. No one in the office suspected a thing. Wouldn't hurt a fly, they said.'

'Well it wasn't the bloody flies that needed to worry,' Jenny said with some venom, 'it was people like my Geoff who had to be concerned.' She shoved her hair behind her ears with some force and I wondered what that meant. It wasn't like she was lying, but then it struck me, the lie was not in the words but in her expression of emotion. She was not upset about Geoff having gone. The lie was the overacting of the anger she was pretending to show.

'And they are sure it's him?' Desiree asked.

'I don't know. I suppose they have to do DNA tests on the knife and that sort of stuff before they will know for sure,' I replied. 'I really don't know too much, and the police aren't saying anything. They asked all of us in the office about him, you know.'

'Really? What sort of questions?'

'Oh, things like if we had noticed any violent traits, had he been acting strangely lately, that sort of stuff. But can we talk about something else. This is all too weird for me at the moment.'

I could tell that they wanted to ask more question but gave in to my request and we turned our attention to the next episode in the life of The Grumpy Crumpets.

CRUMPETS HIT NUMBER 1!

The Grumpy Crumpets' new single, 'Lusting For A Friend' was revealed as the top selling hit this week. The single entered the charts at number 18 two weeks back, then jumped to number 5 last week before snatching the top spot from

Culture Club. The all-girl band have seen their following grow over the past year with their debut album, *Easy Peasy We're The GCs* having fared well, but this could be the big breakthrough they are looking for. Already there is much excitement in the industry about their forthcoming album, *Beyond The Loss* and it is the bookies' favourite to enter the album charts at number 1 when it is released later.

'Lusting For A Friend' has also had some decent airplay in the States and it is rumoured that Sire and Geffen record labels are interested in obtaining the US rights to the group's material.

'We couldn't believe the news when we heard we were number one,' Sara The Bitch said. 'Our fans are just the best. Thank you, thank you for sending us to the top. You guys are awesome.'

A new single, 'Forever Ended Last Night' is due out on 4AD at the end of the month.

'You can't have it going in straight at number 1. It wasn't like that back then. A new entry at number 1 was exceptionally rare, not like nowadays,' I had to patiently explain to my band mates. They wanted a number 1 with a bullet, but I wasn't having it. The only songs that went straight in at number 1 in the eighties were things like the Band Aid single.

Eventually they relented. 'On one condition,' Sara said, 'I want us to knock Boy George off the number one slot. I never liked Culture Club, always thought they were overrated.'

There were no arguments with this as it turned out that none of us liked Culture Club that much.

I was enjoying the way this fantasy was building now. We were slowly moving towards being the biggest band on the planet, but doing things the old way, none of this X-Factor jump to fame nonsense we have these days, but a proper working for one's fame. The bit about the U.S. interest was the start of the next phase. We had just about conquered Britain but now we needed to make it across the pond to really go global and the eighties was a good time for the Brits in the U.S. We had the Eurythmics, Culture Club, Duran Duran and to some extent even Howard Jones and A Flock Of Seagulls doing well there. So, having The Grumpy Crumpets crack that market was not over stretching the imagination.

It was a good evening after we had ditched the talk about my boss and moved on to The Grumpy Crumpet stuff. It also felt good going home and not having to worry about being stabbed.

After a week of wondering what would happen at work, Head Office sent us a new boss. Just a temporary measure they said, until we know what is happening with Guy. We didn't have to wait too long to find out what was happening with him as he was formally charged two days later and not long after that, he was denied bail. There was also talk that they suspected him of being the driver in the hit-and-run that killed Carol.

Our new boss was a woman called Ursula. She was tall, quite skinny, but with a pretty face and alert eyes. Her looks were a bit deceiving as under that innocent looking exterior, she was as hard as nails and had fired three of my colleagues within a month of being there.

Fortunately, she seemed to take a shine to me and I liked her. I worked hard and now 'working late' started to mean what it normally means. We had our hands full as my previous boss had neglected a lot of things, despite the 'hours' he put in.

During the days we would concentrate on new business, but after everyone had left in the evenings, Ursula would go outside, have a cigarette, then come back, kick off her shoes and we'd get down to sorting out the backlog. She would relax a little and often, when we were tackling some really big tasks, would order in pizza for the two of us. We would sit in her office going through the paper work, trying not to let the cheese drip on the documents.

We very quickly built up a friendship and one evening, when we were taking a little break, I told her about The Grumpy Crumpets. She chuckled, then momentarily looked sad before regaining control of her emotions. 'You're lucky to have friends like that where you can just have fun,' was all she said, but I detected more in that comment. Her tone and body language told me that she was a lonely woman. I knew that I couldn't invite her to join The Grumpy Crumpets and was about to suggest we have another side project like me and Tracey had with OCD See? But she sighed and said, 'Okay, so where had we got to with this file?' and we were back working again.

A NEW NUMBER 1

After topping the charts for 3 weeks, The Grumpy Crumpets'
'Lusting For A Friend' gave way to Depeche Mode's 'Master

And Servant'. The latter had been in the charts for 3 weeks and climbed from 2 to 1, giving the Boys from Basildon their first chart topper. The song was the second single from their *Some Great Reward* album and follows up on the number 2 success of their previous hit, 'People Are People'. Dealing with domination and relationships, the new number 1 has an element of the seedy which seems to have captured the nation's more perverse side.

'I know "Master And Servant" never made it to number 1, but it was one of my favourites and, seeing that this is our fantasy, we can put right things that people got wrong back then.' It was surprisingly Desiree and not Jenny who put forward the song to take over from us at the top of the chart. If it had been Jenny suggesting Depeche Mode's BDSM hit I wouldn't have been surprised. But Desiree? I knew that she wasn't Mrs Prim and Proper, but I didn't think she would be that far the other way. On a scale of The Eurythmic's 'Missionary Man' to Depeche Mode's 'Master And Servant', I would have put her down as Cyndi Lauper's 'Girls Just Wanna Have Fun' or at a push Aerosmith's 'Love In An Elevator' although she would have to have had at least three glasses of red before being that adventurous. Jenny was, of course, Depeche Mode's 'Just Can't Get Enough'.

The others didn't seem to think Desiree's choice unusual. Jenny said she didn't mind who took over from us and then brushed her hair behind her ears so undoubtedly she wanted Jackson Browne to have the honours, while I think Sara was a secret Cliff Richard fan although she would never admit that. She did put up a little resistance, suggesting one of Duran Duran's hits, but couldn't decide between 'Hungry Like The Wolf' and 'Wild Boys'.

I would have loved it to be This Mortal Coil's 'Song To The Siren' but as I had got my way in only allowing three weeks at number 1, I felt I would be pushing my luck by requesting my choice for the new chart topper.

I wanted to ask Desiree what it was about the Depeche Mode hit that she liked but didn't get a chance as the conversation moved on quickly to what we needed to do next in the lives of The Grumpy Crumpets.

'Isn't it the track by track review of the album?' Sara asked. 'In that case we need to be coming up with more song titles.'

'Shouldn't we have an album launch first. We could come up with something different like imagined conversations with other stars instead of the usual newspaper reports,' Jenny suggested.

I liked that and said, 'Good idea, but we should really release the second single then we can do the album launch. What about a US tour after the album comes out. If we're going to rule the world, we need to start cracking the market over there.'

'I never realised how into your music you are, Sweetie,' Jenny said, and her smile was genuine. 'I knew you liked the more obscure stuff, but you must have followed those groups really closely to know what we have to do and when. You're a bit of a dark horse, you know.'

I waited for the brush back of the hair to show that she was being insincere, but it didn't come and that left me with a warm feeling even though I wasn't sure if Jenny meant to be complimentary or not. Her 'tell' with her hair may not have appeared because she was being genuine in her sarcasm, but I didn't care just then.

As the evening went on, we moved away from The Grumpy Crumpets and back into the real world.

'Any update on your boss?' Desiree asked.

'My ex-boss,' I corrected.

'Yes, your ex-boss. Have they charged him yet?'

'I believe they have,' I replied. 'From what we've been told, the forensic tests proved that the knife they found was the murder weapon in at least two of the stabbing cases, although they couldn't find his fingerprints on it. They presume he wore gloves.'

'He must have done,' the others agreed. What I didn't tell them was that the police had come round to ask if I could alibi my boss for some of the murders. He said he had been working late with me most evenings since the stabbings started. I explained to them that I hardly ever worked past five thirty.

My father and Bruce Willis were now fighting it out for the starring role in my dreams. On good nights Bruce and I would get up to all sorts of fun, sometimes sexual, sometimes it was just pleasant walks or quiet dinners. Once it was even a day at the fun fair where he won the giant teddy bear for me, but that was after watching a movie on TV, I forget which one, where that's what happened to the characters.

But it was not all Bruce and roses in my dreams. My father would appear some nights, invariably bringing blood with her. It would be like the stabbings never stopped, as if my boss was still on the loose and doing his evil deeds. Some nights I felt like I was drowning in blood, the crimson pools, sticky and cloying, would engulf me and invariably I would wake up gasping for breath only to find that I was still in a dream and my 'waking' only switched me from one nightmare to another as my father would still be there, a threatening violent presence clinging to her and I would scramble to find a way out, trying to get away.

Did I refer just refer to my father as 'her'?

There are chinks in my armour. I can feel them but don't know how to repair them. Things are crumbling, a slow erosion that I cannot stop, and I am scared. I fear what will be revealed. I fear what will be left of me when everything falls apart and I cling to The Grumpy Crumpets, hoping that they will save me.

CRUMPETS DOMINATE THE CHARTS

'Forever Ended Tonight', the second single to be taken from The Grumpy Crumpets' upcoming album, *Beyond The Loss*, has crashed into the charts at number one. The poignant punk rock ballad which talks of loss, has captured the nation and rocketed to the top spot, dragging the first single from the album, 'Lusting For A Friend' in its wake and the band now occupy the top 2 positions of the singles charts. Their earlier singles 'Scratch Your Eyes Out' and 'Putty In my Hands' also re-entered the charts, sitting at number 18 and 37 respectively, while their debut album, *Easy Peasy We're The GCs* celebrated its 70th week in the album charts by climbing 30 places from 50 to 20.

This is the first time an all-girl group has had occupied the top 2 positions in the charts and they are also the first to have 4 hits in the top 40 in the same week. Radio 1 DJ, John Peel, who has been championing The Crumpets for a while, said that he was delighted with the band's success. 'They're a lovely bunch of women and have brought a feminine charm to a traditionally male dominated genre. They deserve all the success and accolades they get.'

The band's lead singer, Desiree Desire, expressed their excitement. 'We're over the moon. We never expected this sort of response. All we can say is wow! Thank you, thank you, thank you.' She went on to add that The Grumpy Crumpets were just sorting out the final details of their tour to promote the album and hoped to advertise these in the next few days.

Beyond The Loss, the second album from The Grumpy Crumpets, is due out next week. John Peel will be playing the album in its entirety on his Friday night show which will also feature an exclusive interview with the four Crumpets.

It was completely over the top, but I needed that. With all that was going on, I needed to immerse myself in a completely self-indulgent fantasy world. It was just a pity that the others hadn't been there to share the success and by the time we would get round to talking about 'Forever Ended Last Night', I would probably have calmed down and not needed the boost as much. In reality, second singles rarely fared better than first ones.

But as a counter measure to my dreams being invaded by my father, I went over the top in a solo fantasy. The press was full of stories about my boss and the difficulties surrounding his case as he had alibis for some of the stabbings but not others. There was speculation that he had been working with a partner and his friends were being investigated. One article suggested that he was part of a group where members competed with each other to see who could notch up the most murders.

I saw a bit of Tracey during that time. She and Jenny were on much better terms, but occasionally they both needed some space and I would get an invite to meet up for a pizza or a curry. She was still interested in the progress of The Crumpets and I updated her. When I told her about 'Master And Servant' being the song that took over from 'Lusting for A Friend' at the top of the charts, she laughed and said, 'I guessing that it was Desiree who suggested that.' I was a little surprised and asked why she thought so.

'Well, because she and Ian are into that sort of stuff.' She looked at me with growing incredulity. 'Oh my god, you didn't know! I thought everyone knew.'

I was truly shocked. 'What? Desiree? You mean she…'

'Yeah, all that whips and chains stuff,' Tracey was enjoying herself.

'How…I mean…how do you know?'

'Oh, Ant told me. He heard noises coming from the art studio one day when he got home early. When he went to investigate, he found the door locked so peeped through the keyhole and saw his dad tied up naked and his mum dressed as a dominatrix whipping him.'

I was not sure what unsettled me the most, the fact that Desiree and Ian were into that sort of *Fifty Shades of Grey* stuff or that Tracey knew words like 'dominatrix' and seemed to find it all quite amusing. I was really quite shaken but did not want to show this so laughed.

'Oh my god,' I said. 'You know I never even suspected. I used to think that Ian might be abusing her, but Desiree dominating Ian? Wow! That's truly amazing. Who would have thought?'

Having semi-laughed it off, I proceeded to slowly move the conversation away from the topic and eventually got us talking about OCD See? I wanted to know if she was still interested in running with that fantasy.

NEW EP FROM OCD SEE?

OCD See? follow up the success of their first EP, 'Remembrance Of Memories' with a new single entitled 'Forlorn Scorn'. The 4 tracks on the new EP are 'Earthwhile', 'Ends To All Beginnings', 'Spacial Doubt' and 'Halfwise For A Daydream'. The duo of Clair da Loon and Tracey Bombhead recruited New Bosses singer Ursula Andrex to add backing vocals and her strong alto voice brings another tantalising layer to OCD See?'s complex sound.

I thought I would add Ursula because I felt sorry for her although she would never know about her involvement in my side project nor the bad joke surname I gave her. Tracey was quite okay with it once I explained about my new boss. Neither of us really liked the band name 'New Bosses' but we couldn't come up with anything better.

I was glad we had resurrected OCD See?'s career, especially as I had felt very uncomfortable talking about whips and chains and domination. The fact that Tracey seemed quite at ease talking about BDSM and even hinted that she would not be adverse to trying it herself made it worse. She quickly back tracked when she registered on my shock. But it got me thinking. She had an arty streak which neither of her parents had, but Ian did and now she showed an interest in this perverse behaviour which, while her mother could be promiscuous, I didn't think Jenny was into that stuff. But Ian was.

It was not the biggest stretch of the imagination to believe that Tracey could actually be Ian's daughter and not Geoff's. I don't think that

Tracey in any way suspected this, but I now needed to satisfy myself, so I arranged to meet up with Jenny.

I asked how things were going with her and Sara, then admitted that I hadn't seen that relationship coming.

'I hadn't either,' Jenny smiled, 'it just sort of happened. We were hugging each other as comfort and next thing I knew we were kissing and, well, that was it. I hadn't ever thought about having a relationship with another woman before. We just sort of fell into it. I think Sara was just as surprised about it as I was.'

I then asked her if she now saw other women in a different light. Did she think she could have a relationship with another woman, Desiree for example?

'Oh no, Sweetie, it's not like that. It's not just physical. But I suppose if it was, just physical I mean, I wouldn't say no to Desi, if it was on offer,' she said with a gleam in her eyes.

'What about Ian?' I said.

'Oh, he's not my type,' she said and firmly brushed her hair behind her ears.

'I didn't mean would you go for him, I meant wouldn't that be unfair on him if you hit it off with his wife?'

'Oh, that. Well, whatever,' she dismissed Ian's concerns with a wave of her hand, but I had my answer.

We were questioned by the police again. They came to our offices and one by one we were called into the boardroom. Ursula had told us they were coming and that we should co-operate with them. They were still working on my ex-boss' alibis and probing the theory that he had worked with someone else or was even part of a group.

Even though I had nothing to hide, I felt nervous. I did not want to let them know about my 'overtime' hours, especially as I had lied to them about it earlier. But they were gentle, double checking dates and seemed happy with my answers. They then asked particularly about the time that his daughter had been kidnapped and subsequently killed. It became clear to me that they suspected him of that too.

It horrified me that he could have been guilty of killing his own daughter, but he was that sort of a man, a vicious predator, so I suppose I shouldn't have been too surprised. It just made me hate him more.

The papers had dubbed him 'The Gentleman Killer' as everyone had been saying how surprised they were as he was such a gentleman, surely he could never have done this. If only they knew what this Jeckyll and Hyde would get up to after hours.

I found myself rather shaky after my interview with the police and felt the early signs of a migraine coming. By late afternoon I knew I was in for a bad one. My head pounded, and I felt physically ill. I stumbled home and collapsed onto my bed as the vice around my temples tightened, leaving me feeling as if my skull was being slowly crushed. My eyes were attacked by flashing pinpoints of light that bombarded them relentlessly and I could find no comfort with them opened or closed.

I took a large dose of headache tablets, not really caring what that may do to me, then lay down again and begged God to relieve me from the pain. I don't believe in God, so I don't know why I bothered. I suppose that, by asking Him for help, it gave me something to blame for my state. If He could cure it, then He must have created it was, I guess, the slightly weird logic I was using. Or maybe I was just desperate to get rid of the pain.

But I didn't need God. The handful of painkillers slowly pried the gripping fingers from my head and I began to feel like I could breathe again. But breathing in seemed to inflate me like a hot air balloon and I began to float around the room as mellow colours started to weave strange patterns in front of me. At times I looked down from the ceiling and saw myself lying on the bed, then suddenly I was on the bed looking up at me crawling across the ceiling.

Things began to spin, and I felt myself spiralling like water down a plughole, but I was going the wrong way, as if I was in another hemisphere. It did not feel right and I grabbed at whatever I could get hold of to steady myself and stop the spinning.

I stared down into the vortex that I was being drawn into and saw my mother and father looming over my sister Cathy. She was lying on a kind of altar. I did not see the blow as this nightmare vision suddenly skipped forward and went from her lying on the slab, a cute smile on her face, to her bloodied corpse staring startle-eyed up at me and my mother standing over her with a knife in her hand, letting the blood drip from the point of the blade onto Cathy's forehead.

This was all wrong. It was not mother who killed Cathy. A mother can never do such a thing. A mother has a special bond with their child. Why did this strange vision get something like this so wrong? I wanted to shout out, to tell anyone who may be seeing the same scenes as me that this was not how it happened. But all I could do was float over my family.

It was as if my vocal chords were trussed up like Ian seen through the keyhole by Ant.

I did not have to battle long with this scene as I must have fallen asleep then. The vision just turned off like a switch had been flicked and everything went black.

The next morning I woke feeling surprisingly refreshed. I got up and went to the shower to wash the blood off my body.

STILL WILD ABOUT THE 'WILD BOYS'

Duran Duran's 'Wild Boys' held on to the top spot on this week's top 40, seeing off the challenge from Spandau Ballet's 'True' which was stuck at number 2 for a second week. The Grumpy Crumpets' new single, 'Forever Ended Last Night' was the highest new entry, coming in at number 8. Also new to the charts were OMD's 'Talking Loud And Clear' and Tracey Ullman's 'Breakaway' which entered at 15 and 25 respectively.

The Grumpy Crumpets' new album, *Beyond The Loss* is due out next week and it is anticipated that it may well knock The Thompson Twins'*Quickstep And Sidekick* off the top spot on the album charts.

There was not much appetite for Grumpy Crumpet talk when we next met at Jenny's. We eventually got round to talking about it quite late in the evening and everyone agreed straight up that the second single could not do as well as the first despite us all saying it had a better title. Sara got her way with the Duran Duran single being number 1 and she also suggested 'True' for two 'because it rhymed.'

I had forgotten the Tracey Ullman song which was unusual for me. Desiree, who had suggested it, had to sing it before I remembered and I felt a bit of an idiot for not recalling. I was supposed to be the music expert. But at least we had the next episode sorted, even though it was not remotely like my original version.

The reason we had been so late in starting our Grumpy Crumpet talk was that we had been discussing the recent night of stabbings which had put a huge question mark over my ex-boss' guilt.

I was a bit distracted while the other three talked about these recent events as the 'vision' of my mother apparently stabbing my sister was still haunting me. Cathy had not been stabbed. She had fallen and hit her head...I think. It was not mother who had killed her. But my memories of that awful day were hazy. They came in waves. I could go for months without being reminded, then suddenly I would be hit with these recollections and they would stay for a few weeks like unwanted guests in my head. And I use the plural, memories, because there was a herd of them, each one different to the other. Some closely resembled others while some were radically different, like this latest one.

My friends didn't notice my discomfort until very late in the conversation, but then they put it down to being related to my boss and the recent stabbings.

'Where there's smoke there's fire,' Jenny said, presumably trying to reassure me.

But Desiree saw through this and said, 'That's not very comforting, Jenny. If he is guilty, as you suggest, and the latest stabbings means he gets off, then Clair will have to work with him again. This is quite serious.'

They continued to discuss this for a bit longer till I eventually said, 'Can we talk about something else? Can't we talk Grumpy Crumpets, please?' The thought of my boss returning to work did not fill me with joy.

In amongst all that was going on, my mind had not forgotten Tracey's revelation about Desiree and Ian and their left-of-centre sexual tastes. I still could not get my head around this, particularly the idea of Desiree being the dominant one.

A part of me really wanted to ask her about it as I was curious to know how it would feel to have so much power over a man, to have them completely at your mercy. I must admit to the occasional fantasy of having my boss...ex-boss...in my clutches like that. Not to give him any pleasure though, only to cause him pain. But I would probably go too far if I did, not stop when he had had enough. This didn't prevent me imagining it. Everything is safe in an imaginary world, as long as it doesn't leak into the real world.

Then there was the question about Tracey's parentage which also played on my mind. Did Ian know? And how could Geoff not have known that she wasn't his daughter? Maybe he had. Maybe he and Jenny just had one of those relationships. After all, he had got Sara pregnant at uni. Jenny would obviously have known that he had slept with her. Or did she? There seemed to be a lot about my friends that I know nothing about and this left me feeling uncomfortable. What else did they get up to? What other dark secrets lurked in the group?

I have always felt like the odd one out as I never married and even now with Ollie and Geoff gone, Sara and Jenny had paired up, so I was still the spare wheel. But these revelations of late were making me feel acutely different and at odds with the rest of the group. I did find myself wondering why they had kept me on as a friend once we left uni and they all got married but could never find a satisfactory explanation.

I started to question what would happen to the group dynamic if Ian were out of the picture. Would Desiree and I team up like Jenny and Sara had? I couldn't see myself having that sort of relationship with her even though of all of them, she was the one I felt closest to. But it was a friendship that I felt, not a sexual attraction and, if I did end up unwittingly in such a relationship – Jenny claimed that theirs had not been planned – would Desiree still want to practise her dominance fetish with me? These thoughts disturbed me, but the idea of Ian being out of the picture was something I could not help fantasising about. I had always found him creepy.

BEYOND THE LOSS – A TRACK BY TRACK REVIEW

1. *Forever Ended Last Night:* The Crumpets kick off their second album in a reflective mood. Written in the wake of the death of Jenny Jangle's husband, this rock ballad talks of love and loss. And with its Jim Steinman-esque production and Desiree Desire's scratchy power-vocal delivery, one can't help comparing it to Bonnie Tyler's 'Total Eclipse Of The Heart'. Poignant, but it's not what we're used to from The Crumpets.

2. *Lusting For A Friend:* The first single from the album and one that fans will be familiar with. This slots in neatly after 'Forever Ended Last Night' and returns us to the Crumpet sound that we are used to.

3. *An Icy Scream:* The song explores the thin line that divides sanity from madness and the fear that one can cross over at any moment. 'I skate through life/the thin ice is all between/a good day out/and an icy scream'. Desire's vocal delivery of this lyric is as brittle as the ice she sings about while Jangle's guitar has a cutting edge that claws its way into your mind. Drummer Clair da Loon is maturing as a songwriter and this is lyrically one of her best yet.

4. *Diatribe of Youth*: Rumoured to have been written by Jangle after a row with her daughter, this rocker explores the generation gap and the relationship between parent and child. It talks of two way hurt when things not meant are said in the heat of the moment. But there is a bit of a tipping of the hat to the wisdom of youth.

5. *Harvey X*: Track 5 finds The Crumpets in story telling mode. There is a slight Dylan-esque feel to the song which is somewhat folky but with a twist thrown in. Harvey X runs a music instrument shop which is a popular hangout for musicians. Harvey loves the instruments but cannot play a note until one day a guitar falls on his head and suddenly he is an aficionado and filling stadiums. Desiree Desire puts on the nasal twang of Dylan as she sings, but all is not what it seems as the last line of the songs reveals that the knock on the head actually had a different effect in real life. 'Harvey X looked down from above/and as the hearse drove away/those heavenly angels asked him to play.'

6. *Two Cups Left Steaming*: A poignant song about the loss the band still feels over the death of both Sara The Bitch's and Jenny Jangle's husbands. It speaks of the emptiness those deaths have left with a sort of *Mary Celeste* kind of eeriness. There is a hollow echo to Jangle's guitar while Sara The Bitch's bass thuds along with a breaking heart rhythm. The drums are slightly jazzy but in a melancholic way while Desiree Desire's vocals are haunting. Interestingly it is Desire who is credited with writing the song and it is her acute observations of her friend's grief that make this an emotional affair.

7. *One To Go*: Clair da Loon takes writing credits again on this upbeat number that lifts the spirit of the listener after the reflectiveness of 'Two Cups Left Steaming'. A bouncy beat is matched by Desire's girlie vocals on this one which give it a bit of an Altered Images feel. Bubbly but not irritatingly so, the song celebrates accomplishment of goals and looks ahead to a final task. It is rumoured that this alludes to the American market which the band are hoping to crack, but those who know the Crumpets well will realise that there is probably

some other hidden meaning to the lyrics, but it's anyone's guess as to what this might be.

8. *Shame Eludes Me*: A cheeky number that tips its hat to the album cover which features the band starkers playing their instruments. There is a freedom in this rushing punk pop track that has all the abandonment of a giggling streaker running through a crowd. These girls can do anything, nothing fazes them. Hand claps accompany a chant of 'Rules are meant to be broken'. One can almost visualise the four Crumpets stalking, vixen-like, up on the listener who is a helpless victim just waiting to be taken.

9. *In A Weird Place*: A Sara The Bitch number which finds The Crumpets in an unsettled frame of mind. The lyrics speak of an uncomfortable situation that one can't seem to escape. This is a clash of sounds that ironically are in harmony with the words in that both try to convey a sense of unease. It leaves one wondering if Sara is really over the loss of her husband.

10. *Easy Peasy We're The GC's*: The album ends on a happy note with this carefree number. It is a gorgeous romp with a catchy tune and sing-a-long chant of the title. It sends out the message that despite all the difficulties these girls have faced, they are still fighting on, taking life by the horns and enjoying it. This is an acknowledgement that there will be ups and downs, but one can still be positive, and this is captured in the line 'Helter Skelter here come lemons, Helter Skelter now there's candy. Life is fine, life is dandy. It's easy peasy with the GCs'.

My ex-boss appeared in a dream. I had been slowly forgetting about him, wiping him from my life but the dream brought back all the awfulness and pain he had caused me with his after-hours' antics. The recent talk about him possibly getting off because the stabbings had continued while he was in jail had brought him back into conversations and, I presume, he felt that this gave him permission to invade my dreams. I was not happy but what could I do? I could hardly go to the authorities and moan that they were not doing enough to protect me from him.

I mentioned the intrusion into my dreams to Ursula the next day. We were going through some old files and sorting out some things related to it.

'Well, don't worry. Even if he does get released, he's not coming back here,' she said. 'From what I've seen since I've been here, he's not been doing his job properly and I've already passed my report to Head Office.'

She stopped suddenly, her face saying that she had said too much. She was not just some fire fighter sent from Head Office, she was an investigator sent to dig and find out if suspicions were correct. They suspected he had been defrauding the company.

My immediate thought when jumping to that conclusion was, 'has he implicated me?' I started to worry that he had somehow covered his tracks by making it look like I was the perpetrator.

Ursula seemed to follow my mental panic and her face softened. 'I shouldn't be telling you this, but the branch has been making losses for a while and we were on the point of sending a team in to investigate when Guy was arrested. We gave him some leeway when his daughter was killed, but things didn't improve. I've not found any evidence of fraud, just poor management, so you've got nothing to worry about. In fact, I have noted how helpful you've been in my investigation and recommended you for a bonus.' She smiled kindly. 'But Guy will not be returning here if he gets off the charges. There's enough evidence for a dismissal.'

I didn't know what to say. This was the first bit of good news I had received in a while and I felt myself well up. I struggled to rein in my emotions, only too aware of what could happen if I couldn't, but as the relief flooded through me, it set my self-control free and I did not have the strength to try and pull it back as it drifted slowly away from me and somewhere far away I heard myself starting to sob. 'He abused me.' My voice was distant, spoken in an echo-ey chamber detached from reality.

It is hard to read a person when you are seeing them through a curtain of tears and a haze of emotions, so I have no idea how Ursula took my sudden outburst. She must have been taken aback at first, too surprised by my emotional meltdown to take on board fully what I had said and what the implications were. It seemed to take an age for her to take me in her arms and comfort me.

'Come on Clair, it's all right, it's all right.' I could feel her hand gently patting me, trying to comfort me back to my senses and I knew I needed to regain my self-control and quickly before I said something else stupid. I drew in a deep breath, pulled all those rogue thoughts and feelings back into me, wrapping mental fists tightly around them, reprimanding them for their reckless behaviour. I felt my breathing return to normal and my body relax while my mind tightened.

'I'm sorry,' I said, easing myself away from her and wiping away the tears. 'I'm sorry, I don't know what happened there.'

She studied my face, a concerned look on hers. Once I was sufficiently calm, she looked at me and asked, 'Who abused you? You can tell me, it's all right.'

The cat was out of the bag and I knew I could not put it back. 'Guy,' I said quietly.

A puzzled look crossed Ursula's face. 'Guy?'

I nodded, but my face must have shown some emotion as she suddenly said, 'It's not that I don't believe you, it's just I thought you had said *she* abused me.'

'The new album is getting great reviews,' our agent told us. He was a good looking guy of about 26 and I am sure he has the hots for me. 'It's highly likely to enter the charts at number one.'

'Oh, it's definitely going in at one,' one of the record execs said. He was also a good looking guy, maybe slightly older than our agent, with the deepest blue eyes you've ever seen. I knew that he had the hots for me.

'But that means we will be knocking The Police's 'Synchronicity' off the top spot,' Sara The Bitch almost gasped.

'We don't mind,' Stewart Copeland said and winked at me, although I don't think Sting was best pleased despite giving Jenny a vague smile. Jenny had been fawning over him since he walked into the room. We were only meeting with the biggest band on the planet to discuss The Crumpets having a supporting slot on The Police's upcoming US tour. 'Synchronicity' had been at the top of the charts there for like a hundred years.

Our agent didn't like the way Jenny was drooling over Sting because he also had the hots for her.

The record exec was not best pleased with the attention Stewart was paying me, but it was a drummer thing, so he didn't stand a chance. Not only did I find Stewart extremely cute, he was also an awesome drummer.

'Bruce Springsteen and Prince have also expressed an interest in having you as their support act,' the record exec said in what was clearly an attempt to interrupt the eye flirting that was going on in the room. Desiree was trying to muscle in on Stewart, while Sara seemed to have resigned herself to not winning with either Stewart or Sting so had been

quite openly showing interest in Andy Summers. We were like school-
girls again and all I could think of was what backstage antics Stewart and
I could get up to after the concerts. Things were about to go huge with
The Grumpy Crumpets, there was no doubt about it.

'Apparently Jackson Browne's agent is also asking if you want to tour
with him,' our agent said, presumably feeling duty bound to give us all
our options, or in a desperate attempt to distract us from The Police.
Little did he know about Jenny's obsession with Jackson and all our eyes
turned to her, imploring her not to change her mind about touring with
The Police.

I imagined the whole Police meeting as I lay in bed the evening of my
breakdown with Ursula. I needed perking up and the only thing I could
think of was to immerse myself in Grumpy Crumpet world. I probably
would have ended up in the sack with Stewart Copeland if bloody
Jackson Browne hadn't come along and ruined things. It annoyed me
that I didn't have complete control of my fantasy. Despite my best
efforts, I couldn't stop the intrusion and it made me hate Jenny because
it was her fault. Jackson Browne was an okay looking guy, but not nearly
as sexy, or as successful for that matter, as The Police.

The unwanted arrival of Jackson's name into my fantasy ruined it and,
despite my best efforts, I could not get The Police to stick around long
enough to spend some quality time with Stewart. I tried to see if Bruce
Willis was available, but he was busy discussing with Ursula how he was
going to drop my ex-boss from a tall building, like he had done with the
baddie in *Die Hard*.

I got up and ran a hot bath with lots of bath salts, easing myself into
the steamy aromas and feeling the heat of the water pricking my skin.
There was no getting away from my earlier breakdown with Ursula and
I knew I had to work through it again or I would never get to sleep.

I had manged to wriggle out of things a little after admitting that my
boss had abused me. I didn't call it rape rather just talked of it as bullying.
I could not admit to the after hours things that had been inflicted on me.
Even with the stabbings hanging over him, I was not convinced anyone
would believe me and besides, he may even use that in his defence to alibi
him for the stabbings, although they had all occurred after I had been
dismissed for the evening.

So instead of giving all the details of what he had actually done, I just
kept to the mental bullying story. I could see that Ursula suspected that

I was not telling her everything, but she didn't push. She was just kind and kept reassuring me that he wouldn't be coming back to work there, even if he got off the stabbing charges.

I grabbed hold of those assurances as I lay in the bath and slowly felt relaxed enough to try to sleep.

Our next girls' night was a few days after my breakdown. In the interim I had worked through the emotions and felt back in control despite reports that the case against my former boss was crumbling. I managed to convince Ursula that I had told her everything about my boss and in my fantasies Bruce Willis and I were back together.

We were at Sara's again and she had cooked a great fish pie. Desiree's choice of red was spot on, even though red is not supposed to go with fish, and we were in good spirits when we sat in the lounge, basking in a post good food glow. Jenny and Sara had really begun to relax into their relationship and Desiree had probably just come from a session of dominating Ian as she seemed to be buzzing with a kind of adrenaline induced energy.

They were talking about the 'lost' album cover pictures, a conversation Jenny had started, and were debating whether we should re-do the pictures. Desiree was against doing so and kept looking at me. Jenny was, unsurprisingly, the one pushing for it while Sara seemed indifferent. I was surprised that Jenny hadn't picked up on the way Ian had been drooling over me when we had posed for those pictures. She's usually quite sensitive to those things, especially when it involved a man she was interested in. I could only conclude that, despite Ian fathering Jenny's daughter, there was no attraction between them anymore, at least nothing from Jenny's side.

I was not interested in going through all that again. It had been enough of an ordeal at the time and, thinking about how Ian had looked at me during the photoshoot made me shudder. It also worried me that it would cause a rift between me and Desiree which was not my fault.

'Where will we get the instruments from?' I asked, hoping that this would dissuade Jenny from her plans. 'That shop closed after the owner passed away.'

'That's a point,' Desiree said and gave me a smile which was the warmest reaction I had had from her since the topic came up.

'There must be some other shops around,' Jenny said, 'I'll find one.' She looked around the group for support and saw that it was not forthcoming. 'Or not,' she said in an offhanded way, but there was an undertone of bitterness. She was the naturist of the group, wanting to take her clothes off whenever possible.

She sat back with a slightly sulky pout and spoke very little for the rest of the evening.

When I got home, I took out Ian's laptop and started searching through his files. I had a hunch and it didn't take me long to find what I was looking for. In amongst his music was a folder called 'Jackson Browne' where I found a good number of image files. Opening them revealed, as I suspected, pictures of Jenny. Most of them were nude shots and looking carefully at them, I realised that they had been shot in his studio. I found some where Jenny had short hair and thought that it was about four or five years back that she had cut it short like that, but it had grown back now. The dates on the files revealed that these sessions went back years. This had been going on for a good while.

I searched through the folder marked 'Duran Duran', wondering if Sara had also been one of his 'models', but there was nothing there, nor was there anything other than music files in the 'Spandau Ballet' and 'Police' folders, but under 'Wham' there were some more. They were not nudes, just some of Sara topless on a beach which looked like they had been taken surreptitiously when we had all gone on holiday together.

This got me thinking and I found the 'New Order' folder and my stomach churned as I immediately saw that it contained picture files. My hand shook as I opened the first one. It was of me during our album cover shoot, but he had caught me fully exposed, as he had done in the next few images. I scrolled through these, feeling annoyed that I had let myself be talked into doing the photoshoot in the first place. As I scrolled through them, the 'album cover' shots were suddenly replaced by the snaps that looked like they had been taken on the same holiday as the ones of Sara. I was rather annoyed by this, but at least I hadn't gone topless back then and was in my one-piece costume. I remember the teasing I had to endure, from Jenny in particular, for not daring to wear a bikini. Given that I was being unknowingly photographed, I was glad that I hadn't given into the pressure.

Scrolling further through the pictures they changed again, and my heart stopped. These were clearly scans of old prints. They were rather grainy and not in brilliant focus, but I would never forget that room. It was the B&B room where we stayed when we had gone up to the New Order concert. The one where Simon had had his way with me after the show, the one where I had 'paid' for my lift home. Although not overly clear, I knew straight away who the couple on the bed were and judging from the angle of the shots, I could only conclude that Ian had been in the cupboard taking the pictures while I was being humiliated.

It took both Bruce Willis and Stewart Copeland to rescue me that night. I concentrated hard on these two men, trying hard to push what I had seen on Ian's computer from my mind. I watched an episode of *Moonlighting* from the box set I had, enjoying seeing a young Bruce again, then followed this with the DVD of The Police's greatest hits and this helped attract the two men into my dreams.

I even managed to get them to be perfect gentlemen with me not, I am sure, that they wouldn't be perfect gentlemen with me in real life if I were ever to meet them, but in my dreams, they wined and dined me, brought me flowers and chocolates, listened to me with bright attentive eyes. They were funny, making me laugh and pampered me till I felt absolutely special.

Had my dreams ended there, I would have had a very good night's sleep and woken up feeling great, the hurt and humiliation from seeing those pictures all but evaporated. But at some early hour of the morning Bruce's neat suit disappeared and changed into the smudged, blood-and-sweat stained vest he had ended up with in *Die Hard*. He hoicked a machine gun over his shoulder, gave me that cheeky grin of his and said that he just had to go and sort Ian out.

I tried to stop him from going, but he ignored me and headed off. I turned to Stewart for help, but he just shrugged and vanished in a puff of smoke. I was left sitting on my own in a posh restaurant with all the customers looking at me as if I had just done a Meg Ryan fake orgasm. That wouldn't have been so bad if all the customers had not been my ex-boss, all staring lasciviously at me.

I did not have to wait long though before Bruce returned, his face, vest and torso were all blood-spattered and all he said was 'Yippee-ki-ay-motherfucker' and winked at me while Desiree's shocked face glared accusingly from behind him.

'Where have we got to in The Grumpy Crumpet saga?' Desiree asked during the next girls' night. She seemed to have forgotten the antagonism she had shown towards me when we talked about re-doing the nude shots for the album cover. She also had no animosity towards me like she had in my dream and that threw me somewhat. I had been expecting her to still be angry at me for sending Bruce to kill Ian, even though I never did, either in my dreams or in real life. But the dream had been so vivid and had felt so real that it made the adjustment to actual reality rather difficult for me and I had to work hard to disguise the feelings it evoked in me.

'The new album had come out, hadn't it?' Sara said.

'Had it?' Jenny replied, 'I thought we were still discussing the cover.'

'The last thing we did was the track by track review. The album was just about to come out,' I said.

'Oh yes, that's right,' Sara said, 'so does the album go straight in at number 1?'

'I vote that it does,' I said after a pause from the others. No one seemed too enthusiastic and I began to panic that they were getting bored with the whole fantasy. Desiree had suddenly gone quiet after Jenny mentioned that bloody cover again. Jenny, judging by the way she mentioned the cover, was still sulking at the fact the we didn't want to re-do the photoshoot and Sara who had been a little slow on picking up Jenny's mood, was doing so now.

I looked round the group, hoping that someone would support my vote.

'I suppose,' Jenny said as I looked at her.

'I guess,' said Desiree when I glanced at her.

'Oh, okay. Go on then,' was Sara's response.

I was getting desperate and was just about to try and encourage them by suggesting something about touring with The Police as in my earlier solo fantasies, hoping that this would entice some interest out of them, when Ian popped his head round the door to see if we wanted some coffee.

I was quite shocked at seeing him as Bruce Willis had supposedly done him in. I was annoyed with Bruce for lying to me and resolved not to let him into my dreams for a week as punishment.

Our conversation, having been interrupted, moved away from Grumpy Crumpet business but I was not really engaging as Ian's appearance had stoked the anger I had towards him over the photos.

Eventually Jenny picked up on my change in mood. 'You sulking because we didn't want to talk Grumpy Crumpets, aren't you? Come on, Clair sweetie, grow up will you. It's just a stupid bloody game. You can't go getting all serious about it.' She was in one of her moods, but I had not realised how bad it was and I was not in a good place to cope with it.

'No, it's not that, it's just…'

'Just what?' she snapped. 'Just that you'd rather be talking about bloody imaginary bands that don't exist instead of doing something exciting with your life. Live a little for god's sake!'

How I hated her at that moment. She had no idea how much The Grumpy Crumpet fantasy meant to me, how much it kept me sane in a world that seemed intent on battering and abusing all who passed through it.

'I'm not sulking about not talking about The Grumpy Crumpets, it was just that I had a nightmare last night, a really vivid one in which Ian had been stabbed by my boss…my ex-boss…like Geoff had been and, well, seeing him just now brought back the dream and the memory of what happened with poor Geoff.'

It was cruel, I know, reminding her of Geoff when he hadn't even come into my thoughts until I started fighting back against her tirade. It was a low blow, but it had the desired effect as she suddenly shrunk back in her chair and reached out to Sara for comfort.

Out of the corner of my eye, I saw Desiree looking at me quizzically. I could sense she was wondering if I was genuine about what I had said, or if I was just using Geoff's death to shut Jenny up. Desiree knew me better than the other two. I turned to her. 'It was horrible, Desi. I woke up screaming and in a cold sweat. I am glad it was just a dream and that he's okay. But you wouldn't have wanted to see what happened in the dream.'

Desiree's suspicion seemed to wane, and I congratulated myself on my acting skills. But, despite my defeating Jenny and placating Desiree, we had left ourselves very little to talk about and ended up going home quite early. There were more stabbings that evening which happened near to my route home.

Stewart Copeland invited me to his place after we finished our meeting. 'Come have a coffee, I want to talk to you about some of the drumming arrangements on your new album.'

I could tell the others were jealous, especially as Sting and Andy Summers had disappeared straight after the deal was sealed, leaving them to the attentions of our agent and some leery record execs.

We drove out to the Copeland Estate in Stewart's open-top sports car. It was a lovely hot summer's day and I loved feeling the wind in my hair as we sped along the country lanes. The house was amazing, a stately mansion. There were servants too. I was nervous as my heels clacked across the marble floor of the entrance hall, but Stewart did not even notice the squeak his trainers made. He was comfortably dressed in his stovepipe jeans and untucked shirt while I worried about being under-dressed for such an elaborate home.

He casually threw the car keys into a small basket on a table and ushered me into a room. There was a huge drum set laid out in front of large French doors that looked out onto a pristine garden with a small pond and fountain. Ducks played merrily on the pond. I must have been gawking as Stewart suddenly started to laugh.

'You get used to it after a while,' he said.

'What do you mean?' I asked.

'The wealth,' he grinned. 'At first it does your head in when you realise you can get whatever you want, but eventually the novelty wears off and you start being sensible.'

'Sensible?'

'Yeah. You start investing instead of just spending. You have to be realistic. Careers like ours do not usually last forever, especially us drummers. Very few bands can keep a career going for more than a few years. If you last a decade, you're doing well. Lead singers can sometimes extend that a bit further, but that's the exception. Can you name any band from the sixties that is still going strong? The Stones? That's about it. And band members? Paul McCartney? John Lennon possibly if he hadn't been killed. Cliff Richard. That's about it and Cliff's a singer, not a band. But who else is still having hits on a regular basis? No, enjoy your time in the limelight, Clair, but be sensible with the money, it's not going to keep coming in at the same rate forever.'

It was odd getting such advice from someone who was at the top of that wave. I thought about the money that was beginning to flow quite freely into my bank account. It had frightened me a little if I was honest. I was never much good with finances and the Royalty Statements that I received confused me so I would just file them away.

I had splashed out on a few new outfits, but other than that, the money was just building. The others, especially Jenny Jangle, were really starting to spend big time. Desiree Desire had bought a new house. Sara The

Bitch had got herself a couple of sports cars while Jenny Jangle was doing everything, mansion, cars, clothes, shoes. She was mad about shoes.

'If you like I can see if my accountant is prepared to take you on as a client, he's really good. Tea or coffee?'

'Tea, please,' I answered.

He nodded, picked up a phone to relay the order. As we waited for the housekeeper to bring our tea, I walked around the drum set admiring it.

'Want a go?' Stewart asked, and I nodded. 'Okay,' he said, 'but on one condition.'

'What's that?'

'You kill Ian.'

Due to my annoyance at Bruce Willis for pretending to kill Ian when he hadn't and the way the girls had been disinterested in progressing The Grumpy Crumpets' career, I had decided to go solo with the fantasy and also to exclude Bruce from my dreams. It seemed only natural to continue The Grumpy Crumpet story where I had left off with The Police wanting us as their support act. It was one I could run with and, unlike the group ones where we 'played' everything out via media reports, this gave me the freedom to get immersed into the private life of a rock star drummer without having to worry about what the others thought. It felt quite liberating and I decided that I would not raise The Grumpy Crumpets at our girls' nights again. If they wanted to continue then so be it, but I wasn't going to prompt.

I went to bed in a good mood. How could one not when one had been invited over to Stewart Copeland's – *the* Stewart Copeland – place and a chance to play on his drum set. And all this after having signed up to be The Police's support act on their upcoming U.S. tour. I thought that I would have had a good night's sleep with pleasant dreams, but my father had to go and spoil things. She came into my dreams and dragged a whole lot of blood, Cathy's blood, in with him.

I looked around, desperately searching for my sister, but all I saw was her blood.

'Where is she?' I screamed at my father, but she just grinned back at me, a nasty evil grin. He knew what had happened to Cathy, I could see it in his eyes and the blood down the front of his dress told me that he had been the one who caused it. My mother…I mean my father…could be like that.

I floundered around in the darkness of the dream, desperately searching for my sister, but found myself slipping in the blood that covered the floor. All the time he watched, seeming to take more and more pleasure in my panic. At the back of my mind I was angry, not because of her laughter or the fact that Cathy was dead, but I was angry that my dream had been hijacked.

Later, when I woke up, I would struggle to understand how I could be so caught up in the panic of what was happening in the dream, yet so aware that it was just a dream. I couldn't figure out how I could be annoyed about the way this dream clashed with my earlier thoughts and fantasies around Stewart Copeland.

Every time I felt I was getting closer to finding Cathy, I would slip and then suddenly feel miles away from her. I became more and more desperate till, thrashing around, I woke feeling hot and sweaty yet icy cold inside. I lay on my bed panting and shivering, my body burning up.

It took me a long while to settle myself, return my heartbeat to normal and get my temperature to match my mood. I pulled the duvet closer around me as I cooled while the confusion in my mind still raged. Who had killed Cathy? I had been convinced that it had been my father, but my dreams were confusing things. I knew somewhere deep down that the true answer lay buried in my mind. But I had locked that memory in a mental strong room, not wanting to face the truth of it. Had my father been the monster that my dreams portrayed him as?

I did not really want to confront that episode from my youth. I turned onto my side, as if turning my back on my family and all it entailed.

The news at work the next day was not good. The case against my ex-boss had fallen apart and he was to be released that afternoon. I felt a cold spike of dread stab at me as Ursula broke the news. We had all been called into the conference room to be told. Ursula went on to explain that she would be returning to head office soon, but despite his release, Guy would not be coming back. They would be sending a new person in to run our area. She looked at me as she said this as if to emphasise the point that I had nothing to worry about and I believed her. But it was not work that worried me, it was outside of work that I was scared of. He could track me down, follow me to my home and continue where he had left off.

Even the thought that I could now report him without fear of losing my job did not help as I knew that I was so programmed not to say anything about 'our little secret' that it would be impossible for me to break out of that habit. His release was shown on the TV news and all in the office crowded around the big screen in the reception area to watch as he told the world how glad he was that this was all behind him and he just wanted to get back to his family and a normal life and put this whole nightmare behind him. He had never done anything wrong and he would never harm anyone. Well that's what I picked up from those around me. I spent that time in the ladies, trying hard not to be sick.

Ursula called me into her office latter to check that I was okay, but by then I had recovered enough to convince her that I was. She thanked me for all my hard work and said she was sure that I'd get on well with Tony who was going to be our new boss.

'He's a good egg, one of our best managers. He'll get this place back on its feet. And he'll appreciate hard workers like you, Clair,' she told me with a smile.

Although not in the mood, I smiled back and told Ursula how much I had enjoyed working with her and how much I would miss her. And I really meant it. She had made going to work a pleasure again after the hell I had gone through. By the time I got home that evening the news about my ex-boss was everywhere, so I ignored the TV and spent my evening just listening to some of my favourite music.

Someone called me Colin in my dreams that night. There was a haze in my mind and I could not see who was talking to me. It was a woman's voice, one that I did not recognise. She said her name was Lydia. Her voice was soothing, a gentle sound, but when she called me Colin it jarred, and I felt myself flinch each time she said it. She was probing, I could tell. Her questions were aimed to get me to talk, but in the dream I could not speak. I felt my tongue lying heavily in my mouth, a useless lump of meat.

It seemed to go on for an age, the dream, all the time this dulcet voice talking to me from inside a foggy light. I could sense my mother just outside the conversation, lurking, listening, making sure that I did not say anything stupid. She could be like that when I was young, always there to make sure that I didn't say anything I was not supposed to.

'Are you Stewart Copeland's wife?' my dream-self asked Lydia, my tongue had loosened, and I was suddenly concerned that I might be up against a jealous spouse who was trying to coax me into admitting infidelity with her husband. I had done nothing wrong, I had not slept with Stewart, although in the fantasy within the fantasy I wanted to and would probably do so. But this dream was encroaching on my fantasies. I didn't like Lydia, she felt threatening, like she knew something about me that I did not want anyone to know.

I shrunk back from her and her questions, not liking this intrusion. Where was Stewart? Even Bruce Willis would do. Come back Bruce, all is forgiven. Why does Lydia call me Colin?

There was no Grumpy Crumpet talk at out next girlie night which was at Jenny's place. Not even a hint of it. Neither was there even any talk about starting up a new fantasy. The conversion revolved almost entirely around Sara and Jenny's decision to move in together. They were like excited teenagers searching for approval from Desiree and me. Desi managed to say the right things and showed enough enthusiasm for them to be happy despite it being quite obvious that she was really quite ambivalent about it. She was a good actor, but I saw through her, I always did.

I, on the other hand, was genuinely pleased for them and said so, but then blew it by asking how Tracey felt about it.

'She's thrilled,' Jenny said, shoving her hair behind her ears with some force. 'We were thinking of having a party to celebrate. I know some of our friends don't approve,' she looked at me then, 'but most do and those that don't, well they just aren't our friends.'

I struggled to work out why she would feel that I didn't approve, but then realised that Tracey obviously did not approve and Jenny must have felt I was taking her side by bringing the topic up, as if trying to get her to admit that there was an issue. It hurt, but I did not rise to the bait. Instead I mustered up some fake enthusiasm and said, 'Excellent idea, count me in.' That really messed Jenny up as the way I said it meant that she would only look silly if she continued to imply that my concern for Tracey meant I didn't approve of their relationship. The fact that I was now planning to have a migraine the day of the party – a revenge on Jenny for her treatment of me – was beside the point.

What I had not planned was the migraine that hit me on my way home. I managed to stumble through my front door and throw myself onto my bed, my skull feeling as if it were being slowly crushed.

The next day there was a huge outcry in the press. There had been five fatal stabbings overnight, all within days of my ex-boss being released.

'*Beyond The Loss* is straight in at number one,' our excited manager told us. 'Apparently the record first week sales for an all-girl group.'

There was a slight media frenzy as all the papers wanted a piece of us and we were going to do *Top of the Pops* later that day. It was all a whirl.

'We're absolutely thrilled,' Desiree said.

'There are rumours that you are going to support The Police during their upcoming U.S, tour. Is that true?'

The hack who asked the question was kind of cute and he had been eying me all through the press conference.

'We're in talks,' Jenny answered, despite the question clearly having been directed at me. We were under strict instructions not to say anything until the agreements had all been signed. We all glanced at Jenny, but she ignored us and continued to grab the limelight.

'I for one am very excited at the possibility of working with Sting. I have admired him for a long time and if this tour comes off it will be a dream come true.'

I could almost imagine Stewart rolling his eyes if he were to hear this interview and Sting being sulky and possibly calling the whole thing off.

Fortunately, another journo diverted the conversation by asking about the album cover. 'Do you feel that you are just using sex to sell your records?'

'Nudity is not sex,' Desiree's reply was immediate and with a straight face. 'Sex is an action. The cover of the album is an expression of the raw nakedness of the emotions expressed in our lyrics. In modern society, being naked is associated with vulnerability and that's where we were emotionally when making this album. The cover art is merely an expression of how we were feeling.'

The journalist, a severe looking woman, was not convinced. 'But surely people…men…will be buying the album simply because of the titillation of the cover.'

'We can't control the emotions and thoughts of others. If someone wants to see the cover as something sexual then we can't stop them. We can only re-iterate that our intention with the cover was for it to be a metaphor for the nakedness of our emotions.'

Desiree was good at nonsense like this and after the press conference ended, the severe looking journalist caught up with us and said that she thought we looked amazingly sexy on the cover and if she didn't have a review copy, she would have gone out and bought it just for the cover. You have to love the press.

The interview moved on to talking about our plans. Were we likely to sign for a major label? Was a UK tour on the cards? Any thoughts about the third album yet? What was happening to OCD See?

To the last question I answered that it was a part-time project to keep me out of mischief when time allowed, but for the moment all my energies were concentrated on promoting 'Beyond The Loss'.

'What do you make of all the recent stabbings?' The person asking the question was my boss…sorry…ex-boss.

The intrusion of reality into my fantasy really threw me. I had been lying quietly on the couch, some rubbish flickering on the telly, while my mind had been engrossed in furthering The Grumpy Crumpets' career. Why could he not leave me in peace? I knew that his recent release had caused this. He had been in my thoughts a lot as I dreaded bumping into him again. I kept thinking he would come to the office to pick up his belongings even though they had all been boxed up and sent to him.

There had been days recently when I could swear that he had followed me home from work and I began to fear that one day he would attack me as I opened my front door, forcing me inside and violating me in my own home.

I was becoming paranoid and started taking different routes home, sometimes adding as much as an hour to my commute and I kept checking back to see if I was really being followed, but I never spotted him and each evening I arrived home a nervous wreck, unlocking the door quickly and just as quickly closing it behind me.

The whole thing was exhausting me. As was my work. Ursula's replacement, a guy called Tony, was a no-nonsense boss. We worked hard, continuing to sort out the remains of the mess Guy had left us, and once we had completed what Ursula had started, we set about re-building the business. There was no time for any misbehaving, no time even for being a little sociable, just hard graft.

One day on my way home, I swear that I saw my old boss walking down the road on the opposite side. I dived into a Boots store and hid behind the beauty products, my heart pounding and praying that he did not come in. Fortunately, he just carried on walking down the road. The next day I got some news that cheered me up no end. A husband of one of the stabbing victims had walked up to my ex-boss in broad daylight and shot him seven times. I felt sorry for the husband, he had done the world a favour but would end up doing some serious jail time. He could hardly have known that it was me who had planted the knife in Guy's office.

Of my three friends' husbands, I think that killing Ian gave me the most pleasure. Ollie's death had been done remotely, spiking his cocaine had been easy, but I had not been there to watch him writhe as the poison took hold and not seeing that surprised look, as he realised what I had done, left me feeling rather cheated by his death. Stabbing Geoff had been a whole lot better. All the anger at how he had cheated on me at uni with Sara and how he had dumped me for Jenny came out as I repeatedly pushed the knife into his soft belly. I didn't tell him why, even though his eye pleaded for an explanation as the blood drained from him. I let him die not knowing why he had been killed. If he was too stupid to realise, then let him die stupid.

But Ian knew. I wasn't going to let him go without making sure he was well aware of how his actions had affected me. Seducing him wasn't difficult. Men who think with their genitals instead of their brains are easy prey. I played on the way he had looked at me during the photo shoot. Told him, when we had snatched moments alone, that I had noticed how many pictures he had taken of me compared to the others and how I felt flattered. I built things up slowly, eventually suggesting a private photo session when Desiree wasn't around. It took weeks to get this far as I had to be careful not to let on to anyone else that I was making moves on Ian as it could have raised questions after I had killed him. It was risky, especially as I had no control over what he might mention to others.

So, I proceeded cautiously. At first, he was suspicious. I had always seemed reluctant about the album cover shoot, he said. He thought that I had been uncomfortable being naked in front of the camera and did not seem to have been enamoured with the resulting pictures.

I admitted that I had not been keen on the whole thing at the time, but for some reason I could not stop thinking about it and had eventually reached a point where I realised that I had just been silly about it all and really wanted to try again and promised that I would not be so nervous this time around. I swore him to secrecy, saying that if the others knew it would just bring back the nerves. I knew that he was unlikely to let Desiree know, he must have picked up on her vibes whenever the photoshoot was mentioned. And what reason would he have to tell

Jenny or Sara unless there was still something going on between him and Jenny. That was a risk I just had to take,

The first session was hard. I did not feel comfortable being naked in front of Ian on my own, but I pushed all that aside as best I could and managed to lose my nervousness by concentrating on poses and thinking forward to what I was planning to do.

At the end of the session he tried to get a bit fresh with me, obviously turned on by what he had seen, but I strung him along, playing hard to get yet giving enough away for him to know that it was not a 'no' but a 'not just yet'.

After the second session, a week later, we had sex despite my abhorrence at having to be intimate with him.

We had two more sessions and each time I got a little rougher in doing it with him, sending out signals that if he wanted to do something a little more kinky, then I was game. I had, after all, had experience of rough sex with my boss. The third time, I mentioned I had heard that he and Desiree were into S&M and was it true?

He was taken aback, but the trap had been baited and he admitted to enjoying being tied up.

'Do you want me to tie you up?' I asked. The softly softly approach had worked. My growing roughness during sex had engendered a level of trust in him and he was now willing to take the next step. He talked me through the process, how to tie the knots, how a 'safe word' worked – the word he would shout out if it was becoming too much – and how trust was hugely important in this whole process and I was to stop immediately if he said the 'safe word'. I don't know if I should have read anything into the fact that his 'safe word' was 'bananas' but couldn't think what it may say about him.

I wanted him to trust me. I wanted him to feel betrayed the way I had when I found the photos he had taken of me and Simon in that B&B room in Manchester. So I played along with his kinky fetish. Having sex with a tied up and, let's face it, helpless man was very empowering as was doing the things he wanted done which gave him pain.

'You're really good, a natural,' he said after our first proper S&M session. I had struggled to stop when he had shouted out 'bananas' as the pleasure of inflicting pain on him was addictive. I had to remind myself that he was actually enjoying it and that helped me to stop.

I had a fine line to tread. The longer I took to complete my task, the greater the risk that someone would find out about us and that would cast suspicion over me when the police investigated, but I wanted to build up his trust and, dare I say it, his love for me so that my revenge would be even sweeter.

I numbed my mind and body to what I was putting it through, constantly reminding them of the ultimate goal.

After nearly two months of this, I finally felt I was ready to make my move. I had Ian tied up naked on a chair in his studio and had been applying some rather painful torture, the kind I had learned he really liked. Once I had him cooking, I whispered that I wanted to show him something. He grinned lasciviously as I dragged a small stool in front of him, put my laptop down then, as it booted up, aroused him some more till the computer was ready.

I had made a slide show and had used Frankie Goes To Hollywood's 'Relax' as accompaniment and rigged up some speakers for better quality sound. It seemed the perfect soundtrack to what I wanted to do.

The show started harmlessly enough with some pictures of the four Grumpy Crumpets on a beach in our bikinis or rather the other three in bikinis and me in a one-piece. Then I had taken some selfies of me in various stages of undress till I was eventually naked. I kept touching him as the show progressed, keeping him turned on. When the pictures changed to the ones of me totally naked he grinned up at me and at that moment I hated him so much I just wanted to smash his skull in. But I had planned something else, so I moved behind him and cut a good length of packing tape and, while his eyes were glued to the laptop screen, quickly stuck it across his mouth and wrapped the rest around his head. That was the first indication he had that something may be amiss. But I smiled sweetly at him and, with a flick of my head, indicated that he should carry on watching. The time was getting close. I moved behind him again and cut another length of tape then, just as the photos of me in the B&B room started, I moved in front of him, taking care not to obscure his view of the screen. It took him a few seconds to realise what he was seeing and a few more seconds for the panic to set in as he realised what I was about to do, He struggled against his restraints, his head shaking back and forth while he sucked in air nosily through his nose, muffled cries trying to escape from behind the tape across his mouth. I leaned forward and whispered in his ear, 'Frankie says relax' and put the new piece of tape firmly over his nose.

'I can't believe we've been at number one for ten straight weeks,' Jenny said as the charts were released. 'That's amazing.'

'And *Easy Peasy We're The CGs* is at number 7,' Desiree added, studying the copy of the fax of the new album charts.

Not only were our albums doing well, the singles were all in the top 100 with the new single, 'Two Cups Left Steaming' debuting at number 15 which was not at all bad for the third single from an album. What pleased me more, however, was that the two OCD See? EPs were at 74 and 92 respectively. I had never thought they would make the main charts, but people were scrambling for anything Grumpy Crumpet related. We were being recognised in the streets now, so were going everywhere by car. We had all employed drivers – I hate the term chauffeurs – who would drop us off right in front of the building where we were going and pick us up there again. We all had large houses and the money just kept rolling in.

Things were also going well with the preparations for the US tour with The Police and interest in The Grumpy Crumpets was growing on the other side of the pond. A number of the radio stations there had picked up on *Lusting For A Friend* and it was starting to get some decent rotation on their playlists. The latest *Billboard* charts had shown it entering at number 70 while *Beyond The Loss* was at 103 and *Easy Peasy We're The GC's* was at 188 on the top 200 album listings. Our agent had managed to line up a few interviews and a handful of television ones as we moved around the country. The plane tickets – first class – had been booked and…

'Colin.'

The plane tickets – first class – had been booked and…

'Colin!'

Why does Lydia call me Colin?

The plane tickets had been booked and the hotels – fancy five star ones – were being lined up.

'Colin, look at me.'

I don't like Lydia, she is not welcome in my fantasies. Why does she keep trying to intrude?

Watching Ian struggle against his restraints as his body was slowly starved of oxygen was exhilarating. His fighting grew more frantic as he became more desperate. He knew now why he was going to die but still did not have the decency to apologise for his actions, panicked moans were all he could manage. He was using the fact that his mouth was taped shut as an excuse. 'How could I tell you I was sorry when I was gagged?' I could just hear him saying. Pathetic! That is no excuse! Besides, I did not want to hear his feeble apologies. There was to be no mercy, no forgiveness. I slapped him across the face with some force and he sucked hard against the tape stuck over his nose and mouth so I slapped him again. In the grand scheme of things, I suppose that it did not take him too long to die, but those few minutes were deliciously satisfying.

At last the twitching stopped and his body flopped forward limply, only held on to the chair by the restraints. I turned off the slide show and the silence that filled the room after the throbbing beats of 'Relax' was a shock to the system and took a little of the edge off my adrenaline rush but was not enough to spoil the elation I was feeling.

I worked quickly to sort things out, grabbing the memory card from his camera, then cutting him loose. Disposing of his body was going to be the tricky bit but I had planned this. A few weeks earlier I had found a large suitcase that someone had fly tipped and which I had rescued. The sides were a bit torn, but most importantly, the wheels were still working. A good quantity of packing tape had seen to the tears. I fetched the case from the car and, with some difficulty, managed to squeeze Ian's body into it. He was not the biggest guy but was still pretty heavy and I struggled to load the suitcase into the boot but eventually managed it. There was a risk that I would be seen doing this, but Ian and Desiree lived on a quiet street and I had pulled the car up close to the door, so I was not easily seen.

I returned the suitcase to its original fly tip home and then to celebrate, went out and stabbed five more people.

My dreams are playing tricks on me again. I am searching for my sister Cathy. She is lost and I am frantic. I am pushed from one faceless person to the next. 'Go away, we don't know a Cathy', 'There is no one here by that name, sod off!', 'Bugger off, don't bother us with your questions.'

It's a hostile environment and I feel scared and vulnerable, but I must find Cathy. Desperation begins to grab at me, tightening around my throat like the hands of a strangler and I gasp for air. Lines blur. I don't know if my panic is for my sister or for myself as I struggle for breath.

I wake up, but it is only into another level of a dream, I am in bed but there is a weight on top of me and I can feel hands pressed around my throat. I cannot see my assailant, but I know it is my boss...ex-boss, come for revenge. The weight of his body, the strange grunts that he used to emit, the sour smell of his breath, all tell-tale signs.

But, my mind reminds me that he is dead, he cannot be here, and I relax into the attack, trying to draw pleasure from the power of the knowledge that this is just a dream. The grip tightens around me, an angry response to my brazenness. I half laugh, half gasp and change.

I am now Cathy and the hands that threaten to end my life are those of my father. I cannot be Cathy for she is dead and the hands – small feminine hands but with surprising strength – cannot be my father's hands for he too is dead. But I cannot relax now that the dream has changed. I must fight to save Cathy from my father. I start to struggle, thrashing out, trying to scratch at the hands that hold me.

And then I come out of the dream, gasping for breath and pulling at the sheets that had become entangled round my neck. I free myself and lie exhausted from the fight, feeling the air slowly refilling my lungs and the dream slowly fades in spurts, aftershock spasms make my body twitch involuntarily, but they diminish, and I am left feeling lifeless and drained.

They took five days to find Ian's body and I really felt for Desiree during that time. She was frantic with worry and then, when her worst fears came true, she seemed to just crumble inside and collapse into herself.

But I was there for her. Comforting and helping her though the grief. I took time off work to be there. The boys, Ant and Pete, weren't much use as they skulked around the house, moody as hell, and quite frankly numbed into inaction by the loss of their father.

Jenny and Sara did their bit too, coming around and offering their support, but they silently acknowledged that I was closer to Desiree than they had ever been, so they helped but didn't try and take over.

Tracey came round a few times as well and was good for the boys. Desiree would stop worrying about them on those evenings and then she could concentrate on her own grief.

One evening Tracey persuaded Ant and Pete to go out to a movie with her and Jenny and Sara, who had been around for most of the afternoon, decided to give us some space. We polished off two bottles of red, or rather Desiree managed a bottle and a half while I had a couple of glasses. It was then that she admitted her little secret about their S&M fetish, going into a little too much detail for my liking.

There was no guilt or shame in her confession, just a sense of loss and I found myself recalling the power I had over Ian as I built up to killing him and the thrill it gave me. But then Desiree began to talk about what she would let Ian do to her and I couldn't understand how anyone could get pleasure from being willingly hurt like that.

But I kept my neutral face and let her talk. 'Oh my god, I don't know why I'm telling you all this, you must think I'm some sort of pervert. Promise me you won't tell the others, not a word. They would never understand, but I know that you do. I wouldn't have this sort of relationship, the kind I had with Ian, with just anyone, you know. It was our special bond. It was a unique understanding between him and me.'

'I am not sure I understand,' I said gently, 'but you know me, I won't say anything.'

She smiled sadly, acknowledging her trust in me. I wish she wouldn't do that. It will make it harder to kill her when the time comes.

There was a short UK tour planned before we headed off to the States. Just five shows, one in Edinburgh, one in Manchester, one at the Birmingham NEC and then two nights at the Hammersmith Apollo. All of them sold out in minutes. Unfortunately, we had no time to add on any extra shows, but promised our fans that we would do a more comprehensive tour once back from the States. We were also getting requests for shows across Europe as well as the Far East and Australia. It was hectic.

Stewart Copeland came to the Edinburgh gig and I let him take over on drums for one song. The crowd loved it, but the other girls were jealous of my growing friendship with him. Jenny was the worst. We had got the names wrong, we should have had Jenny the Bitch, not Sara, although Sara could do her fair share of bitchy too. Maybe we should have had Jenny the Queen Bitch and Sara the slightly less Bitchy, but neither name rolled off the tongue.

Stewart was flying out to America the next day so didn't stay too long after the gig and, as the other three had ganged up on me, I was side-lined at the after-show party and ended up being cornered by a leery promoter who, I was convinced, the other girls had told that I fancied him.

I had a rule that Clair da Loon would never stab anyone, that was strictly a real world thing. I wanted Clair da Loon to be unsullied by anything I ever got up to, but as this fantasy developed, the urge to break the rule grew to the point where I terminated the fantasy and went and took my frustrations out on some poor unsuspecting bloke who had the misfortune of walking home alone that evening.

It seems that the more I kill, the more Lydia tries to intrude into my life. I have told her that I am not Colin, but she insists on calling me that. She is also becoming more than just a voice. I get vague, wispy views of her face. It is a kind face, shoulder-length hair, bright alert eyes, lips always immaculately lipsticked in bright red and soft unblemished skin which I have a strong urge to caress. She looks kind, but I don't trust her. I don't know what she wants. Why does she try and muscle in on my thoughts?

I summonsed up Bruce Willis. We hadn't met up in a while and he had grown a moustache like the one he had in that film '16 Blocks'. I never liked that look, it didn't suit him, and it rather spoiled what was otherwise a pretty good movie. At least he wasn't drunk in my dream, unlike the cop character he plays.

'What's with the chick?' he said nodding his head in the direction of Lydia's ghostly face. I didn't really like him using the term 'chick' but let it slide.

'I dunno,' I said.

He nodded and looked thoughtful for a moment. 'You want me to get rid of her?' he asked.

'Rid of her? How?' I asked, worried that his definition of 'getting rid of her' had a sort of permanence to it.

He drew a finger across his neck. 'The usual way.'

'No Bruce, that's not your usual way. It's only the characters you play that do that sort of thing. You need to be able to tell the difference between fiction and reality,' I responded.

He roared with laughter at that and I didn't know why.

I met up with Tracey. She was heading off to uni soon and I was hoping we would fit in a last OCD See? single before she went. We met at our usual pizza joint and it was better than I expected as we managed to get a whole album done while also having a good chat. She admitted that she was pleased to be moving out of home. She and her mum were getting on fine, but she felt awkward with Sara moving in.

'I don't have a problem with their relationship,' she told me. 'It's good to see that mum's happy and it's not that I don't like Sara, although she can be a bit bitchy sometimes, but I've nothing against her. I guess it's more that I've got nothing for her. It feels like we just accept each other, no love, no hate. And, I don't know, I suppose I worry that because there's no love then things could degenerate, and I end up hating her and I don't want that, I don't want to hurt mum. Does that make sense?' She smiled sadly, and I nodded.

'I think I can see what you're saying,' I said.

'And sometimes I feel in the way. Don't tell mum I said that, she'll only deny it and try and make me feel bad about saying it, but I am in the way. I can see it in the looks I get when I decide not to go out in the evenings. It should be the other way round. I should be the one wanting to be left at home alone with my boyfriend but...'

'You have a new boyfriend?' Tracey had broken up with the one who had rescued me when I had been knocked out at Sara's that time. I hadn't heard that Tracey had found a new guy.

'No. No, I don't but I'm at that age where if I did have one then I would want to be left at home alone, you know what I mean?' Her smile was happier this time.

I nodded and smiled back.

We talked about boys for a bit, Tracey telling me about the ones she was interested in and those who were interested in her and how, if she drew a Venn Diagram of the two groups there was no overlap.

'I'm sure you'll meet someone nice at uni,' I said. I was glad that she was heading off. I would miss her, but at least this way I didn't have to kill her.

'Colin, you need to talk to me. I cannot help you if you do not talk to me,'

I just want Lydia to go away.

I played Stewart the OCD See? album soon after we joined The Police in LA and he loved it.

'It's very different to The Grumpy Crumpet stuff,' he said, 'but I can tell that it's your drumming.' Now that was a compliment.

We were in his hotel room – no, it was nothing like that – and he had a ghetto blaster that he was playing the album on. He studied the CD case. 'Love the song titles,' he said and read through them, '"Dawn of a Dream Backwards", "Leftover Oblivion, "Return of The Out Of Reach", "Unfurl to the Half-light", "Subwise", "Inner Datacore Drill", "Days of the Outer Limit", "Fidget Against", "Daylight Murze", "Leaning Shewards", "Dim Telk Gone Green"'. He looked up a little puzzled. 'What does murze mean?' he asked.

'It's a contraction of murky haze,' I answered.

'And telk? What's that?'

'I don't know. It was something that Tracey came up with.'

'Tracey Bombhead?'

I nodded.

'She's Desiree's daughter?'

'No Jenny's but...' I stopped just in time.

'But what?' Stewart asked sitting forward. He had picked up that I was holding back something juicy.

'Oh nothing,' I said but I knew that I would have to tell him, the look on his face was already breaking down my reticence.

'It's just...well, I have no proof, but I suspect that Tracey is actually Ian's daughter.'

'Ian? The one they found in the suitcase?'

I nodded and put on a sad face.

'He was Desiree's husband, wasn't he?'

I nodded again. I wanted to remind him that he had been the one who had told me to kill Ian as he seemed to have forgotten, but then I remembered that this was a fantasy and it was not Stewart's fault that he had called for Ian's murder. It was me, the puppet master, guiding his words.

The LA hotel room melted, and I was on my couch staring at the TV which was showing another home-makeover show. The sound was on mute.

I sighed. The loss of my fantasy hit quite hard as I was needing to be perked up. I had spent the afternoon with Desiree, nursing her through a particularly bad episode of her grief. It was almost as if she was suffering from withdrawal symptoms from her domination fetish. The fact that the police had been around to return her S&M paraphernalia and Ian's dark paintings which they had taken as part of their investigation, hadn't helped. They were still treating Desiree as a suspect, but she had her bridge club as an alibi for the time of the murder so, despite their suspicions, they couldn't tie his death to her. She was too caught up in her grief to worry about me watching the way she lovingly caressed the quite bizarre and frankly rather frightening equipment that had been returned.

I had hoped that a little time with Stewart would have made me feel better and it had for a bit. While we were talking about the OCD See? album I had been fine, but it had returned my thoughts to Ian and that had ruined things.

I sighed and turned off the television. I was tired, and it was bedtime, but Lydia was telling me to take my meds before I could go to sleep.

'Can anyone remember where we got to with The Grumpy Crumpets?' Sara asked out of the blue about two months after Ian's death. That took me by surprise. I thought everyone had forgotten about our little band. I also had the problem that I had continued with the fantasy and was already on tour with The Police where the others, if my memory served me correctly, were still in the early stages of the release of 'Beyond The Loss'.

'You seriously want to resurrect that nonsense?' Jenny asked and with one hand pushed her hair behind her ear, giving it a second stroke, which may just have been because it didn't settle comfortably with her first effort, or she just wanted to reiterate the 'lie' in the dismissive tone of her voice.

'Why not?' Sara asked, 'You know that it was The Grumpy Crumpets that helped me recover after Ollie's death.' I saw Jenny bristle, but Sara went on before Jenny could say anything. 'I just found that it brought me closer to you guys.'

That did the trick as Jenny visibly relaxed. 'You're such a sweetie,' she said and leaned over and gave Sara a kiss on the lips which lasted just long enough to make Desiree and me feel uncomfortable. They had been intimate in front of us before, but that was just holding hands or the occasional snuggling up to each other on the couch. This kiss was the next level up. We didn't say anything, but Sara was left looking sheepish while Jenny gave her smug 'I'm in charge' look and reiterated the point by saying, 'We'd just released the new album and it had gone straight in at number one. We were about to head over to the States to tour with Jackson Browne.'

'The Police,' I said. I was not going to capitulate on that one.

'The Police? I thought we had decided on Jackson Browne,' Jenny said, shoving her hair back with both hands.

'No, it was definitely The Police,' Desiree said and that swung it. No one wanted to argue with the recently bereaved, but it didn't stop Jenny giving me a glare.

'The Police? Oh, okay,' she tried to sound gracious in defeat. 'Fine, but I want to be the one who gets off with Sting okay?'

That was fine with me as long as I kept Stewart. Sara was happy with having Andy Summers while Desiree said it was too early for her to be getting into another relationship just yet.

'We should have chosen a four-man band to tour with,' Jenny said, 'then we wouldn't have this problem.' She hadn't really taken Desiree's point on board. 'Queen or Duran Duran maybe.'

'There were five in Duran Duran,' I retorted, unable to stop myself.

'Well then, I could have two and you guys could have one each,' Jenny said without missing a beat, a cheeky gleam in her eyes.

'Well Queen wouldn't work either,' Desiree said.

'Why not?' Jenny asked.

'Because Freddie Mercury was gay so there would effectively only be three.'

Jenny was momentarily stumped, but then came back with 'Wasn't he bi? I mean Sara and I are in a relationship but that wouldn't stop us having sex with a man now would it?'

Sara looked hurt, but Jenny didn't notice.

'Same-sex,' I said to distract her.

'Same sex with man?' Jenny looked puzzled.

'No, they're called same-sex relationships now, not gay relationships.'

Jenny just shrugged,' I don't know why they call it that, it's very different sex. You should try it yourself sometime Sweetie, shouldn't she love?' She turned to Sara for support while I kicked myself for making things worse.

'Depeche Mode.' Desiree came to the rescue.

'What?'

'Depeche Mode. They are a four-man band. We could tour with them.'

'Or maybe we could just bump Jenny off, go down to a three piece and then we would be perfectly matched to The Police.'

I don't think I actually said that. I hope I didn't say that aloud. It had felt like my thoughts were being prompted and the only person who seemed to be trying to prompt my thoughts these days was Lydia.

Jenny was really putting a spanner in the works. I knew what she was up to. She was jealous of my relationship with Stewart and was therefore trying to move us away from touring with The Police. She would happily have shagged all five Duran Duran members and all four of the Queen guys too, all in one night if she had the chance. She could be quite the slag if she wanted to be.

I was angry at her for trying to come between me and Stewart so vented by stabbing nine people that evening in what the police – the law enforcement officers, not the band – would describe as the most vicious attack yet. The nine represented the total of the Queen and Duran Duran band members. In my mind I was getting rid of the competition. With those nine out of the way, Jenny couldn't keep suggesting that we swap touring partners. One of my victims even had a Freddie Mercury moustache and I took great pleasure in sticking the knife into him.

I slept well that night, enjoying Bruce Willis' company. My sister, Cathy, was there too and it was nice to see her again after so many years. She had not aged, still the innocent ten-year-old that I had known and loved and still with that wide-eyed wonderment that she had for life.

I could sense the presence of one of my parents but could not work out which one it was, my mother or my father. The sinister presence was a light undercurrent in the air, just taking the edge off the warm feelings I had about seeing Cathy, but not spoiling it. At the time I didn't think of it, but afterward, when I woke up, I struggled to understand why I could not remember which of my parents had been the abuser. I could recall that one of them had been responsible for the death of the other as well as the death of Cathy. But which one had been the violent one? It bothered me that I couldn't recall who had caused me so much pain. Surely it was not something one should forget so easily. I looked around, hoping to find a prompt for my memory, but all the walls of my room were blank, white. It was not how I remembered my room to be and I did not feel comfortable in this place. I reached up to scratch an itch on my chin and felt rough stubble. At first I thought it was Bruce Willis' chin that I was touching, but I knew that I was deceiving myself.

'Lydia!' I muttered.

She was good, whoever she was. She had climbed into my dreams and was slowly turning me into this Colin character that she kept calling me. I needed to up my game in order to keep her at bay. I shut my eyes and withdrew from the Lydia/Colin dream.

THE POLICE LIVE @ COMISKY PARK, CHICAGO

Last night, British band, The Police, kicked off their US tour to promote their new album, *Synchronicity*, at the home of Chicago baseball, Comisky Park. Ably supported by Ministry,

The Fixx, A Flock Of Seagulls and The Grumpy Crumpets, the three-piece from across the pond certainly gave credence to their 'biggest band on the planet' tag that has been touted for a few weeks now. The album had already spent three weeks at the top of the *Billboard* charts as has 'Every Breath You Take' on the singles charts. But oldies like 'Roxanne', 'Walking On The Moon', 'Don't Stand So Close To Me' and 'De Do Do Do De Da Da Da' were greeted with as much enthusiasm as the new material.

Charismatic singer Sting had the crowd eating out of his hands and with the help of some expert lighting and pyrotechnics, The Police gave Chicago a night to remember.

While it was The Police's night, mention should be made of upcoming all-girl group, The Grumpy Crumpets, who played their part in preparing the crowd for the main act. The punky foursome from London, England, shimmied through a slick and sexy set with sultry lead singer, Desiree Desire, seducing the audience into the fractious world they created on their album *Beyond The Loss*. Expect big things from this band.

We only got to bed at three after the gig. Not only were we buzzing from our own performance, but The Police had been awesome as we watched from the side of the stage. Even Jenny had got excited and, if she had been wearing a skirt instead of her trademark blue jeans, I reckon she would have whisked off her knickers and thrown them at Sting. But that was something she only did later, judging by the noises coming from the other side of the screen that she and Sting disappeared behind in the dressing room after the show.

I at least waited till we got back to Stewart's hotel room before dispensing with my underwear.

Work was not too bad under Tony. He was tough, but fair, driving us to perform better, but never asking the impossible. We still had a lot to sort out from the Guy days, but slowly things were coming right, and the backlog of mess was being sorted.

There was rarely any time for chit-chat but one evening when just he and I were left in the office, he asked me how I was doing. I could tell from his tone and his body language that he was leading up to something but I wasn't sure what.

'Fine,' I answered him. 'I think I'm just about there in sorting out the paperwork in this filing cabinet and I hope to be done by the end of the week. Then I'll start on that one.'

He nodded. 'That's good news, but I was really just checking that you were okay, you know, personally. Ursula mentioned that you had not been treated very well by Guy. I just wanted to make sure that you were doing okay. I know I'm pushing everyone to get stuff sorted and it's important that we do this, but I can't do it without you being on board. You will let me know if you think I'm pushing too hard, won't you? I do sometimes over do things, my wife…my ex-wife will tell you that. That's why she's my ex-wife I guess.'

He looked so sad at that moment that I just wanted to take him in my arms and mother him. I don't have much of a maternal instinct, but Tony certainly brought what little I had out in me that evening. He seemed like a lost little boy who needed guiding.

'Oh. you've got the balance just right,' I was almost gushing. 'We all know that we have a lot to sort out, our jobs depend on it. And we're a good bunch here, we'll get it done.'

He smiled now and nodded. 'Thanks, I appreciate that.' And then he left and went back to his office.

I found it difficult to do any Grumpy Crumpet stuff that evening. I kept thinking about that moment with Tony when I had felt all motherly towards him. The last person I had felt like that towards was Cathy and I guess what happened to her had jaded my view of motherly feelings, to the extent that I had closed myself off from those kinds of emotions. But in that moment – and it was just a moment – I had let my guard down.

I knew it was not any sort of feelings I had for Tony – I was pretty neutral about him – it was his sense of being lost that got to me. But he was not the kind of guy to show much emotion. The moment, however, had got me thinking about Cathy too much for my liking. I had tried to forget all the bad times, the times when she, or I, were subjected to the abuse we had to endure. I so wanted to forget the scared look on her face or, even worse, that lost questioning look as if to ask, 'why is this happening to me?' I could never answer that look. How could I give any sort of reason for behaviour that stemmed from things that happened before we were born? We were just collateral damage as our father…or was it our mother?…waged war on their demons.

The memories of the abuse are hazy, the details unclear. But the memories of the effects of the abuse, no matter how hard I tried, were still crystal clear whenever I let my guard down or whenever, like tonight with Tony, I am suddenly reminded of it. I desperately needed the distraction of The Grumpy Crumpets, but I couldn't bring them up in my mind. It is too late to call any of the girls to meet up for a drink, so I am stuck with my thoughts. I am tempted to talk to Lydia as a distraction, but even she is not there. My hand tightens around the handle of my stabbing knife. I am being left with no option.

The revival of The Grumpy Crumpets with the girls was short lived. At our next get together there was no mention of it at all and I began to realise that the dynamic of the group had shifted so much that it was unlikely that we would ever really explore that fantasy again. For that matter I was unsure if we would ever play the fantasy game again, Grumpy Crumpet or otherwise.

Jenny and Sara were forming a tighter alliance which was beginning to feel like they were wanting to exclude me and Desiree from their lives. Desiree had reacted by trying to form a closer link with me. I was not averse to the latter and must admit a certain sense of relief at the former. There was something about Jenny in particular that was disturbing me. In a strange way she was beginning to dominate Sara. It was little things at first, but it had now begun to border on mental abuse the way she ordered her around. There were times when Jenny's tone of voice, or the way she commanded Sara to do something, made Desiree and I exchange glances.

Sara was always the one who needed to fit in, so she meekly accepted whatever Jenny threw at her and this just egged Jenny on to worse things. It began to be unpleasant being around them and Desiree and I found ourselves making excuses not to meet up with them although we never said anything to each other.

'Why don't you guys come around anymore?' Jenny asked me when we bumped into each other in M&S one day. The scary thing was that she had no idea how unpleasant things had become. She seemed genuinely saddened that we appeared to be avoiding her and Sara and had that puzzled look as if to say, 'have we done something wrong?'

Of course I should have said something. I should have sat her down for a coffee and told her, gently, that the way she was treating Sara was not on, that Desiree and I were concerned about how she was dominating her and how it was making things very unpleasant and uncomfortable for us.

'It's just been so hectic at work,' was my response. 'You know we've got this new boss and we have to sort out all the nonsense that the previous guy left, you remember, the one you fancied? Well he wasn't any good at his job.'

'But he was pretty hot, wasn't he?' Jenny brightened up.

'Yeah, I guess.' I really didn't want to talk about him, what he had done to me still left scars. But at least it had distracted Jenny.

'Such a pity what happened to him, wasn't it?'

No, it was not a pity. The bastard got what he deserved.

'Yes, terrible.'

'Well, you guys must really come round again. Soon. We're missing you.'

I hate it when the other person is at fault, yet you are the one who ends up feeling guilty.

'Yes, we will.'

Maybe if we were still doing The Grumpy Crumpet thing, I would have been more enthusiastic, but I managed to sound genuine enough.

'Colin, tell me about Jenny. What did she do to you?'

I am not going to answer Lydia and look at the corner of the ceiling. There is a dusty spiderweb there. They don't clean this place properly. There is no spider in the web as far as I can tell. He, or she, left ages ago. This is the spider equivalent of a haunted house.

Lydia sighs. Not loudly, but enough for me to hear. Very unprofessional. She's not supposed to show her frustration in front of me, she's meant to be patient.

'Clair, tell me about Jenny. What did she do to you?'

At least she got my name right this time. I cannot remember telling Lydia anything about Jenny, or about any of the others for that matter. In fact, I cannot recall ever having answered any of her questions.

I look at the spiderweb again. It is not going anywhere. They obviously never dust this place. Well, not properly anyway.

Lydia looks very pretty today. Her eyes, alert as ever, have a slight softness to them. Her lips are bright red, perfectly lipsticked, the make-up clearly defining them. I can picture her smoking – although her hands are not smokers' hands and she does not smell of smoke – but rather she wears a gentle perfume that has a note of lavender. I can imagine her with a cigarette between her lips, her delicate fingers gently holding it there.

It's Freudian, they'll tell you. A visual metaphor for sex. I disagree…I would disagree if it didn't make me feel…feel what? Turned on? Why would I feel turned on by the thought? I am Clair da Loon, the drummer in The Grumpy Crumpets. I should not have sexual desires for other women. I am Clair, Clair da Loon, the drummer in The Grumpy Crumpets. Men, like Colin, they are the ones who should be turned on by Lydia.

I look at the spiderweb, then at Lydia again, Lydia with her sexy mouth aching for a cigarette. I feel a stirring in my loins and look at my hands. They are men's hands. But I am Clair, Clair da Loon.

'Jenny,' I sigh, 'Jenny was my mother's sister.'

Beyond The Loss had jumped up the charts in the US. It was now at number 17. The Grumpy Crumpets merchandise sold out at the last concert and they had to make an emergency order for more. The crowds were going wild when we played our set. Sting was getting even grumpier. He thinks we're stealing his limelight. But Stewart is great. We're sleeping together now, Stewart and I, but we're being discrete. So far, the others have not picked up on this.

Beyond The Loss is at number 2, held off the top spot by The Police's *Synchronicity*. Tickets to our concerts have become the hottest property in town. There was a story of someone paying $20,000 for a ticket to the New York show. We've had three radio interviews this week and our songs are everywhere, on the radio, in the shops, blaring from cars. MTV has the video of 'Lusting For A Friend' on constant rotation. The schedule is gruelling, but we live on adrenaline. Stewart is an amazing lover, he can go all night.

Beyond The Loss has finally knocked *Synchronicity* off the top spot. Sting is not talking to us and Stewart finds this hilarious. The press are scrambling for stories about us – 'What's your favourite food?', 'Who are your influences?', 'What was the first record you bought?' 'Are there plans for a new album?' Jackson Browne came to our gig and wrangled a backstage pass. He and Jenny disappeared off together. That really pissed Sting off. We also had John Taylor from Duran Duran come along one night. Sara bagged him. It was good to see her getting a bit of action. I think I am falling in love with Stewart.

I binged on Grumpy Crumpet fantasy after the session with Lydia. I am struggling with her. I know she is just a dream, an intrusion into my life.

I don't know where she has come from, or how she gets into my dreams, but they are becoming more intense. Lifelike almost.

She hasn't managed to put me off The Grumpy Crumpets, but I have noticed that Bruce Willis doesn't come round anymore. She seems to have scared him away. I laugh out loud when I have that thought. Bruce the tough guy, Bruce the John McLean of *Die Hard* who single-handedly fought off a gang of vicious thieves. How can he be scared of little Lydia? She is so petite and doesn't seem like she could hurt a fly.

But she's a mind person. She digs into places you don't want anyone digging into and I guess that's why Bruce doesn't visit anymore. He doesn't go in for all the emotions and feelings nonsense. He's a tough guy. Tough guys don't need help. I miss him, but at least I have Stewart to keep me company.

I really don't want to visit Jenny, but I feel that Lydia is trying to drive a wedge between me and her. No, not just between me and her, but between me and all the girls – Jenny, Sara and Desiree. She's like a jealous lover, Lydia. I can't spend time with my friends. I must spend all my time with her. What right does she have to demand this? I hardly know her. I won't succumb to her. So I visit Jenny, not because I want to but because I cannot let Lydia win.

'It's good seeing you guys again. It's been so long.' Jenny seems genuine in her gushing as she ushers Desiree and me into their sitting room. Sara is there putting out some nibbles and she is just as pleased to see us. I feel a little guilty for having avoided them.

'Sara's cooked up a right treat for us tonight, haven't you my love.'

Sara nods and smiles. It's a warm smile but it is tinged with a note of…something…I can't quite put my finger on what exactly the emotion is. It feels sour, or poisoned. I am not sure if it is aimed at Jenny or at us. I need to make an effort to feel happy being here. I cannot let Lydia win.

Desiree has brought the wine and the first glass of red goes down quickly. We all feel a little nervous. Jenny is treading on eggshells, trying not to do whatever it is that she thinks Desiree and I have a problem with. Sara is battling to make things look normal, to show us that there is nothing wrong in their relationship. I am still on my mission to stop Lydia getting her way. It's only Desiree who has nothing to prove and she is the most relaxed.

We chat generally. 'How have things been going?', 'What are you up to now?', 'Have they wound up Ian's estate yet?'

The mention of Ian doesn't faze Desiree. She's adapted quickly to widowhood, quicker than either Jenny or Sara did. Strangely this makes me think that her relationship with Ian was closer and more genuine than Jenny had with Geoff or Sara had with Ollie. I began to think that both Sara and Jenny's relationships were superficial, more an act than an emotion and therefore when the two men were gone, the show had to go on, they had to continue the act that they loved their husbands, so they overdid things. Whereas with Desiree, I get the sense that she and Ian were genuine soul mates. Yes, they had their weird fetish, but the intimacy and trust they must have built up through their sex games created a very strong bond. Desiree's grief when Ian died was so much deeper than either Jenny or Sara experienced. Her grief was personal and not to be flaunted in order to gain sympathy. But Jenny and Sara were just continuing an act, a part they were playing.

This thought swirled round in my mind as the evening went on, but I could not bring myself to feel guilty about killing Ian. What he did to me in Manchester was unforgivable. Desiree was collateral damage in this one and I had to stop myself feeling regret at what I had done.

The wine slowly broke down our inhibitions and Sara's food – a delicious casserole – mellowed us further so things began to feel a little like the old days. I half hoped that The Grumpy Crumpets would be resurrected but given where I had single-handedly moved the fantasy on to, I didn't want the others dragging me back and then probably setting us off in a different direction to where I had gone.

But there was no Grumpy Crumpet talk or even any sort of hint at starting another fantasy game. We talked about work, about the latest films we had seen, Sara gave us some insights into how she had made the dinner and Jenny gave us Tracey's news.

Quite late in the evening Jenny had a brainwave.

'We should go on a holiday together, maybe hire a villa in Spain, something like that. We deserve a break. What do you guys think?'

I wasn't sure myself, but both Sara and Desiree immediately enthused about the idea, so I had to pretend that I was also excited by it.

We set about deciding on where to go, I wasn't that keen on Spain as I remembered the photos on Ian's computer. His voyeuristic pictures made me not want to go anywhere near where they had been taken.

'What about Greece? One of the islands?' I suggested.

'We could do Crete or Malta.' Desiree was also keen on seeing something different.

'South of France? Nice or Cannes?' Sara was also up for a change.

We were all a bit nervous that Jenny would put her foot down and insist on Spain, but she was open to all suggestions and didn't push her hair behind her ears except once and I believe that was genuinely because her hair was getting in her face.

Despite all the talk of other places though, we eventually were worked round to agreeing on Spain as Jenny subtly manipulated us in that direction. She had been getting sneakier of late. At last we decided that Sara and Jenny would look to see what villas we could hire, Desiree would find flights and I would see if I could get the time off.

I felt quite happy when I went to bed that evening. It would be nice to get away with the girls for a bit.

'You can go,' Lydia said, 'on one condition.'

'What's that?' I asked.

'That none of them come back. You must get rid of them while you are away.'

Lydia is only a dream, I tell myself without much conviction, but I know that the time is right and agree with her that Jenny and Sara should not return from our holiday, but I am reluctant about giving up Desiree.

I won't be able to take my favourite stabbing knife with but am sure I will be able to find something when we get there.

CRUMPETS EYE EUROPEAN TOUR

Following a very successful tour of the US as The Police's support act, The Grumpy Crumpets have announced a string of European dates taking in 23 cities and headlining a number of festivals.

The band, whose album *Beyond The Loss* recently spent 4 weeks at the top of the US album charts, have seen growing global success with the album also topping the charts in Germany, France, Belgium and Australia while going top 5 in The Netherlands, Austria, Italy and Spain.

'The US tour was an amazing experience, the people there just took to us and The Police were something else, really supportive,' the band's lead singer, Desiree Desire said. 'We are really excited about touring Europe. None of us have travelled there much, other than a holiday to Spain, so we are looking forward to experiencing new cultures and seeing the sights like the Eiffel Tower, the Berlin Wall and the Leaning Tower of Pisa.'

'We are really knocked out by the level of support we have there,' bassist Sara The Bitch added, 'so we want to give something back to the fans. It's gonna be great.'

'And,' lead guitarist, Jenny Jangle, adds with a gleam in her eye, 'we've managed to persuade Jackson Browne to support us.'

Browne, who has been very successful in the States has not yet cracked the European market in the same way and will be looking to this tour to boost his global fanbase.

Meanwhile rumours still continue to circulate about The Crumpets' drummer, Clair da Loon and Stewart Copeland from The Police, as the two were spotted going into a restaurant in Mayfair together last night.

I had to give Jenny her time with Jackson Browne. Call it a condemned's last meal if you like. Of course she'll never know about it, but then it's her own fault for not continuing with the fantasy. At least she'll die happy in my mind. Despite all her nastiness, she is still my friend.

I planned to have Duran Duran at one of the festivals for Sara's enjoyment and Depeche Mode for Desiree's but hadn't yet worked out the details. I was still reluctant about giving up Desiree but had quickly got used to losing the other two.

Whenever I think about what I have to do to Desiree, my dreams end up being full of visions of my sister, Cathy. Poor thing. She looks so frightened in the dreams and I feel so helpless, unable to comfort her. I tell her of my plans and she smiles when I talk of killing Jenny and Sara, but gets really agitated when I say I must get rid of Desiree too, so I don't mention Desi anymore.

I can feel the presence of one of my parents, the one who killed Cathy and my other parent. They come into my dreams, a sinister intrusion, still trying to keep me away from Cathy. But I am strong now, stronger than them. I can even sense now that it is my mother was the one who did so much damage to our family although I am still not one hundred per cent sure. It doesn't seem right that a mother would do such a thing to their own child, unnatural almost, but I am more and more convinced that it was my mum who did it.

I think about going to the library to check out the newspapers as I recall that the story of Cathy and my father's, or possibly my mother's, murders did make the news and, if my unreliable memory serves me correctly, it was the brutalness of the killings that attracted press attention.

When I do try and remember, I recall a photograph of me on the front page, presumably because I, the frightened 12-year-old, survived the ordeal. What exactly the ordeal was, I can't say except that there was a lot of blood and my sister and one of my parents were dead.

There was a documentary on TV the other night about PTSD. That's what Lydia says I am suffering from. She keeps asking me about Jenny. Not Jenny Jangle of The Grumpy Crumpets, not Jenny my friend, but Jenny my aunt. She keeps making out that Aunt Jenny is the Jenny in the real world and that Jenny my friend is the dream, but I know she's just trying to confuse me. You shouldn't confuse people who are suffering from PTSD should you?

Despite my confusion, Aunt Jenny is becoming clearer in my mind. She was my mother's sister...I think. I have a vague hazy picture of her in my mind. I can't say with any conviction whether she looks like my mother's sister as my memory of my mother is just as out of focus. Aunt Jenny doesn't look too dissimilar to my friend Jenny – tall, slim, light brown shoulder length hair. I can't really recall her face though.

But she is a dream. Like Lydia. She is just a creation of my imagination and not as interesting as Jenny Jangle. I don't want to talk about her anymore. She is just a figment of my imagination. Go to hell, Lydia! Go to hell and stop messing with my mind. I am not Colin. I am Clair. I may be suffering from PTSD from what my mother...or maybe my father...did, but I know who I am. I am Clair. I am not Colin!

The police are struggling with the level of stabbings. There is real paranoia on the streets and it is becoming more difficult to find victims as there are more police about and people walking on their own late at night are becoming harder to find. I have started travelling further from home in order to find people to stab. It is tiring as I get home later than I used to, but I need to keep stabbing. It keeps me from losing it. I managed to get five tonight.

There is nothing quite like a nice hot bath after an evening of mayhem. The heat slowly soaks away the adrenaline, leaving one feeling slightly euphoric, but in a laid-back way. I close my eyes and let the water caress my body, imagining it to be a lover.

I'd like it to be Bruce Willis or Stewart Copeland but am too relaxed to put in the effort to give character to my lover and there is something exciting in this mysterious partner who stays with me as I dry myself off and climb under the duvet, still naked.

I drift off to sleep slowly, feeling consciousness falling away like snowflakes. Then I sense a dream rushing towards me like an oncoming train. I try to turn and run back up the slope I have just descended, try to run back to consciousness, but I am trapped in the dream which overtakes me with terrifying speed.

I can't understand the dream. Cathy, poor little Cathy, is scared. She is shaking and crying, her tiny arms held up, trying to protect herself as she begs me to stop.

Stop what? I don't know what I am doing to cause her so much anxiety. I would never do anything to hurt her, yet I hear a laugh in the dream and it echoes in my head. I know that laugh. It is my mother's laugh. It has to be my mother's laugh. Surely. I plead with the dream to make it my mother's laugh, but the dream keeps making it mine. Why would I laugh at Cathy when she is so scared? Why would I laugh as someone rains blows on my poor little sister's body, beating her senseless?

The plans for our holiday are beginning to come together, I had no problem getting Tony to sign off my leave. We had just about sorted out all the mess that my ex-boss had left, and he had been pleased with my work. Jenny and Sara – well mostly Sara I surmised – had found a lovely villa for us to stay at and Desiree had got us a good deal on the flights. The only downside was that it was bloody Spain again.

It's not that I have anything against Spain or the Spanish, it's just the memories of Ian and the pervy photos that put me off the place. But I smile and play along, acting like I'm pleased with the choice.

'Looks great!' I say when Sara shows me the pictures of the villa on her laptop.

'It's even got a pool,' she says, flicking on to the next image.

'Nice,' Desiree sounds genuine.

'Nice? It's bloody amazing,' Jenny comes back into the lounge with a tray of champagne flutes. 'To celebrate our holiday,' she says as she offers the glasses around.

The bubbly quickly goes to my head and suddenly Spain and the villa with its deep blue pool all seems great. I can almost see the colour of the water in the pool slowly turning pinky red with the blood of my three friends and it starts to excite me.

We talk about sunbathing on beaches, walking in the hills, picking up Spanish waiters, eating good food. It's going to be a great holiday. I start to wonder how good the Spanish police are and how much I will have to do to cover my tracks. It won't be easy as suspicion will obviously fall on me. That's going to be the tricky bit.

'You all right Clair?' Desiree's looking at me with a puzzled face.

'Fine, why do you ask?'

'You just had this really strange look on your face, all concerned and serious,' she smiles nervously at me and Jenny and Sara stare too, Sara seeming to become a little frightened. I force myself to relax. I had not realised that my thoughts were starting to show through and I cannot afford to tip the girls off.

'I'm fine. Really. Just a bit of heartburn,' I say, putting my hand to my chest, 'happens every now and then.'

'Oh, you poor thing,' Jenny immediately goes into mother mode, 'I'll go get you something.' She's up and off before I have a chance to object, but the medicine is far less damaging than letting them have any hint of what I am planning.

'Better?' Jenny asks a few moments after I have swallowed the Rennies.

I nod and thank her. I need to be more careful.

I stare at the cobweb in the corner of the room, the spider equivalent of a haunted house. But it is not the web that is haunted, it is my mind. I try to convince myself that I am Clair. Any Clair would do. Preferably Clair da Loon, the drummer in The Grumpy Crumpets, but at the moment even Clair, the friend of Jenny, Sara and Desiree would do. But my anatomy is betraying me.

I am convinced that it is the medication that Lydia keeps making me take that has caused me to doubt who I am. A recent exploration of my body has told me that I can't be a Clair. I may be a Colin as I have the necessary equipment to be one. But my mind still wants to be Clair.

I think back to the night before when Jenny gave me those heartburn pills. Were they really heartburn pills or is Jenny a secret agent working for Lydia?

'How are we today, Colin?'

I am too tired to fight with Lydia at the moment so give in to being called Colin. I shrug a response. I love her lips, the way she manages to get the lipstick just perfect, giving a beautiful shade and shape to them. I could get completely distracted by those lips, watching them move as she talks, the words that come from there a mere murmur in the fuzz of my fascination. I watch as a tiny thread of saliva forms between the upper and lower lip, a silky thread as delicate as the spiderweb. I imagine myself shrunk down to such a small size that the thread of spit becomes like one of those ropes that you climb in the gym and I am pulling myself up, up, up.

But up to where? I don't know. The ruby red upper lip looms over me, large like a painted roof of a huge cavern. I start to swing on the rope, back and forth, back and forth, higher and higher until at last I let go and fly into Lydia's mouth and am swallowed up by her, becoming one with her. Damn, she is so sexy.

'Tell me about Sara Green.' Her words send me tumbling back out of her mouth, past the silky rope of spittle, across the desk and into my seat. I stare at the spiderweb, anger boiling inside me. How dare she interrupt my thoughts? I want to lash out at her but my restraints forbid me, biting into my wrists till the pain causes me to force myself to relax. The restraints remind me of Ian and how I killed him.

'Sara Green?' I sigh. 'She was a teacher?'

'Yes.'

I shake my head, trying to get rid of the image of the school teacher who had sprung up in my mind.

'She shouldn't have got involved. She should have just left me alone.' I can't decide if the twinge I feel is remorse or just heartburn.

GRUMPY CRUMPETS RELEASE SURPRISE SINGLE

The Grumpy Crumpets surprised the music world by announcing the release of a newly recorded single. 'The End Comes Too Soon' was written by Clair da Loon while the band was touring the States as The Police's support act. The song was recorded at a New York studio on the eve of their final concert.

The tour was hugely successful for The Crumpets and it helped to propel their album, *Beyond The Loss* to the top of the charts in the US. The new single is presumed to be about the end of the tour, although there are rumours that da Loon is planning to leave the band after their upcoming European tour.

We were unable to get hold of any of the band for comment as they are manically rehearsing for the tour which will include shows in Paris, Munich and Rotterdam. The tour will end in Barcelona.

It is unusual for a band to release a non-album track as a single just before embarking on a tour, but a spokesman for 4AD, The Crumpet's record label, said that da Loon had insisted on the song going out and quoted her as saying that it captured a feeling at a moment and delaying it would lose the moment.

'The End Comes Too Soon' will hit the shelves on Monday and it will be interesting to see how it fares as it will only be released to the radio stations on the same day.

If the girls had still been doing The Grumpy Crumpet thing, they wouldn't have agreed to this little episode. But they gave up on it, so I have complete control of the destiny of the group now. They would probably have read the same thing into the song title that the imagined journalist did, but I knew what it really meant.

The song would go straight in at number 1, sales based purely on our reputation and it would be the pinnacle of our career. No other act during the pre-streaming era would manage to see a song go straight in at number 1 with absolutely no prior airplay.

But, as the title suggested, it would be The Grumpy Crumpets' swan-song. Yes, sales of our records would soar when news of the tragic death of Jenny, Sara and Desiree hit the headlines. All big acts have a surge in sales in the wake of a death.

I thought I would feel sad about the imminent demise of The Grumpy Crumpets, but I had to come to terms with it, recognising it as something that was necessary for me to move on.

I am not sleeping too well. Excitement at the upcoming 'European Tour', both for The Crumpets and for the four of us, keeps my mind racing. How am I going to fit all the concerts in? Am I going to be able to do justice to the fantasy tour before I end everything in real life? Will real life last long enough or will Lydia ruin everything and steal it from me?

Thoughts churn and clash as I try and relax my mind, hoping to drift slowly off to sleep. I feel a migraine coming on but am too warm and cosy in bed to go and take something for it. I need to go out with my knife again.

But I am saved...sort of saved...as I drop suddenly into a dream.

Cathy's bloodied body lies on the floor in front of me. My mother, and this time it is clear that it is my mother, and Aunt Jenny stare at it, mild smiles play on their lips. Somewhere, just outside the spotlight of the dream, someone plays 'Clair de Lune' on a piano. I know that it is my father playing, even though I can't see him. He always did like that piece of music.

I look down at the carving knife in my hand. A dark crimson drop of blood forms on the point, growing, slowly at first but, as it expands, it gains momentum. I can see my reflection on the shiny surface of the drop. I know it is me, even though I do not recognise the features.

Why am I holding the knife? I did not stab Cathy. I couldn't stab her, she was my sister. It must have been my mother...or Aunt Jenny...it could not have been me. I must have picked up the knife after they did it. Yes, that must be it. I look across at my mother and aunt, but they have changed into my father and Sara Green, the teacher. Despite my father being in the spotlight now, the piano keeps playing 'Clair de Lune'. I hate that piece of music.

'I got this one at Zara's,' Jenny holds up the bikini she had bought. I hadn't even thought of swimwear. It had been so long since I last needed any and wondered if I still had my old one piece and whether it would still fit me? I sighed inwardly, thinking that I had better go shopping for something. I didn't really want to spend money. Things were a little tight, what with having to pay for the holiday.

'Of course I won't be needing this,' Jenny added, holding up the bikini top, 'but I had to buy them as a pair.' She gave a naughty laugh then carelessly threw the top aside. She was drunk.

Sara had over indulged too. She had been quite good since Ollie died but had been slowly slipping back towards full-blown alcoholism of late.

'Doan do that,' she slurred at Jenny.

'What?' Jenny asked, looking around as if she could see what it was that Sara was objecting to.

'Doan...' Sara had to think hard to find the words, 'doan throw stuff.'

Jenny looked around again, her face saying that she had already forgotten throwing her bikini top on the floor behind her.

I looked across as Desiree and she rolled her eyes. This was not going to end happily, and it made me worry about what our holiday was going to be like.

'Throw what stuff?' Jenny eventually gave up looking. But Sara had passed out, her head slowly dropping till it landed gently on the armrest of the settee. Jenny stared at her for a long time, her look changing from amusement at her silly actions to one of anger at Sara. She got unsteadily to her feet and walked out of the room without saying a word.

I looked across at Desiree. She was a little bit tipsy but sobering up quite quickly given what was unfolding in front of us. We made Sara comfortable on the settee then I went to see where Jenny was. She had passed out on her bed, her bikini bottom clasped in her hand. I folded the duvet over her then found a blanket which I took back to the lounge and, with Desiree's help, we wrapped Sara up.

'You go on home,' I said once we had sorted everything out. 'I'll stay here and make sure that they are okay.'

'You sure, Sweetie?' Desiree said, and I nodded. I could tell that she was relieved that I had offered. It was a Friday night, so I didn't have to go to work the next day.

I packed Desiree into a minicab then went back inside feeling slightly breathless with excitement. In the kitchen I found a large carving knife and made my way to the bedroom. Jenny still lay on her stomach as I had left her. I pushed the duvet back, then gently eased her over on to her back. She moaned slightly but didn't wake. I then proceeded to undress her, leaving just her knickers on. She had a wonderfully flat stomach which I had always envied. I ran my hand over it gently, loving the warm smoothness, my fingers feeling the blood circulating just below the soft surface.

I took the knife and let the tip of it moved gently over her exposed throat, then down across her chest, between her breasts, right down her belly till it reached the top of her knickers, then back up to just below her ribcage where I stopped.

It would not take much now. A bit of force, in and up. If you get it right, you cut the aorta and death comes quickly. The urge to do it was great and I let the knife hover, feeling my heart pounding in anticipation. But the time was not right, the place was not right.

I pushed the point of the blade against her skin, just enough to leave a small nick, but not enough to draw blood, then sighed and put the knife down on the bedside table, gently kissed her forehead before tucking her up under the duvet. I picked up the knife and went through to the lounge and slit Sara's throat.

'Your wife came to see you today, Colin,' Lydia watches me for a reaction.

'My wife?'

She nods. 'Yes, Desiree, your wife. But you were having one of your turns.'

'My turns?'

'You zone out, as if you are living in a dream.' She watches me, waiting for my response.

I stare at her for a long time before responding, 'This is the dream. Where I was when I "zoned out", that was real life. This is the dream.'

She is not fazed by this, she just nods. Her lips are, as usual, immaculately made up, but for some reason it's her eyes that attract my attention this time. I had never really noticed the eyeliner before and something about it fascinates me. The dark rims accentuate the light blue of the eye, drawing me in, inviting me to converse with her soul.

'Why do you say that this is the dream?' She is a seductress, a tease. Her eyes seduce but she does not want to expose her soul to me. She manipulates. She wants my soul and offers nothing in return.

'Because there feels real. Here feels fake, dreamlike. There I am a person, here I am tethered, like an animal.' I gesture to my restraints. 'Here I am not free. There I can do what I like.'

Lydia nods slowly. 'And what do you do there that makes you feel free?'

I look at the cobweb in the corner and imagine a large deadly spider slowly descending on a silk thread, down, down, down, till it lands on Lydia's cheek. One bite and she's writhing, trying in vain to fight off the poison that shoots around her body.

But no spider comes. The web is deserted. Not even the ghost of a spider haunts it.

'What do you do in what you think is the real world?' she asks again.

'I kill people,' I reply.

I could have sworn that I had slit Sara's throat wide open. I can even remember the blood going all over the place, remember giggling at the thought that Jenny would have a hell of a time trying to get her carpets clean.

But when Sara moans and turns over on her settee, it wakes me and, as my mind begins to focus, I slowly recall pulling the blunt edge of the knife across her throat as she slept. I feel relieved as this was not the right time or place. I ease myself out of the chair where I had fallen asleep and go through to the kitchen. I put the knife away and make myself a cup of tea then check on Jenny before going back to the lounge to settle. I try to think Grumpy Crumpet thoughts but am too tired and I let myself drift slowly back to sleep again.

If I do dream, I don't remember anything of it and wake as the sunlight starts to brighten the room. I'm disoriented at first, but then remember where I am. The chair was comfortable, but I had slept at a funny angle and my neck was stiff and sore. I eased myself up and stood for a minute slowly moving my head from side to side to ease the pain, then went through to the kitchen.

The kettle had just boiled when Jenny came in. She was just in her knickers and her hair looked slightly dishevelled, but she still looked amazing, despite her hungover condition.

'God, my head hurts,' she said, showing no sign of surprise at my being here. 'Strong coffee. Black, please,' she said and went and sat in the breakfast nook, her head in her hands.

I made the coffee and sat down opposite her. She nursed her mug for a while before getting up enough courage to take a large gulp.

'Woah!' she said, her eyes opening wide, 'that's bloody strong.'

I smiled at her and she started to giggle, then groaned. 'Don't make me laugh, it hurts.'

After a moment she took a sip of the coffee, the caffeine shock of the initial gulp making her more cautious.

'Ah, that's hitting the spot,' her voice was slightly husky like Bonnie Tyler or Kim Carnes. She contemplated her mug for a bit, then asked, 'did you put me to bed last night?'

'Sort of,' I said, 'you went and fell onto you bed, I just undressed you and tucked you in.'

She nodded a thanks, then said, 'And Sara?'

'She passed out on the couch. I couldn't move her, and it was too difficult to undress her, so I just put a blanket over her.'

'Thanks Sweetie,' she smiled gingerly. 'You are a true friend.' Then after some further study of her coffee she asked, 'Did I do anything stupid last night?'

I shook my head. 'You did throw your new bikini top away. It landed near the display cabinet if you really want it, but you did say that you wouldn't be needing it.'

She burst out laughing and immediately regretted it. 'Don't make me laugh,' she moaned again, then when she had settled asked, 'Anything else? What about Sara? Desiree? God it was a big night.'

'Nope, Sara was a bit miffed at you throwing your bikini top but that's about all. Otherwise we just spoke a lot of nonsense. I packed Desiree into a minicab, she was quite tipsy, not really in any shape to be of much help looking after you two.'

Jenny smiled at this. 'Thanks,' she said with genuine warmth, 'You are a real sweetie.' She scratched absent-mindedly at the little nick I had given her with the knife, and a puzzled look came over her face as she stared down at her chest. I could almost hear the thoughts ticking over in her mind as she tried to work out where this little injury had come from.

Slowly something formed in her mind and her expression changed from puzzled to a rather frightened one as she stared up at me. Then she looked across at the kitchen counter where the knife I had used yesterday sat in the knife block where it always sat. That didn't seem to satisfy her though.

'You okay, Jenny?' I asked as innocently as I could.

'What? Yeah. Fine. Hungover, but otherwise okay. I think I'm just going to check on Sara.'

I had my final evening dinner with Stewart Copeland at a fancy restaurant in Chelsea. He was quite the gentleman and his cheeky schoolboy grin had me all aquiver.

'Love the new single,' he said. 'Hopefully you weren't thinking about us when you wrote it.'

'Nope,' I shook my head, then added, 'Well in a way I was. I was having so much fun on tour that I didn't want it to end.'

He smiled and nodded. 'Me neither, I'm going to miss you while we're in Australia.'

'I'll miss you too,' I said putting my hand on his. We sat like this till the waiter brought the food, Stewart talking about the drumming and rhythms on 'The End Comes Too Soon'.

'After our tour, I'm planning to go to West Africa and study some of the drummers there. They have these amazing polyrhythms which I want to try and understand. I've got a few contacts. You fancy coming along with me?'

'I'd love that,' I said, but knew that I would never get to make the trip. The Grumpy Crumpets' career would be over by the time Stewart returned from Australia and I would have finished with the fantasy. I supposed that I could have continued it with a solo career and also a relationship with Stewart, but that did not feel right.

Drummers have an amazing sense of rhythm and Stewart is one of the best around. He proved it in bed that evening. In the morning we said our goodbyes.

Lydia looks tired today, but it's a healthy tired, as if she had been up all night making love. It makes me jealous thinking that she may have been with another man. And not just any man, but one wjo means a lot to her. She has the look of one in love. It is a good thing that I have the restraints on as the anger inside me threatens to control my actions. I clench my fists and push my wrists as hard as I can against the straps, hoping that the physical pain will ease my mind.

'Are you okay, Colin?' she has picked up on my agitation, but I don't care.

I glare at her, angry at the intrusion into my inner thoughts. It is not fair that I am held here by these straps and cannot escape from her probing. She is free to go off and have sex with her lover, but I am a prisoner.

She is unmoved by my glare. 'Do you need something? Water?' she asks.

I shake my head and wish that the restraints could be tightened further.

'The last time we spoke you said that you killed people in your other world. Who do you kill?'

'Did you have sex last night?' I don't want to answer her questions.

She's good, but not that good. For just a nanosecond a look of irritation mixed with embarrassment passes across her face, but it's gone as quickly as it arrived.

'Do you really kill people, or just imagine it?'

Afterwards, I saw what she did. She deflected my attempt to make her feel awkward by appealing to my ego. I had said with all my macho bravado that I killed people. I wasn't going to back down on that now. Besides it was true. In real life I killed people, why should I deny it in this dream world?

'I kill people,' I answered with some force. 'I stab them mostly. I go out at night and hunt them down and stick my knife into them as hard as I can. And I killed Ollie, Geoff and Ian.' I suddenly feel mightily proud of my achievement. 'Poisoned Ollie, stabbed Geoff and Ian...well Ian got special treatment.' I smile as I remember Ian thrashing around, eyes bulging as he suffocated with the tape over his nose and mouth.

It occurs to me that there is nothing stopping Lydia from doing to me what I did to Ian. I am already strapped to the chair, all she needed was a bit of tape and I could be the one struggling as I was starved of oxygen. I could almost picture it and in a strange way the thought excites me.

'You killed Ollie, Geoff and Ian?'

I nod proudly as she gives me an odd look.

'Ollie as in Father Oliver, the priest?'

'What?'

'And Geoff as in your brother Geoff?'

'No. What are you talking about?'

'And Ian, that's your father's name. Are you talking about him?'

'No! You are trying to confuse me,' I am almost shouting.

Lydia is unmoved by my outburst, she just looks at me, waiting for me to answer her questions and I know she's beaten me. Every time I lose my cool it means that she has got under my skin. It means that I am starting to be persuaded that she is not lying when she says that this is the real world and the world where I am Clair is an imagined one.

I force myself to calm down. 'Oliver was Sara's husband. He practically raped me. Geoff was Jenny's husband, he cheated on me when we were at uni and Ian was a sleazeball. He hid in a cupboard and took pictures of me when one of his mates forced me to have sex so that I could get a lift home from Manchester after a New Order concert. Ian was Desiree's husband, but he got what he deserved.'

There's quite a lot for Lydia to take in, but she absorbs it quickly.

'When you say that Ollie practically raped you, that was you as Clair?'

'I am Clair,' I say with some force.

'And Geoff dumping you and Ian taking those photos? You were Clair then too?'

'I *am* Clair.' I want to wake up now. I am tired of this dream with Lydia asking all these questions. 'I am Clair da Loon and I am the drummer in The Grumpy Crumpets.' I had hoped to keep The Grumpy Crumpets from Lydia, but she tricked me into revealing them to her. The effect on her though is quite funny. She has no idea what I am talking about.

'The Grumpy Crumpets? What's that? A band?' She is trying to gain lost control.

'It's only like the biggest band on the planet. Our album knocked The Police off the top of the charts in America.'

'The Police? As in the band? Like Sting and The Police?'

I scowl. 'No, The Police as in Stewart Copeland and The Police.'

'I see. So you as Clair fancy Stewart Copeland rather than Sting?'

I don't answer.

'So who else was in The Grumpy Crumpets? Ollie? Geoff? Ian?'

'No, it is an all-girl group. It's me, Jenny, Sara and Desiree.'

Lydia nods. 'You said that it *is* an all-girl group. It's still going?'

I nod. 'But not for much longer. I am going to kill them. I am going to kill Jenny and Sara when we tour Europe.'

'And Desiree?'

I pause. In this dream world Desiree is supposed to be my wife, I am supposed to be Colin and Desiree is Colin's wife. A man shouldn't kill his wife.

'And Desiree,' I say but without much conviction.

Jenny and Sara are jittery around me. It's as if my antics that evening when they were drunk and passed out somehow sunk into their subconscious. I am a little annoyed as I was sure that they would not remember any of it afterwards.

We are at Desiree's and I am being super sweet to try and put them at their ease, even though I feel an acute unease around Desiree myself. I feel nothing, except eager anticipation, about getting rid of Jenny and Sara, but the thought of killing Desiree is not sitting well with me.

The dream with Lydia hasn't helped. The hesitation of that Colin character in answering about killing Desiree has seeped into my thoughts and is causing me doubts. But how can I not. I won't be able to get rid of Jenny and Sara but leave Desiree. It is going to be hard enough getting away with killing all three. Leaving one as a possible witness, or possibly one who may end up suspecting me, was problematic.

'You two have both lost a bit of weight,' I say to Sara and Jenny. 'You're looking beach body ready already.' I turn to Desiree. 'And you always look fantastic. I wish I had a body like you guys.' I look down at my stomach. I don't have too bad a body if I am honest, but this is about getting rid of the suspicious feeling that I am sensing.

'You look great yourself, Sweetie,' Jenny pushes her hair behind her ears with both hands. She is a sucker for compliments, especially when it comes to her figure, but completely insincere in her praise for me.

'Yeah,' agreed Sara, 'I hope that you're at least going to wear a bikini this time. I remember that one-piece you wore last time. It never suited you.'

My ploy is working.

'Well, to be honest, I haven't even thought much about swim-wear. I can't even find my old costume. I'll have to go shopping soon.'

'Or you could just sunbathe in the nude,' Jenny laughs.

'Not at the beach, it's not a nudist resort you've booked us at, tell me it's not a nudist place.' I feign horror.

'No, not on the beach, but you could around the pool at the villa.' Jenny's grin is slightly leery, but in an over the top kind of way.

'Don't mind them,' Desiree says, putting her hand on mine. 'I can take you shopping on Saturday if you like. I'll help you pick out something suitable.'

'Thanks,' I say, although this isn't helping my resolve regarding Desiree and a day out shopping with her is just going to make things more difficult.

I give Jenny and Sara warm hugs before they leave and sense that I have gone a long way to overcoming their concerns about me.

I don't head straight home, rather getting the minicab driver to drop me off a few tube stops away and, once the cab has disappeared, find three lone walkers for close encounters with my favourite knife.

Cathy was an amazing kid. No matter what life threw at her she could still smile. She was better at hiding the abuse than I ever was. I used to get into trouble for being moody or restless in class. 'Why can't you be more like your sister?' the teachers would scold.

It was hard to sit still when your bottom was so bruised that you could not find a comfortable way of sitting. But because I never smiled like Cathy did, my restlessness was seen as bad behaviour while Cathy's was just regarded as 'the exuberance of youth'. The teachers never had a clue, never suspected and mom and dad were brilliant at coming across as loving, caring parents. They were also very good at ensuring that any outward signs of their abuse were kept well hidden.

There was one teacher who suspected. She tried to get me to talk, but I knew I couldn't. I could not betray my parents. They must have found out though as that teacher did not last too long. She was apparently out walking on the cliffs – something she loved doing and often spoke about – where she lost her footing and gravity did the rest.

The memories confuse me. I do not remember my mother and father as both being complicit in the abuse. I always thought it had been one or the other and, of late, I had a strong suspicion that it was my mother who was the perpetrator. I was almost convinced that she had been the one who killed my father. But today's memories have them acting together. If that was the case, then who killed my father?

CRUMPETS BACK ON TOP

The Grumpy Crumpets returned to the top of the singles charts with their new hit, 'The End Comes Too Soon'. Despite receiving no airplay (the single was only released to the radio stations the same day it hit the shelves) the song sold well based purely on the band's reputation and outsold the new Madonna hit which had been the bookies favourite to take the number 1 spot until the Crumpets announced the surprise release.

Sales of the band's two albums were buoyed by this bold move around the single and *Beyond The Loss*, their second album, bounced back up to number 9, while their debut, *Easy Peasy We're the GCs* re-entered the charts at number 43.

'The End Comes Too Soon' is a haunting tune which sees Desiree Desire's voice at its heartbreaking best while Jenny Jangle lays down a bassline that is not too dissimilar to that on The Police's 'Every Breath You Take'. There are further signs of the Crumpets recent 'intimacy' with The Police in the drumming. Clair da Loon's rumoured affair with Stewart Copeland seems to have influenced her rhythms and experts in the field are excitedly talking about it. The likes of Phil Collins, Queen's Roger Taylor and Cream's Ginger Baker have all been quoted as saying it is the best drumming they have heard on a pop record of late.

The Crumpets embark on a major tour of Europe soon and have already had to add extra dates at a number of venues due to the high demand for tickets.

Shopping with Desiree was fun. We headed out early and had breakfast at a lovely little café. It was a beautiful morning, warm with the sun shining and we sat outside where they had a few tables and chairs. Desiree flirted with the waiter who was a good-looking guy about half her age, but who got flustered by her advances, leaving us giggling like schoolgirls.

We trawled the shops, Desiree buying herself a beautiful summer dress, a sexy evening outfit, a second bikini because she was unsure about the one she had bought last weekend and three pairs of shoes while I umm-ed and ahh-ed.

By the time we sat down for lunch she had loads of parcels while I had still not decided on a single item.

'Right,' she said as we waited for our food, 'I'm giving you three shops to find something or I'm going to buy the first bikini I find in your size and you'll just have to make do with it. You'll bankrupt me if I have to go into too many more shops,' she laughed looking at the bags that surrounded us.

In the third shop after lunch I found something that would do. I was convinced that Desi would carry out her threat and knew that if she did, I would end up with something skimpier than I was prepared to wear.

We had a lot of laughs, but when we sat down for a coffee before heading home, she seemed to deflate.

'What's the matter?' I asked.

She tried hard to smile but couldn't bring herself to.

'I don't know,' she sighed, tears gathering in her eyes, 'I have tried really hard to shake off this mood, but I'm really struggling with this going on holiday together thing. The last time we did so Ian was still alive. So were Ollie and Geoff. I keep thinking about it, of how drastically our lives have changed. I miss them, all of them.'

She wiped away a tear that rolled down her cheek.

I looked at her a little quizzically. I could understand her missing Ian, but never thought that she was that close to the other two.

She gave an unexpected laugh. 'Damn, we were good at hiding it,' she said, her voice slightly husky with emotion.

'Hiding what?'

She looked at me for a long time then said, 'Promise me you will never, ever tell the others,' she was dead serious.

'Tell them what?' I was confused.

'Promise me,' she said with a bit more force.

'Desi, this is me, Clair that you're talking to. You know me. You can trust me. If you tell me something in confidence, you know I won't say a word. I promise.'

After a moment's contemplation she nodded. 'Yes, of course I know I can trust you. It's just that this is pretty big. It could destroy my friendship with Jenny and Sara.'

I nodded and she looked around as if checking that our friends were nowhere near.

'We used to have sessions together, sex sessions. The four of us. Me, Ian, Ollie and Geoff.'

A spider has moved into the web. I can just about see it moving around up there. I wonder if it is the same one that built the web that has returned, or if it is a new one. I imagine there having been four spiders who lived there, then they go away on holiday and only one comes back. It's like a black widow spider.

'Do you like spiders?' Lydia has followed my gaze. It annoys me that she wants to know my every thought.

The dreams are becoming clearer, more real. I am seeing Lydia in high definition these days. She started out as just a voice – like radio. Then came blurry images, not quite black and white, but certainly very muted colour. Slowly this changed to the grainy colour images of 70's television. But now I can see every little detail, the fine powdery dust of her make-up foundation, the tiny clumping of her mascara, barely perceptible as she is very good at applying it, the slight crow's feet that bring laughter to her eyes and the small ridges on her lips – those marvellous lips – that one never notices when you just glance at someone. But now I see everything.

'I'm not scared of spiders,' I answer.

'I didn't ask if you are scared of them, I asked if you like them.'

'Same thing,' I say and shrug. She gives me a look that says she's not amused by my answer.

'I like black widows,' I say. I have never actually seen one and to be honest don't really know anything about them other than that they are used as metaphors for husband killers.

Lydia raises an eyebrow. 'Black widows? Interesting choice.'

'What about you? Do you like them?'

It's her job not to answer my questions, so she asks, 'What attracts you to the black widow?'

I shrug, 'I don't know. I just like the name.'

'Does it have anything to do with your friends,' she consults her notebook, 'Jenny, Sara and Desiree?'

'Why would it?'

'Well they are all widows.'

I think about this for a moment. 'They didn't kill their husbands. They are not black widows.'

She nods, then says, 'I suppose not. But what about you? Do you think that you are like a black widow in your other world, the world where you are Clair?'

I shake my head and laugh. 'You can only be a widow if you have been married. I have never been married.'

'Not as Clair?'

'Nope.'

'But you are married to Desiree...as Colin.' She is hesitant to remind me that I am Colin and I can understand why. I have reacted angrily to her when she has called me that, but I am beginning to realise that there may be some truth in this. What if I am actually Colin and the whole Clair thing is a dream? Why would I dream such a thing? Why would I dream that I am a woman if I am a man in reality?

I think for a moment, then say, 'I'd like to see Desiree, my wife, if I can. Please.'

It has become harder to feel that I am actually Clair as the dreams of Colin and Lydia become more focussed and are happening with more regularity. I wonder if I am going mad and think about seeing a psychologist, but I know I cannot. Psychologists get into your head and I don't want anyone rooting around in there. They would probably find out about the people I have killed and my plans to kill. They would most certainly try and stop me doing it.

I become a bit touchy-feelie with my friends, the physical contact helps to bring a reality to them that Colin and Lydia want to destroy. I don't think Jenny notices, nor Desiree, but I can feel Sara's eyes on me, watching. They are jealous eyes. She thinks I am trying to steal Jenny away from her, I can tell. I debate whether to continue to taunt her, but decide not to rock the boat, let her live out her last days in happiness and have no reason to hate me when I kill her. I turn my attention to Desiree, but this doesn't help me in my resolve to kill her. The physical contact creates a bond between us that it doesn't with the other two. So, I stop patting her hand as I talk. But this brings me back to thinking about Colin and Lydia.

It is a week to go before we head off to Spain. I can't wait.

Stewart has gone to Australia for their tour there and I am missing him already. We are really busy rehearsing for our upcoming shows, especially the new song, 'The End Comes Too Soon', as we haven't played it live before. Desiree has no problem with the vocals, she nails them every time we run through it. She's even worked out a little dance routine to go with it. Sara seems okay with the bass part and she and I have got the rhythm section sorted, but Jenny is struggling with the guitar bit. It is a tricky one, I will admit, but it's sort of her own fault as she was showing off when we recorded it. Took her a huge number of takes and a lot of studio wizardry to get it right, but now she doesn't have the luxury of 'takes' and technology in a live show.

She has stormed out twice in frustration, blaming me and Sara for not getting the rhythm right, but we both know that we were spot on, it was her who was not getting it right.

Both times Sara went after her to calm her down. This left me and Desiree hanging around together waiting for them. It was a difficult time for me as it blurred the lines between reality and the Grumpy Crumpet fantasy. My guilty feelings about wanting to kill her in real life kept leaking into the imagined scene of the rehearsals and made the conversations stilted. I tried to will Jenny into getting the guitar piece right so that we could just get on with the preparations for the tour and I could ignore real life for a bit, but my growing hatred of Jenny kept tripping her up in my fantasy.

In frustration I just assumed that this whole issue was sorted and shut down the fantasy, feeling very unsatisfied. It was already quite late in the evening, almost too late to go out with my knife, and to be quite honest, I didn't really feel like the effort it would require.

I decided to have a hot bath instead, hoping the warmth and aroma of the bath salts would calm my mind. At least Lydia wouldn't interrupt, she's a 9 to 5 girl so never comes in the evening.

I started having vague notions of others who flit around just outside of my consciousness. Shadowy figures whom my mind tells me I should view as sinister or malicious, but I can't bring myself to think that of them.

One of these shadows is more a scent than a being, a pleasant perfume that gets mixed up with my bath salts. I call this formless odour Nurse. Now and then I feel Nurse's gentle touch and I long to see her clearly, put a human shape and face to this smell, but my mind refuses to allow that to happen, as if it knows something about Nurse that I don't, as if it fears that seeing Nurse's face would somehow have bad effect on me. My mind is protecting me.

Cathy is back in my dreams, but it's not a Cathy I recognise easily. She looks different, older. She's also not the defenceless little girl who had come to me in the past. This Cathy is tough. There is almost a violence about her that scares me. Mum and Dad are there too, barely. They are vague impressions of a presence, but I can feel their fear. Again, this does not fit in with what I know. I am not even sure if my dream is one of Clair's or one belonging to Colin.

The flight to Spain was an early one, so we slept over at Jenny and Sara's the night before. I was excited but didn't want to show it too much. The girls were also excited but had no qualms about showing it. Desiree was a good actor, covering up the pain she had revealed to me when we had gone shopping.

There was not too much wine, we couldn't afford to oversleep, so it was a simple dinner, followed by coffee, then off to bed, Jenny and Sara together to their room, Desiree insisting on taking the sofa and I got Tracey's room. I had not thought about Tracey for a while now. She was doing well at uni by all accounts and I wondered if she had formed a little group of friends as we had done. I tried to imagine her and her mates discussing their imaginary band. Would they go for the name OCD See? or would one of the others in the group be stronger and insist on some other name?

Better still, perhaps they would form a real band, not just a made up one.

I had to think about this. I didn't want my thoughts to meander on to the pain I would cause by making her an orphan. I wasn't that close to Sara's two. Tango and Sprite, that was what she called them when she was in The Grumpy Crumpets. And Desiree's boys? I struggled to remember their Grumpy Crumpet names. Pierre and Antoine, wasn't it?

Tracey was Bombhead, I remember that with no problems. But this is not helping me sleep as the thought of those kids becoming orphans lurked in the background. I decide to come up with another OCD See? album to take my mind off the kids.

Track listing for *Twilight Merging*, OCD See?s second full album:
1. Comfort Wakes Defiant
2. Here, Here, Gone
3. Straight-Faced As An Echo
4. Sweetblade In The Depths
5. Cut Fast, Dream Later
6. She Lies Within The Lies
7. Changefast Temporal Blues
8. Diving Plungewards
9. Slaughterous Interloper
10. …

I stopped there. It was not helping. While I was quite proud of the song titles that I made up, they were not quite as good as what Tracey came up with. Hers were more surreal, untainted by the violence of my life.

I got out of bed and went quietly to the kitchen and made myself a cup of tea. While I waited for the kettle to boil, I took the knife, the one I had pretended to cut Sara's throat with, out of the wooden block. It was a really good knife and I would have loved to take it with me to Spain, but I knew I couldn't risk it. I ran my finger very gently over the blade, feeling the acidic sharpness that tingled in my fingertips, the power I held in that simple kitchen utensil knotting my stomach with anticipation.

I heard a stirring in the living room and had just replaced the knife when Desiree walked in.

'Sorry, did I wake you?' I whispered.

'No, I was struggling to sleep. That couch is not as comfortable as I thought it would be,' she smiled. 'How about you?'

'Oh, I often struggle to sleep when I'm not in my own bed. You want some tea?'

She nodded and settled herself in the breakfast nook while I made the drinks, then joined her.

'How you feeling, you know, about Spain?' I asked. 'You going to be all right?'

She thought for a few seconds, then nodded slowly. 'It's going to be difficult, but I should be okay.'

We sat in silence for a moment, then I said in a very soft voice, 'if it's any consolation, I'm struggling with this trip too.'

'Why?' she asked, looking up suddenly.

'Well, I don't really want to say, but...you promise not to mention this to the other two?'

She nodded solemnly but her eyes showed eager intrigue.

'Well, last time we went to Spain, Ollie raped me.'

I am not supposed to see the news, but Lydia always forgets to hide her newspapers. She carelessly has them sticking out of her bag and I can usually make out the headlines. The level of knife crime in London has been a hot topic for a while now. Today's headline is about a woman who was raped.

I'm struggling with The Grumpy Crumpet fantasy. Thoughts are not coming easily. I want to bring Stewart Copeland back, but that doesn't seem right. And it's no good bringing out a new single or album as we've just released 'The End Comes Too Soon' and any other new release would seem forced. Looking back, even 'The End Comes Too Soon' was a little too over the top and I'm regretting it a bit now.

I know we're supposed to be heading off on the grand European tour, but I don't know quite where to begin with that. For some reason Meat Loaf comes into my mind, I can't remember if I had heard one of his songs recently or if Sara had made some for us in the last few weeks. But I can't bring myself to include him in my fantasy. He scares me too much.

I know that I should be trying to get some sleep, but my mind is still racing. Desiree had been shocked by my confession about Ollie, but not as shocked as I had been. The scary thing was that I had no idea if it was true or not. I could not work out if I had just made it up, or if it had really happened. I know he had forced himself on me that evening when Sara got so drunk that she passed out. But I hadn't pushed back, I had let him have his way so I suppose that technically wasn't rape even if it had felt like it.

Remembering that night at Sara's put me into a spin about Spain now. If Ollie had it in him to do what he did when Sara passed out, then I wouldn't put it past him to have done the same, or worse, way back when we were all on holiday together. But I could not remember and that worried me.

Desiree had believed me. Something in her eyes differed with her words as she kept asking me if I was sure. It was as if she knew it was true – which her eyes said – but her words said she couldn't believe it.

I had been my usual convincing self and it didn't take long for the suspicion in her eyes to convince her mouth and she was offering me all sorts of sympathy.

I could only conclude that there was something in the way Ollie had been when she was having 'sessions' with him, Geoff and Ian that made it easy for her to convince herself of his guilt. Did he show a particular kind of violence then? She went to bed looking rather pensive and somewhat sad but hugged me saying that we two needed to look after each other while on holiday.

I let her take Tracey's bed and curled up on the sofa. She was right, it wasn't very comfortable, but then neither were my thoughts.

The woman sitting opposite me is strangely familiar, yet I don't feel like I know her. She smiles nervously, unsure what to say, unsure what to think. She is quite pretty, short blonde, almost spiky hair, alert blue eyes, a smooth, pale complexion and a small, neat mouth that was permanently in a pout as if she wanted to kiss the world. Her lipstick, however, is not as prominent as Lydia's. Hers is a muted pink that makes her lips merge with her face. I would like to see her with Lydia's style of make-up. I think it would suit her.

They tell me that she is my wife, that she is Desiree. That I had asked to see her. They say that it will help my memory. I did not know that there was anything wrong with my memory. But when I see this Desiree now, this woman with the indistinct lipstick, this woman whom I am supposed to be married to, I do not recognise her. They are trying to trick me, I think.

Then I see the pain in her eyes. She wants me to recognise her. She is willing me to remember her, not for my sake, but for hers. She reeks of loneliness and despair, of desperation and woe. I feel like a complete bastard for not remembering her. I wonder why I am still restrained. I would not harm Lydia, nor this woman. I pull at the straps that stop me from moving, not hard, not so it looks like I am fighting them, but rather as a gesture to show that all I want to do is reach out and touch this

Desiree's cheek gently with the back of my hand. And I do want to touch her, just as I want to touch Lydia. I crave the softness of a woman's skin, but I am denied.

'How are you doing, Colin?' she asked. She sounds just like the Desiree in Clair's world except that she does not have the same confidence. This Desiree's voice is timid, searching warily for words, frightened of saying the wrong thing, scared that she may, just by a careless sentence or tone of voice, set me back in my treatment.

I can feel Clair shudder within me, feel her trying to fight. 'Do something, anything. Try and lash out. Shout. Scream. Do not let them take me away from you,' I hear her voice verging on the paranoid and I am scared about what she would do. Clair kills people. She goes out on stabbing sprees. She murdered her friends' husbands. What would she do to me?

I feel my wrists pull hard against the restraining straps, feel the leather painfully eating into me. Somewhere in my mind I know that this cannot look good, that it must seem that I want to attack Desiree. 'It's not that,' I want to scream, 'I don't want to harm her, I want to escape from Clair.' I know that I must fight this, I must calm down, I must show them that I mean no harm. But I cannot help myself and continue to struggle.

I feel like I am losing the battle with Colin. The dreams where I am him are becoming more intense. The details are vivid and the feelings more real. I wake with a bad headache and pray that it will not turn into a migraine. I am supposed to be going to Spain today.

Desiree is in the shower, so I find my headache tablets and take them before checking the time. It is 4 a.m. The cab to the airport is due at five so we still have time. I make tea for everyone, then quickly tidy the lounge and wonder briefly which of Sara or Jenny's kids would be the ones to take all this stuff away when they came to clear out the house after their mothers are dead.

Sara and Jenny emerge from their room ready to go and Desiree takes so long in the shower that I have to rush my ablutions. But we are ready and chatting away merrily by the time the cab arrives. The ride to the airport feels surreal. It's overcast and gloomy, making the streets dull and drab. It feels like we are driving through treacle despite the speed with which the cab moves down the empty streets. I try to think of Spain and the sunshine there. The warmth of the light that lifts the spirits and eases the aches out of the body. I am now eager to get there and feel that release from the gloom.

I am hoping the sunshine will somehow exorcise my mind of the memories of what Ollie did, memories both remembered and those just hinted at. I am also hopeful that Colin will not come with, but I know that this is wishful thinking. Colin is with me all the time now. He and Lydia. They are no longer just voices, they are real, almost as if they are in the cab with us.

I join in the girlie chatter, trying to at least relegate Colin to a muted presence. Jenny is full of beans, excited about the holiday, talking about the food we will eat, the beaches we will go to, the clubs where we will get drunk and dance the night away.

Sara's 'need to fit in' excitement is plainly obvious. She's saying all the right things, making all the right gestures, but there is something underneath all the show which belies her excitement. Jenny doesn't see it, refuses to see it.

Desiree is doing well at hiding her thoughts. She chatters away with us, but I can see that what I told her about Ollie was haunting her words. It is a barely perceptible reservation in her enthusiasm but I am grateful to her for not letting on to the others that anything is wrong. I have a week in which to find a suitable knife and to pluck up the courage to include Desiree in my final plan.

My wrists still hurt, but this is small change against the agony that wracks my mind. I want to recognise this Desiree whom they say is my wife. I want to be free of the restraints. I want to know why I am here. Why do they restrain me? Am I a violent person? I do not feel violent. I do know that Clair is violent. But she is a dream, she cannot harm Lydia or Desiree, my wife. They are scared of her though. Maybe that is why they restrain me. Maybe they think that Clair can somehow reach out through my dreams and stab them like she does the people in her world.

Clair knows about Cathy, but, like me, the memories are unclear. And, like me, her memories of her parents and what they did are hazy. I cannot picture my mother and father but I know that they existed. Lydia said that my dad's name was Ian, same as the husband of Desiree whom Clair killed in that rather perverted way.

They will bring my meds soon. Those pills are slowly killing Clair and she can feel it. She is fighting, but I know she will lose. The meds make me feel funny, as if I am not myself…or is it that I am more like myself, but that self has become a stranger to me?

I stare at the ceiling. It is a very dull ceiling which offers nothing, reveals nothing as if designed deliberately not to distract one from one's thoughts. Slowly Cathy comes into my mind and with her there is a vague drip-fed memory that crystallises by degrees. Cathy had a friend called Clair. Mum and Dad thought she was a bad influence.

ITALIAN CRUMPETS

All-girl pop-punk band, The Grumpy Crumpets, headed off to Rome today for the first leg of their European tour. The band has already sold out in all the major cities across the continent and their album, *Beyond The Loss*, and new single, 'The End Comes Too Soon', are at number 1 in many of the countries they will be visiting.

Drummer, Clair da Loon, has also announced a surprise new OCD See? album called *Twilight Merging* which features new vocalists as Tracey Bombhead, who provided the vocals on previous releases, was unavailable at the time of recording. Going under the names Tango and Sprite, OCD See? once again provides a mystery about the vocalists' identities although it is rumoured that the pair are brother and sister. *Twilight Merging* is due for release in a week's time.

After their Italian gigs, The Grumpy Crumpets will move on to Lisbon before flying up to Paris, then on to Rotterdam, Oslo, Copenhagen and Stockholm. This will be followed by concerts in five major German cities, Prague, Budapest, then through Austria and across into Spain to end the tour in Barcelona.

'We are really looking forward to meeting our fans in Europe and hope to give them a great show,' the band's lead singer, Desiree Desire, said at a press conference last night. 'We have good memories of our last tour there, although we were hardly known back then.'

When asked if they would start work on a new album after the tour, Jenny Jangle, the band's guitarist, said that they hoped to take a holiday before heading back into the studio. 'It's been flat out for the past couple of years and we need to recharge our batteries before embarking on any new projects.'

While all this sounds positive, there have been some rumours circulating that this will be the band's last tour. Sources close to The Crumpets say that there is a major rift between Jenny Jangle and Clair da Loon, the group's main songwriters. Some are concerned that the pressures of this tour will do irreparable damage to the group and that the OCD See? side project of da Loon's is actually an escape route.

Time will tell if there is any substance to these rumours. There are also stories that concerts will be recorded for a live album and video to be released at the end of the tour. But whatever happens afterwards, the tour is expected to be the event of the year in the music calendar. Watch this space for developments.

I had to do some Grumpy Crumpet fantasy on the plane for two reasons. Firstly, despite their initial excitement – real or put on – the other three fell asleep almost as soon as we settled into our seats, an early sign that we're not as young as we used to be. But the more pressing reason was that I sensed Colin thinking about Cathy and he had now remembered Cathy's friend Clair. That Clair is not me…I think. As sisters Cathy and I were friends, but it's a different kind of friendship.

I worry that Colin, having remembered that other Clair, will steal Cathy away from me and give her to that Clair.

I am also getting the feeling that Colin sees Cathy as someone evil. How dare he. Cathy was a victim. Cathy was killed by my mother…or my father…or both of them. My parents were abusive. I am sure of that…I think.

My memory is betraying me. I want to be confident that at least I know who was good and who was not, but Colin has planted seeds of doubt and I hate him for that. He is taking me over by degrees. His thoughts and feelings are becoming my thoughts and feelings, although I sense in him the same uncertainty that has plagued me for so long.

I hate not knowing the truth. I hate this feeling of being Clair but not fully Clair. I hate this Colin half-mind that inhabits my thoughts. What if I am just a figment of Colin's imagination? He could kill me off in an instant should he so wish. But I sense reluctance in him to do so. He is clinging to something in my world, something that is preventing him from dismissing me completely. And I know what that something is. I saw the way he looked at Desiree, the Desiree who is supposed to be his wife. It is the name that connects them. He is protecting the Desiree in my world because of her name. If I can keep my Desiree alive, I can stop Colin from dismissing my whole world and me along with it. I cannot kill Desiree. Even getting rid of Jenny and Sara will damage my hold over Colin, but I cannot stop myself now. Jenny and Sara must go. I need to satisfy my bloodlust, but for the moment, I think I can resist getting rid of Desiree. I need to work harder at getting Colin under my control before he takes me over.

Lydia says we are making good progress. She says, her perfect lips parting and re-joining as she talks, that it is good that I asked to see Desiree. It shows that I am reaching out. I nod and wonder what it would be like to kiss those lips of hers. Is it wrong of me to think of kissing Lydia while we talk about Desiree who is supposed to be my wife? I say 'supposed to be' as I can only take their word for it because my mind still cannot acknowledge that this woman is my wife.

I do want to see her again though, this Desiree. There is something about her, something that tells me there may be a connection. With Lydia, all I can concentrate on is her lips, but with Desiree, despite her being less attractive – though not unattractive – I could conjure up a picture in my mind of her body, the shape of her breasts, the colour of her nipples, even her most intimate parts come to me as old friends. I know her body in a way that I could never know Lydia's.

'There seemed to be some spark of memory when you met with her this time,' Lydia says, watching me closely, analysing my reactions.

I nod slowly, not wanting to give too much away, but knowing it was useless to lie.

'What is it about Desiree that you remembered?' She leans forward, her lips slightly parted as if she knows the answer and the thought of Desiree naked excites her. Or am I fooling myself? Am I just having a little sexual fantasy about Desiree and Lydia. Although not graphic, it is just the idea of it that gives me a knot of excitement in my stomach. I explain, in detail, what I had remembered about Desiree, about her body, watching for any signs in Lydia that she is turned on by this. I am like a lecherous old priest getting excited by a young woman confessing her sins of the flesh.

But if she feels anything she is good at hiding it. She nods and takes notes, blushes only slightly when my descriptions move below the waist, but she maintains her composure and doesn't stop me talking. I begin to wonder if she will tell Desiree what I am saying. Or would she spare her these details so as not to upset her further by saying, 'all he remembers about you is your body.' Desiree would be hoping for so much more, a recognition of her mind, our love – for surely we must have loved if we got married – of a relationship that goes far deeper than the physical.

Or is Desiree the kind of woman who would snort and say, 'Typical male, only thinks of one thing.' Maybe that's how I was before all…all this, whatever this may be. Maybe all I wanted from Desiree was sex. But then why would she come here to help me regain my memory? Why would she sit here, searching my face, her looks begging me to remember her, her as a person, not her as a body?

When I finish my description, Lydia sits back, watching me closely. She clearly was not aroused by my descriptions and I feel a little disappointed. 'Well that's a good start, Colin,' she says and smiles. I can see that she is trying to work out if she should let me near Desiree again.

'I'd like to see her again if I can,' I ask. 'I know there is more to the relationship than bodies. I can feel it,' I say in the most reassuring tone I can find.

'We'll see,' she says.

That night I dream of Cathy. The smell of sex crowds my dream and I see the body that I have described to Lydia, but it belongs to Cathy not Desiree. This is wrong. Cathy was my sister, I should not be intimate with a sister, but I am not the aggressor here, I am the victim.

The air is warm, bordering on hot when we arrive in Spain. The sky is a brilliant blue and the light almost dazzling. It is most welcome after the lukewarm grey half-light of London. The cardigans come off revealing rather pasty shoulders peeping out from thin strapped dresses – Sara's rounded, slightly plump, Desiree's quite beautiful, almost porcelain. It is only Jenny's that have some colour, a light brown either rubbed on, or burnt on by a session or two on a sunbed. Hers are a little bony – wiry is the word sometimes used – and lightly sprinkled with freckles.

The dark glasses are on, giving my friends a middle-aged-chic look which Desiree and Jenny pull off with some aplomb while Sara could have managed if she hadn't gone for sunglasses that looked like sunflowers. There is a forced joviality in the taxi as they try to hide their regret at having slept on the plane. Jenny's already flirting with the taxi driver, sitting up front, trying to communicate with him through flashed smiles and a mixture of elementary Spanish and baby English. I am squashed in the middle between Desiree and Sara, their hot hips and thighs pressed up against mine. I can feel the sweat dripping down my back, but my face at least gets the breeze from the open windows.

Memories of our previous trip come back to me, memories of sitting wedged between Ian and Oliver, Desiree siting up front, while Jenny, Geoff and Sara went in a separate cab. I recall the way Desiree kept looking back at me, an excitement in her eyes which I took to be because we were on holiday, but with my knowledge now, it has taken on a rather more sexual nature, as if she were imagining me with Ian and Ollie in some sort of sordid threesome.

The thought comes quickly and stabs painfully at my mind. I feel betrayed and glance across at Desiree to see if she recalls the moment like I do, but I cannot read her, not with her sunglasses on. If she was remembering like I was, her demeanour does not reveal it. She is sitting forward watching Jenny flirt, a half-smile playing on her lips.

She catches me looking at her and her brow wrinkles as if to ask, 'What?'

I smile quickly to cover up my thoughts but the puzzled look I get in return tells me I have overdone things.

'I was just trying to remember how we travelled last time,' I say, hoping that this would explain my expressions. 'I remember we had to use two cabs, was it girls in one and boys in the other, or were we mixed?'

She smiles now. 'You do come up with the strangest of things,' she laughs, then thinks for a moment. 'Wasn't it you, me, Ian and Geoff in one cab and the others in another. Yes, I remember now. I was up front and you were in the back…' she trails off as she recalls something.

'Oh yeah, now I remember,' I say, not allowing her to linger too much on her recollection, 'but it was Ollie, not Geoff in the back with me.' I can tell that I have hit a nerve as she turns and stares out the window.

'Yeah, it was Oliver, you're right.' Her voice drifts back to me.

'I told you that you can't trust her,' Colin's voice bubbles up in my head and I feel my body tense up. I knew it was foolish to hope, but I had thought that going to Spain may just allow me to escape from him, from the voices and images of his world that were encroaching on mine, growing stronger all the time.

'You all right?' Sara asks, saving me from a prolonged intrusion.

'Fine, just a little cramp in my leg but it's okay, we should be there soon.' I smile although inside I am seething, mad at the way Colin has planted a seed of doubt about Desiree in my mind. He wants them all dead – Jenny, Sara, the taxi driver…and Desiree.

He wants me dead too.

I am allowed to see my wife again, and it is hard to separate her from the Desiree in Clair's world. I know I cannot be free until all in that world are dead. I have no control over that Jenny, that Sara, that Desiree. But I can influence Clair. Her world is shrinking as she kills off those around her and I am now down to the last three. They will be the hardest to get rid of.

Lydia says that they represent those closest to me – Jenny the aunt who tried to help, Sara the teacher who had concerns and Desiree, dear Desiree, who took a broken and abused man under her wing and nursed him back to normality, a normality that was shattered by an event that we need to remember so I can start to heal properly. That is, of course, if I can trust Lydia.

I notice that they have finally got rid of the cobweb in the corner of the room, it is a bit like an old friend has been taken from me. I had been feeling a bit like that web – old, abandoned and gathering dust, of no use to anyone or anything. The corner appears cold and clinical now, devoid of any personality.

Desiree looks nice sitting opposite me. She's had her hair done, and the new shape compliments her soft features. I find myself noticing her eyes, pale blue pools and I think of the song 'Pale Blue Eyes', but not the original by The Velvet Underground, rather a cover version by Paul Quinn and Edwyn Collins. It's probably because that was the version I got to know the song through. Even having heard the original at a later date, I prefer the cover. The Velvet's version was icy, cold and metallic, as if the owner of the eyes were an enemy, an opponent. Paul and Edwyn, however, are in love with the owner of the eyes as theirs is a gentle song of adoration. I have not thought of music for a long time, at least not a thought of my own. I have, of course, had it thrust on me by Clair and her Grumpy Crumpet nonsense, but as I recall 'Pale Blue Eyes' it feels right, as if music was a part of me…is a part of me, something at the core of my life.

'What is it?' Desiree asks, leaning forward. Has she seen some flicker of my past in my face?

I smile and start singing, watching as a tear comes to her pale blue eyes. It feels good, so I carry on singing. The tears start to run down her cheeks, but she doesn't try to wipe them away, she is too happy to want to obliterate this outward sign of her joy. I want to reach out and gently gather those tears, bottle them up as a memento of a precious moment. But I can't because of the restraints. I look down at my wrists, an involuntary glace as I don't want to be reminded of my condition, I don't want to spoil the moment. It takes me a moment to realise that there are no straps holding me to the chair. Somewhere far away I hear my voice trail off, the song seeming to float away from me slowly, a departing echo. I reach up and brush a tear from my own cheek.

Jenny lies naked on the sun lounger, her eyes hidden by her sunglasses, her skin glowing with sun cream. Sara and Desiree are topless, neither brave enough to go that extra step and that's more sensible. Although we don't expect any intrusions, one can never tell if someone may just turn up – the pool guy, the holiday villa rep, the gardener. If you're topless, you have two hands and two things to cover. If you're naked, well, you just don't have enough hands.

Still, it's great to be lounging by the pool, feeling the warm sun on one's skin. I had expected them to comment as I stepped outside in my bikini feeling hugely self-conscious, and I wasn't let down. Jenny lowered her sunglasses, looked me over them and gave a wolf-whistle. Sara smiled, somewhat lasciviously I must add, and said, 'Well, well aren't we being daring?' I hated her sarcasm.

At least Desiree was kind. 'You look amazing, honey,' she said with some warmth. 'I told you that the pale blue would suit you.'

Jenny started singing 'Pale Blue Eyes', but it sounded funny, as if the sound was coming from somewhere else, so I hurriedly laid my towel on the recliner and applied my sun cream, trying hard to ignore her.

I looked at my friends, slightly sadly, as I knew they would not be around for too much longer. I wondered what would happen to me once I had done the deed. Would I just cease to be? Would Colin keep me on in some secret chamber of his mind, or would I just slowly fade away like a memory that time erodes until it is no more?

I had tried hard, I felt. I had fed him naked women. Sexy naked women. I had even stripped off myself for that album cover photo shoot. At the time I had not really understood what had driven all that, but as Colin's thoughts had intruded more and more into my world, I realised that I had sub-consciously been trying to seduce him with these images and thoughts. I had even sorted out Jenny and Sara becoming lesbians in an attempt to feed his sexual fantasies and try and make him hold on to my world. But I was losing the battle. I blame the meds that bitch Lydia is giving him. They steal away his ability…no, make that his desire, to fantasize.

They are affecting me too. I am struggling to keep the Grumpy Crumpet dream going. It's those drugs they give him. They have slowly corroded my dreams and are now working on me. But I'll keep fighting, keep killing, keep the sexual images going for as long as I can. I will feed the warped mind of Colin with images of lust, blood and success in the small hope that he will let me stay.

I like Clair. She's feisty and kind of sexy in her own sort of way. I think Lydia is jealous of her. Her lips, her perfect lips, always go into a tight, thin line when I mention Clair. She's not too keen on the others either, Jenny in particular. Jenny is the exhibitionist. Now that is one sexy body. I sometimes wish it was Jenny and not Clair that I had the main connection with, but I can't complain. At least it's not with Sara. She's a bit too bitchy for my liking.

If I had to play, snog, marry, kill with them, excluding Clair, of course, it would be snog Jenny, marry Desiree and kill Sara. Desiree is nice. She's not as stunning looking as Jenny, but she's still beautiful. What she has over the other two is temperament. I know that Clair has created this kinky sex aura around, but I just can't imagine her actually doing all that sort of stuff. In fact, I think she's not too dissimilar to my Desiree.

There are days now when I am well aware that I am not Clair and she is not me. Our worlds are dividing in slow motion, like two giant spaceships in a sci-fi movie. But we are still attached by cords and hoses and whatever connects those spaceships. Some days I cannot remember anything about what is happening in Clair's world.

Lydia says I am doing well. Lydia says that it is good I can now tell the difference between Clair's world and mine. Lydia says that it is good to have sexual desires, but that I should try and re-direct them from Clair and her friends to Desiree, my Desiree. Lydia says a lot of things, her immaculate lips moving, forming the words, caressing them before setting them free.

I have begun to notice that when we talk about Clair, Lydia pushes her hair behind her ears. The gesture is familiar, but I can't work out from where. I have not noticed my Desiree do it. Maybe it is one of the nurses that looks after me when Lydia is not around. But Lydia is clearly not a fan of Clair. I have begun to suspect that Lydia fancies me.

I am still not sure if my restraints exist. Some days they are there and other days not. Is it that they sometimes put them on me and other times they don't? Or is it my mind that causes them to appear and disappear? I want to ask Lydia, but don't trust her to be truthful.

She asks me about Cathy. I don't want to talk about Cathy. Cathy is the one thing that is common to me and Clair. Yes, there are names that are common between our worlds, but Cathy is the only one who is the same person in both worlds. Although in Clair's world she is a victim and in mine she is the aggressor. I don't want to talk to Lydia about Cathy.

CRUMPET ROME-ANCE

The Grumpy Crumpets kicked off the first leg of their European tour with an awe-inspiring show at the Olympic Stadium in Rome. Packed to capacity, the good-natured crowd were treated to an energetic performance from the Female Fab Four. Sexy, Sultry, Stylish and the drummer took to the stage in a blaze of lights, a barrage of sound and a deafening roar from the crowd. They immediately launched into firm favourite, 'Scream Till You Bleed', with Desiree Desire prowling around the front of the stage in a tight fitting black catsuit, meowing and purring her way through the refrains and then howling out the chorus along with the seventy thousand fans.

They followed that with 'Putty In My Hands' which had Desire reaching out to the crowd, inviting them into her clutches and they were hooked. They'll do anything the girls want.

And the girls want to get 'Down And Dirty', the funky, sex-drenched track from *Easy Peasy We're The GCs* complete with heavy breathing and orgasmic hiccups from Sara The Bitch and Jenny Jangle to accompany Desire's bedroom vocals.

The new single, 'The End Comes Too Soon' calms things as the crowd are not as familiar with it, but the delivery of this haunting tune draws them in, Desire's silky voice echoing around the venue, weaving itself magically into every fibre, lighting up the lighters while the thudding bass keeps time with every heartbeat. When the song finishes, there is a moment of stunned silence as the crowd absorbs and tries to comprehend the sheer beauty of what they have just heard,

and then they erupt into the biggest cheer of the evening so
far.

I love those moments of stunned silence after hearing a particularly
beautiful rendition of a song and you sit, just for a second, in that
suspended state, your senses clinging to the quickly fading memories of
intense pleasure. I remember feeling that way the first time I heard
Everything But The Girl's 'The Night I Heard Caruso Sing'. Not only is
the tune hauntingly beautiful, but the words are about the very feelings
the song evokes in one. For Ben Watt, who does vocals on the track
rather than Tracey Thorn, it is Caruso who stirs his feelings. For me it
was Ben.

I get those same feelings immediately after a stabbing. All the excitement and energy that goes into the act and then that moment of sated
bliss as the beauty of what I have done sinks in.

Colin says that he is horrified by my actions. That's what he tells Lydia.
But I know him better than she ever will. I know that deep down he
secretly loves it. There is a part of him, a part that he even tries to hide
from himself, that has the same bloodlust that I do. He won't admit it,
but those feelings are there. It is only our first evening in Spain, but I am
already missing the thrill of going out with my knife. I will have to find a
decent one quickly, I need to keep my hand in for the main event.

But I must finish off The Grumpy Crumpet fantasy first. The time has
come to end their illustrious career. It needs to be something that leaves
a mark. A tragedy like the plane crash that sealed Buddy Holly's legacy,
or suicide that made sure Joy Division's Ian Curtis and Nirvana's Kurt
Cobain are immortalised. I am not too keen on the idea of choking on
one's drug excess vomit *a la* Jimi Hendrix. I need to come up with
something big, and soon. I feel that I must conclude The Crumpet's saga
before I turn my hand at sorting out the real world...or at least my real
world.

Clair is right. There is something that repulses me about her violence, yet
at the same time it fascinates me. There *is* something deep inside me that
I try to fight against. It is a part of me that I do not like, yet as I sense
that I am losing Clair – she will tell you I am getting rid of her – I feel
this part of me grow. It is a part that is embedded in my DNA that is
slowly, painfully surfacing. I am scared of this part of me, it has a sinister

power. I know now that, like Clair controls all that happens to The Grumpy Crumpets, I control all that happens to her and her world.

I can, should I choose to, let her friends live or die, I have that power. Lydia says I must kill off everything in that world. Get rid of it, it is just a fantasy, all in my mind. Only I have the power to free myself from that world and the best way to do it is to kill off the characters who live there. She wants me to kill Clair too, but I think that's going to be a step too far. I just need to control her better once she has sorted out The Grumpy Crumpets.

The problem is that she does not want to be controlled. She likes her freedom. She likes being able to kill at will. My meds give me greater control over her, but I don't think I will ever be completely rid of her.

Desiree came round today. She looked nice, but still struggles to know what to say to me. I'm sure that Lydia has primed her on what not to say. 'Don't mention Cathy,' I can hear her instructing, 'it'll only set him off.' I can't think why Desiree would want to mention my sister. She never knew her. All that…that stuff with Cathy happened long before I met Desiree. I'm guessing that Desiree knows all about it, even though I've never spoken to her of those days. I could never bring myself to burden her with all that. It's pretty horrid stuff and Lydia will tell you that I'm suffering from PTSD. Seeing your parents being killed by your sister is bound to have an effect on one.

Sara's busy being sick in the bathroom. Jenny is so drunk, she's not making any sense and will probably pass out on the couch any minute now. I think that Desiree is having sex in the pool with the young man she picked up at the club. She's also high on something, probably ecstasy or maybe cocaine. But I don't want to go outside and check up on her. I suppose goody two shoes Clair will have to sit up and make sure that neither Jenny nor Sara do a Jimi Hendrix on us. I'd hate for something else other than my knife to bump them off.

It was a pretty hectic night out. Started off okay with dinner at a restaurant, then we went on to a bar and finally the club. We're in our late forties and early fifties for goodness' sakes, we should know better, but I guess this was the first time they had let their hair down since Ollie, Geoff and Ian were killed. It was around one in the morning that I eventually managed to herd everyone into a cab, Desiree sitting on her young man's lap while Sara and Jenny snogged each other between drunken renditions of 'Y Viva Espana' and bouts of giggles.

Back home they had staggered inside, still singing, but Jenny had soon slumped onto the couch, slurring and mumbling in a barely awake state while Sara had dashed off to the loo.

Desiree and her young man snogged passionately in front of us for a while before she led him outside to the pool, a trail of clothing letting us know what they were up to.

Sara sobered up a little when she returned, and I made coffee for the two of us, but she fell asleep before drinking it. Jenny had passed out by this stage. I took the mugs into the kitchen and washed them, ignoring the sounds of passion coming from outside although I could not help but marvel at Desiree's seemingly insatiable need and the young man's stamina. To take my mind off the pool antics, I searched the kitchen drawers to see if there was a suitable knife that would serve my purposes. It was the first opportunity I had had since arriving to do a thorough check.

It was tempting, if I could find a decent knife, to do the deed that evening, framing Desiree's young man in the process. It wouldn't be too difficult. Sara and Jenny were sitting ducks, then I could go out and turn the pool session into a threesome, drug the young man – I still had some of the spiked cocaine that I had sorted Ollie out with – then finish off Desiree and plant the murder weapon in the young man's hands, making it look like he went on a killing spree before the cocaine finished him off. I would be the frightened survivor who was lucky that the young man had picked up a bad batch of drugs from his dealer.

Trouble was I couldn't find a decent knife. It was all rather frustrating as this seemed a perfect opportunity. At least I could enjoy my holiday for a bit longer.

She's playing with me is Clair. The 'off screen' sounds of Desiree in the pool, coupled with the excitement of maybe, just maybe, going on a killing spree with her friends as victims, was a game to drag out her existence. What man would walk away from such a charged scene? The hint at making up a threesome in the pool was a particularly good touch.

I didn't mention the scene to Lydia, but I can tell she's disappointed in me, like she can sense that I am procrastinating. She says I'm making great progress, but her lips go into a tight line and she pushes her hair behind her ears with some force. She thinks that I am deliberately clinging to Clair and her world, but I'm not. Clair is playing a blinder. She is clinging to me, making it difficult to want to let go as she throws titillating scene after titillating scene at me. I have no doubt that we will catch Desiree and her young man 'at it' and there will be more nude sunbathing. All the while the tension and excitement around actually killing everyone will keep me keen. The anticipation of the thrill is intense and keeps her from actually going through with it. Once she does the deed, she will have no hold over me and there will be nothing to look forward to in Clair's world.

I watch the spider. It has made a new web in the corner of the room and is sitting waiting, it's body tense with anticipation as a fly buzzes close to the silky threads that could trap it.

'I want to talk about Cathy today,' Lydia is being a bitch. She knows I don't like talking about Cathy. Just her name brings back memories of terror. But there is far more to it. The name stimulates something in me, or should I say someone, a presence that stirs, as if summonsed when the name is mentioned. It is very unsettling.

Okay, it's time to finish off The Grumpy Crumpet saga, so here goes:

CRUMPET CATASTROPHE

The world has reacted in shock to the breaking news that 3 members of The Grumpy Crumpets were killed when the overhead lighting rig came crashing down onto the stage at their Barcelona concert, instantly killing Jenny Jangle and Sara The Bitch. Desiree Desire suffered major head injuries and was rushed to hospital but died a few hours later. Only Clair da Loon survived, the rig destroying her drum set, but miraculously leaving her unharmed but in a state of shock.

It is unclear what caused the accident and an investigation is underway.

The four girls met at university where they formed The Grumpy Crumpets. Their first album *Easy Peasy, We're The GCs* quickly catapulted them to stardom, the punky pop sound, combined with their sexy image, drew a following from both young adolescent boys who fell in love with them, and girls who were attracted by the success of The Crumpets in a male dominated industry.

'We are in complete shock,' a spokesman for 4AD, the band's record label, said. 'They were wonderful people, full of energy. You always had a good laugh when they came into the office.'

Many fans at the concert were treated for shock although fortunately there were no injuries in the crowd. 'At first we thought it was part of the show,' one concert goer said. 'It was only when people started running on stage in a panic that we realised something was wrong. People just started crying. No one knew what to do. It was just horrible.'

As the news broke across the world, fans have flocked to concert venues where the band has played or to record stores to hold vigils.

'It's unbelievable that something like this has happened,' said Sting from The Police. 'We had a great time touring with them in the States, we just can't believe it. Our thoughts are with their families.'

Jenny Jangle (real name Jenny Levine), leaves an 18 year old daughter, Tracey who, it is rumoured, is the mysterious Tracey Bombhead, the voice on the OCD See?'s debut EP.

Sara The Bitch (real name Sara Green) leaves a son and a daughter while Desiree Desire (real name Desiree Anderson), is survived by two sons. All three women lost their husbands in the past few years as the band rose to fame.

News of Clair da Loon is that she is unscathed, but clearly devastated by the tragedy.

And so the grand career of The Grumpy Crumpets comes to a dramatic end. I guess that our records sold massively in the few weeks following our demise, number 1 hits all over the world. Then we would settle down to being remembered as legends, probably having greater status than if we had continued to churn out records till we ran out of creativity and faded into the annals of rock 'n' roll history. Our two albums would consistently feature in 'best of all time' lists. There would be a memorial concert and OCD See? would have some success, although Clair da Loon would become more reclusive, adding a mystique to her persona and being highly respected to the degree that she could release an album of burps and farts and have the critics fawning all over it.

I felt quite at peace as I ended the illustrious career of the greatest band that never was. I had done this while sitting up, making sure that Sara and Jenny were okay, then had eventually gone off to bed while the sounds from the pool suggested that the young man was struggling to keep up with Desiree.

She's a shrewd one is Clair. Connecting my wife's name with a nympho-maniac in her narrative, trying to drive a wedge between me and my Desiree. 'Stay with my world,' she is saying, 'here Desirees are sex mad women who will satisfy your every desire. Not like your Desiree. Sure you two "do it" occasionally, but there's no excitement there, no real passion or experimentation, it's all purely missionary with the lights out. Hold on to my world and I'll give you a woman to satisfy you.'

She is right. My sex life with Desiree was pretty bland before I ended up here. Clair's hints and, more recently, her blatant efforts to try and convince me that her Desiree is a better sex partner than mine has teased out the memories of my Desiree. And while I enjoy the fantasies and antics of the Desiree in her world, I know that my Desiree is right for me. She could have deserted me when I was put in this place, but she has stuck by me. The other one, the one in Clair's world, for all her sassiness and sexiness and kinkiness, is not a loyal woman.

I am glad to see my Desiree and gladder still that there are no restraints to stop me from reaching out and holding her hands. She smiles sweetly at me, tears welling up. She wants to talk but is scared that opening her mouth would free the sobs that are gathering inside her. I smile to let her know that it's okay, she doesn't have to say anything. We can just have this moment of holding hands. I want to tell her that I am nearly there. The Grumpy Crumpets are no more and Clair is on the verge of ridding me of the Jenny, Sara and Desiree of her world. Once they are gone I know that Clair will have no hold over me and she will just fade out of my life. I want to tell Desiree all this, but something warns me not to. There is a barely perceptible crumbling in my own life. I can't quite put my finger on it and wonder if it is the meds that Lydia keeps feeding me. Are they designed to break me down and then rebuild me? And if so, what, or who will I be rebuilt as. I am not sure if I trust Lydia, but for now I have this moment with Desiree and I will cling to it.

She is beginning to open up to me. She tells me about the antics that Scratch, our cat, is getting up to. I had forgotten about Scratch. He was a funny cat, affectionate as hell when he wanted to be, almost to the point of irritation, but if in a mood, could be as aloof or, in some cases, angry as a petulant child.

We chuckle as Desiree tells me how Scratch has become obsessed with watching *East Enders*. Desiree never watches the show herself, but sometimes the TV was left on while she made her dinner and if she dared turn it off, or change the channels while *East Enders* was on, Scratch would literally have a hissy fit.

It was once Desiree had gone that I recalled why we had named our cat Scratch and the scar on the back of my hand only reminded me of the blood that had ended up putting me in this place. Lydia has always hinted that I had slit my wrists, although she never mentioned it outright. But it wasn't me, it was Scratch and his sharp claws that did it. Lydia wouldn't believe me if I told her that truth. Neither would Desiree.

Don't be fooled by what Colin says, it wasn't Scratch. Why do you think blood has featured so much in my life? All that stabbing I do is to satisfy his bloodlust. He cannot get enough of it. He is the one who drives me on to the kill. How could I not have seen this before? I always thought it had something to do with Cathy and my parents, but it is Colin. Cathy is there in the picture, she is a presence, both to me and him. She has something to do with all of this, but from where I stand, it is Colin who is the puppet master, the one who wants the blood. And I will give him what he wants. I just need to find a decent knife. Tomorrow I will go into town on my own and find something.

The noise from the pool has stopped and I hear Desiree and her young man go to her room. It's quiet in the house now, except for the sound of Sara snoring. I left her on the couch where she had collapsed. There was no need to put a blanket over her due to the heat, so I had just slipped her shoes off and moved her into a more comfortable position. I was reminded of the time she passed out and Ollie and I carried her up to her room. I remember too what Ollie did to me afterwards. I expect the feelings of anger to well up in me again but find myself surprisingly calm.

Even forcing myself to remember the Manchester trip, what Simon did and Ian's part in it does not illicit the feelings I expect it to. Neither can I recall the sense of satisfaction I had watching Ian struggle against the restraints as he died in front of me.

I am no longer able to feel. It is as if my emotions have been drained from me and I am left a shell, merely a person without meaning or emotion. I am a puppet and Colin pulls my strings. I will do whatever he demands of me, I have no choice. My mind says that I should be angry that I am no longer able to feel, that I no longer have control, but I do not have it in me to feel any rage.

I must confess that I will miss The Grumpy Crumpets fantasy that Clair created. It was fun feeling part of the rise to fame of the imaginary group. And the affair that her alter-ego, Clair da Loon, had with Stewart Copeland was a nice touch. As my life as Colin comes more and more into focus, I recall having been a fan of The Police. I even remember being impressed more by Copeland's material after the band broke up than with any of Sting's solo stuff.

Another consequence of me remembering more of my life as Colin is that I am starting to feel guilty about my fascination with Lydia's lips, and I put this down to re-establishing a link with Desiree. I still think that Lydia fancies me a little. But she's a professional and has not let her emotions get in the way of doing her job. She has never denied me access to Desiree.

I do wonder if I had led her on in any way, either by something I had said, or by a look. Or is she in love with me for my mind? The thought strikes suddenly and I almost laugh at the idea that Lydia may be in love with Clair, not with me. But then I begin to wonder how Clair would deal with that. She would want to use it to her advantage, create steamy scenes between her and Lydia, with lots of attention being given to Lydia's lips. Oh yes, that's a fantasy I could go for, but it would have to be my fantasy. Lydia could not climb into Clair's world just as Clair cannot come into mine.

I want to spend some time fantasising about Clair and Lydia, but Cathy gets in the way. It is an unwelcomed intrusion into my thoughts which seems to come out of nowhere and it catches me unawares. But once I have adjusted myself and my thoughts, the intrusion is not what I expected it to be. My usual recollections of my sister were of someone evil, someone who killed, someone not too unlike Clair. There always seemed to be a bloodlust attached to my thoughts of Cathy, but this time the intrusion is more of an experience than a memory and I do not feel the aggression that I usually associated with her. Rather there is a sense of helplessness that verges on desperation. And there is hurt, deep hurt. Cathy is a damaged being.

I find myself choked up, sobs catching in my throat as the intensity of the feeling sharpens. 'You were too young to know, too young to understand,' Cathy's voice reaches out to me from somewhere deep within these sensations. 'I tried to protect you, but I failed. I am so sorry.'

'Are you okay, Colin?' A nurse pulls me back into my world.

The house is completely quiet now. Sara has stopped snoring and Desiree and her young man have exhausted each other. I walk quietly into the lounge area where Sara and Jenny are passed out on the couches. I feel a sort of tingling excitement and yet at the same time a sense of dread and hollowness. I know that what I am about to do will fill me with adrenaline and give me huge amounts of pleasure, but at the same time will probably mean the end of my existence. I am, I now know, just a figment of Colin's imagination, a personality occupying his mind. A squatter if you like. But he wants to evict me. His mind is made up and I know I have no control over my actions anymore. I am Colin's puppet.

In some ways it makes me feel better knowing that it is not me who is about to kill my three best friends. I am merely the murder weapon. I am being manipulated and have no control over my actions. I also get a strong sense that Cathy is here with me. It's more than a presence of a companion, it is as if she is part of me. She has been here before. Not here as in this villa in Spain, but she has been in this situation, walking around a house and there is murder in the air.

I stop and stand over Jenny. She is in a deep sleep, her breathing heavy. She will not wake immediately as I put the pillow over her face and by the time she does, I will have too strong a grip for her to do anything. I picture her long legs flailing helplessly as she panics, completely unaware of who is doing this to her. It won't take too long. Not as quick as the knife, and it robs me of the pleasure of seeing her face as she dies. But needs must.

When the deed is done, I look down at her, the faint light from the street lamps, supplemented by a bright moon, throw a soft light onto her face as she stares absently at the ceiling, a look I find disturbing, so I gently close her eyes and it is better. She looks serene now and I kiss her gently on the forehead.

Sara is next. She is a bit more difficult as she is lying on her side and half wakes when I try to roll her onto her back.

'Hmmm? What?' she slurs.

'It's okay, Sara,' I whisper, 'I just want you on your back, I don't want you suffocating.'

'On my back?' she half giggles. 'That's how Jenny likes me. Don't tell her, she's very jealous of you. She always worries that I will leave her for you, so shhh! Do it quietly.' She pulls me to her, her lips trying to find mine.

'No, no,' I whisper gently and pull back. 'I just don't want you suffocating. You're drunk.'

Her eyes have remained closed and I wonder just how conscious she is of what is happening.

'Hmmm. That's a pity,' she says, her voice thick with sleep and alcohol. 'I really like you, Clair.'

I have her on her back now and, not wanting to hear more of her talk, I smother her quickly. That just leaves Desiree.

It is just a thread that keeps me connected to Clair's world. A name. As long as Desiree, her Desiree, is alive, we will remain connected. But Clair has crossed the Rubicon. She cannot go back. How could she leave Jenny and Sara dead in the lounge and let Desiree live? She must go through with it all.

It feels wrong though. There is no blood. That is not how it happened. I know there was blood. Lots of it.

Lydia is pleased, almost smug. The corners of her immaculate lips are raised ever so slightly, hinting at a suppressed smile. She knows she should not show emotion, she should not rejoice in death, but she can't hide her feelings completely.

What she doesn't realise is that she too must die. And so must I. I am beginning to sense that sorting out Clair and her world is just the first step. My world with my Desiree and, dare I say 'my' Lydia, is just another step. I don't know how we will die as there is not the violence in my world that there is in Clair's and that may make it more difficult to get rid of me. I am the calm between two storms.

I smile back at Lydia, a smile that says I know more than her. I understand more than her. And she senses this as her smile fades.

'What are you not telling me, Colin?' she asks, her lips forming a stern line. She thinks I am chickening out. 'You are doing so well. You have got rid of Jenny and Sara, now you must follow through with Desiree and Clair. They are figments of your imagination, they are hindering your recovery. Take that last step. Desiree and Clair must go.'

I smile at her and nod, then say, quite matter-of-factly I might add, 'So must we.'

Colin is beginning to get it. I have struggled through and know I must let go of them. I am almost there with Clair, little Clair who was the youngest. She never really had a chance to understand what they were doing to her. She went so calmly into the washing machine and only started to scream when it was too late.

And Colin, tough little Colin. He was only nine, but he tried to stop it, tried to open the washing machine door, but he pushed him back with such force, the poor little mite. I do not think I will ever truly rid myself of that horrible cracking sound as his head hit the kitchen floor. He never got up.

After dealing with Colin and Clair, he came for me.

I am trembling almost uncontrollably, and I don't know why. I have killed many times before. I have just suffocated Jenny and Sara, but that is not what is causing me to shake. I do know what is causing it, but I am trying to deny it. I do not want to kill Desiree. In fact, I want all the killing to end. I am tired, so tired. My limbs feel heavy, my steps laboured. I am propelled forward by some force outside my control. Something is pushing me towards Desiree's room.

I feel Cathy's presence again. I don't think I will ever get to know what she was about. Was she one of the good guys or one of the bad ones? Colin thinks she was a bad one, but I cannot help seeing her as a good one. Each step is laboured and wrought with indecision. Did Cathy do right or wrong? Was she good or bad? One step – good, one step – bad. Good-bad-good-bad. I feel the dilemma tearing at her. She does not know herself.

'Good,' I tell her. 'Good, good, good.' I seem to gain strength as I override my doubts. 'Good.'

I stand in the doorway of Desiree's room. The pale moonlight – serious moonlight, that's what David Bowie called it – the serious moonlight casts a cold emotionless light across the bed. The young man is not there. I had not heard him leave, but he must have crept out while I dozed, probably exhausted and wondering how a woman twice his age could wear him out like Desiree had. I smile at the thought.

She looks quite beautiful and calm, sleeping in the blue-black light. And yet her beauty cannot prevent a wave of revulsion as memories of Ollie and what he did to me suddenly hit. I know that it is the light that causes this recollection. It is the same steel-grey light that seemed to freeze the room, that room in Spain so many years back, where he came quietly, his hands grabbing at me, his voice threatening me, 'If you tell anyone, I will kill you. This is our little secret.'

The words echo in my head as I feel violated and helpless again, as if I am being abused all over again. I don't know why, but the only way I can escape from this is to go through with my plan to kill Desiree. The shame, hurt and fear has become almost unbearable and I am trembling so much that I can hardly move, but force myself forward, picking up on the earlier thoughts of Cathy. 'Good,' I say and take a step forward. 'Good, good, good.'

The pillow is over Desiree's face before she can even sense that I am in the room. She struggles fiercely, more than Jenny or Sara did, and I have to summons all my strength to keep the pillow in place until, after what seems like an age, the kicking and jerking of Desiree's body stops.

I expect a calmness to descend on me, but instead the room begins to swirl. Faster and faster and I feel like I am drowning. This is not how I expected it to end. I had hoped I would fade out gently, not be suffocated in a strange vortex. From somewhere far away I hear myself scream.

Desiree is not my wife, she is my mother. The thought comes to me from Cathy. I am free, finally free of Clair. *We* are free of Clair and this allows Cathy to fill the vacuum. She is bombarding me with thoughts and memories that blur and clash. Questions and unknowns collide with half remembered facts, or are they facts at all? It is as if she is mining my mind, searching for what is real, looking to rob me of any scrap of information that will corroborate Clair's assertion that she, Cathy, was good.

I want to help. I want to feed her with whatever information I have that can help her. She is my sister. I want to put her mind at rest, but my head is hurting. It is a sharp pain at the back of my head that throbs loudly, almost preventing me from thinking.

Desiree was…is my mother, not my wife. This one thought is in sync with the pain. It pulses in time to the throbbing. I grip the sides of my chair, my wrists unrestrained, but seeming to be held there by pain.

I now understand why Clair was so reluctant to include Desiree in her final killing spree as she was our mother. But she is no more. Clair is no more. Clair did not kill my mother. She killed a memory, although I am still unclear about the memory. There is the violence that linger. The violence of Clair's world and, I sense, a violence in Cathy.

I know there is violence in Cathy, but it is not as overt and 'out there' as Clair's was. It is an internal thing, something she has bottled up to the point of self-harm. I see these things because I have spent time with

Lydia. Some of Lydia has rubbed off on me – unfortunately none of her lipstick, I wouldn't mind that rubbing off on my lips. No, it is more her ability to probe, her way of getting to the cause of things. She sometimes frightened me with the way she seemed to know what I was thinking or feeling even before I knew what I was thinking myself.

So I can see the internalised violence in Cathy which she is aware of herself, but she cannot yet see if she was a perpetrator or a victim. She will know soon. She is slowly recalling what happened. I want to help her remember, but my head hurts too much and I know I have no time left. I want to see Desiree one more time, to let her know that I know. To call her mum one last time. I can barely think now because of the pain. I need to lie down.

I stand in the middle of the room, exposed on all sides, vulnerable to the senses that can attack from any corner. The details are my enemies and my friends. In one corner there is the cobweb that Colin said we were not to disturb. It was a spider's house, he said. How would we like it if someone destroyed our house? Dear little Colin, a sensitive soul. Caught him wearing mum's lipstick once.

And there on the counter was the knife block which Clair was fascinated by. We had a job keeping her from them. She was too young to understand the damage they could do. She just liked the way the light would catch the sharp blades. Mum would get hysterical whenever Clair managed to get hold of one. The washing machine is no longer there. They had to take that for evidence.

The air in the house is stale and dust laden. They tell me it has been ten years. I would have been twelve at the time. I had long hair back then. Aunt Lydia told me that I was forever pushing it behind my ears.

'You should cut it short,' she would say. 'It would look nice and not get in your way.' But I would freak out and sulk whenever anyone threatened my precious hair. I wear it short now. The people at the hospital said I asked for it to be kept short which I can't understand. I remember liking my hair long. Clair was the one with short hair.

The chair I found mum on has gone as well. She was tied up naked on it, her lifeless eyes staring accusingly at me. I recall her screams which suddenly became stifled. He had stuck tape over her mouth and then suffocated her once he had had his way. I only hope that Clair and Colin did not have to witness it.

I had walked quickly into the kitchen when I first arrived. The little door to the cupboard under the stairs was too much for me. Even the short walk up the hallway had been filled with the claustrophobia and fear that the cupboard re-awoke in me. The thin door could only slightly muffle the sound of mum's screams as I hid in there, fearing for my life. I know I should not feel guilty. What could I have done to save her? I would have been completely defenceless and would have suffered the same fate as Clair and Colin.

I hear a noise, or think I hear a noise and my heart thuds loudly in my ears.

'Daddy?' The word forms in my mouth, but I don't let it escape. I cannot trust my feelings. I do not know if it is a good or bad thing this sense that my father is close by. I feel a strange disconnect between what is, and what is just thought. I want to cry out. I have only just reclaimed my life from Clair and Colin, but now feel as if I am coming and going, fading in and out. I am but a dream within a dream.

'Daddy?' I whisper the word.